A *Strand* of Doubt

A Strand of Doubt

DONNA GUSTAINIS FULLER

WALNUT SPRINGS PRESS

For my grandchildren, Jenika, Kierra, and Charly. May you always have the courage to follow your dreams.

Walnut Springs Press
4110 South Highland Drive
Salt Lake City, Utah 84124

Text copyright © 2014 by Donna Gustainis Fuller
Cover design copyright © 2014 by Walnut Springs Press
Interior design copyright © 2014 by Walnut Springs Press

ISBN: 978-1-59992-928-6

Acknowledgments

Just as it takes a village to raise a child, it takes a village to raise a book. I would like to thank my villagers.

For Linda and Walnut Springs Press: thanks for believing in me.

My two partners in writing: Julia for her enthusiasm and inventive ideas, and Christine for making us believe we could be authors and not being afraid to say "Yuck!"

For all the women who passed through our writing group: Jenn, Mandy, Betsy, Liz, Jacque, and Lizy.

For Mary Lou, who taught me to seize the trout.

Finally, none of this would have been possible without my husband Darrel and our children: Jenn & Kyle, Nate & Ashley, Nick & Kristy, Mandy, and Jace. They were and are my biggest cheering section.

Prologue

Aunt Karen's red-rimmed eyes and Uncle Vince's trembling lip told her more than words. Something was wrong—terribly wrong. Jana's entire body began to shake. With her legs unable to support her weight, she sat quickly on the bed and held her stomach. "What is it? What happened?"

As Aunt Karen crossed the room, her mouth moved yet no sound escaped. She closed her eyes and dissolved into tears before reaching out to Jana.

Just outside the door Uncle Vince stood with his hands stuffed into his pockets. Jana watched this giant of a man shuffle from one foot to another, a tortured look distorting his features. He crossed the room, patted his wife's hand, and crouched in front of Jana. "Darlin' . . . your . . . your parents . . ." A sob caught in his throat. "Your parents were in an accident."

"No! That can't be true. They just left an hour ago on the cruise ship." Jana jumped up from the bed and began searching for her shoes. "Take me to them." She slipped her feet into a yellow pair of flip-flops.

Vince approached her from behind, rubbing her shoulders. "Darlin', they're gone. They didn't survive. It's all my fault, if only I hadn't—"

Jana broke away from him and ran the block to the beach. As her feet hit the sand, she struggled to remove her flip-flops before she fell to her knees in the surf. The freezing tide swirled around her legs, numbing her body and soul. A voice registered in the back of her mind, but she managed to push it aside.

A young man crouched in front of her, his jeans soaked by the water. "Are you all right, miss?"

Through her tears, she focused on his brown eyes.

"Let's move out of the water before you freeze." He helped Jana to her feet and guided her to a dry spot on the sand, reaching down to grab her flip-flops on the way. He removed a towel from his shoulders and wrapped it around her shaking frame.

They sat this way for several minutes before her quiet words pierced the early evening air. "I come here when I need to think." She grabbed a handful of sand and watched the grains flow through her fingers. "If only I could travel back in time and stop them from going. The accident wouldn't have—"

Uncle Vince's white Toyota Highlander disturbed the peace when it skidded to a halt in the sand. He jumped from the driver's seat. "It's all right, young man. We'll take care of her." Uncle Vince rushed by him and scooped up the sixteen-year-old like a small child. "It's all right, darlin'. We're here for you."

Aunt Karen moved into the back seat of the SUV, and Uncle Vince deposited the towel-wrapped girl next to her. He climbed back into the vehicle and punched the accelerator. Jana watched the Good Samaritan holding her yellow flip-flops as he faded into the distance.

One

"I want to talk to Coleman. Now!"

Jana's back was to the man as he stormed into her office. She shut her eyes tightly and recoiled. *Okay now, Jana. Keep calm. Keep calm.* She took a deep breath while deliberately opening and closing her fists before spinning toward the intruder.

"I'm sorry, Mr., uh . . ."

"Willis, Trevor Willis. And I said NOW!" He slammed his fist on her desk.

Jana flinched and her shoulders stiffened, but she retained her composure, a smile frozen in place. "As I started to say, Mr. Coleman is not in right now. May I help you?"

"No. You may not help me. I'll wait." Sarcasm seeped from each crisp word. He dropped his six-foot-plus frame into a chair, plopped his feet on the coffee table, folded his arms, and glared.

Jana studied the stranger from behind slightly lowered eyelids. *So, this is the infamous Trevor Willis.* She judged him to be around thirty, but from his long list of accomplishments, she would have imagined him to be older. The old cliché "tall, dark, and handsome" popped into her brain. Every black hair was in place, with the exception of a single lock on his forehead that refused to be tamed. His green eyes were as intense as his mood.

In vain, Jana attempted to suppress a smirk. Trevor clenched his jaw as he pushed himself up from the chair to approach her. Slamming his hands down on the heavy mahogany desk, he spat, "And what, may I ask, is so funny?"

She pushed back her chair and stood straight, looking as fierce as possible at five foot one, plus heels. "I'm very sorry, Mr. Willis, but you look like a little boy who didn't get his way." She mustered her courage. "In addition, you will have a long wait, because Mr. Coleman is out of town. Finally, if you are unable to be civil, I will call security and have you escorted from the premises."

Their gazes locked for an instant before Trevor threw his head back and burst out laughing. "I am so sorry." A chuckle escaped as he glanced upward and took a deep breath. "I guess I was being somewhat childish." He winked at her. "Well, maybe a lot childish. Forgive me?"

Still shaking from the exchange, Jana stammered, "Of . . . of course, Mr. Willis."

He sat at the edge of her desk and read the nameplate. "Miss Clawson, I'd feel so much better if we could start this encounter all over again."

She put her hands up with a slight shrug. "By all means. I wouldn't mind forgetting the entire incident."

Trevor stood, turned on his heel, and exited the office, only to poke his head around the corner a moment later. He pointed his index finger downward, turning it in a circular movement. "Turn around, the way you were when I first came in."

Jana rolled her eyes and shook her head.

A minute later, he knocked on the door, greeting her with a smile. "Good morning, Miss" —he glanced at her nameplate again— "Clawson. I need to see Mr. Coleman. Is he in?"

Smiling at his exaggeratedly cheerful tone, Jana played along. "I'm sorry, Mr., uh . . ."

"Willis. Trevor Willis."

"I'm sorry, Mr. Willis, but Mr. Coleman isn't in the office right now. Is there something I can do for you?"

"You can start by calling me Trevor."

"All right, Trevor, what can I do to help you?"

"Your boss promised delivery of a prototype to my customer by yesterday at closing. As of this moment, they are still waiting, and not very patiently. In fact, they chewed me out, something that hasn't happened since I lived with my parents and came home after 2:00 AM."

"I'm sorry, Mr. Willis—"

"Trevor."

"All right." Jana sighed. "Trevor. I talked to your secretary this morning. We sent it by courier last night. They brought it back today. Apparently the purchase order had the incorrect address. I was about to call the delivery service to pick it up again."

"No!"

Jana's head jerked up.

Trevor shoved his hands into his pockets and kicked an imaginary speck on the floor. "I'm heading there right now. I'll take it over in person." His smile reassured her.

"All right. Do you want it sent up here, or would you prefer it to be delivered to the front desk?"

"I'll wait here." As their eyes met, he crossed his arms and gave her a crooked smile. "The view is much better."

Uncomfortable with his scrutiny, Jana turned to place a call to the shipping department. Trevor moved to the edge of her desk and casually glanced at the various papers there. She scooted over and covered her current project with a manila folder.

He lifted a framed picture from her desk and touched both smiling people. "This must be your mother. You look just like her."

Jana smiled. "Yes, it is. It was taken soon after my parents met. Mom would've been about my age at the time."

He blinked a couple of times, causing Jana to scrutinize his expression. "Are you okay?" she asked.

"Must be an eyelash or dust in my eye." He bent down toward her and looked up. "Can you see anything in there?"

She leaned close enough to examine his eyes and caught a whisper of his musky aftershave. "Nothing but some brown flecks, but they look like they belong there."

"Well, it's gone now."

Her attention returned to the computer screen in front of her, while he grabbed a handful of M&M's from a bowl on the coffee table. He threw the candy up in the air, one at a time, and caught them in his mouth.

A young man with Frankenstein-like ear buds protruding from his head delivered the box in question, dropping it on Jana's desk.

With a forced smile, Trevor reached into his wallet and pulled out a twenty-dollar bill, handed it to the boy, and patted him on the back. "Thanks for getting it here so quickly."

"Sure, whatever." The youth shrugged, then flicked his head back with a teenage gesture of acknowledgement. He shoved the money into his pocket and headed toward the elevator.

"Now, Miss Clawson, apparently I was doubly wrong. Number one." Trevor held out the index finger of his left hand and touched it with his right. "In the address on the purchase order, and number two—" he added another finger "—in thinking you were unable to help me. I can see why Vince is able to leave without worrying about day-to-day operations at the office."

Jana blushed. "Thank you, Mr. Wil—"

His eyebrow rose.

"Okay. Trevor."

"Since I owe you a double apology, will you do me the honor of having lunch with me?" His hand in the air silenced the response ready to fall off Jana's tongue.

"Purely as a peace offering?" He tilted his head to the side, his eyes pleading.

"Call me Jana. And well . . ."

Trevor pounced on the slight hesitation. "All right, Jana, I'll pick you up at noon. Have Coleman call me. Bye!" He grabbed the prototype and retreated to the elevator without giving her a chance to decline his offer.

She remained at her desk, staring open-mouthed at the closed elevator doors.

———◆———

Vince Coleman wiped his sweaty palms on his suit pants and faced a man enveloped in shadow. "I have the latest prototype ready. I'm routing it through Willis's company—less suspicion that way."

The shadow shuffled some papers. "Good. How long before the final product can be shipped?"

"After you let me know what changes are needed, I'd say we could have the first fifteen out in a few months." Vince glanced toward the exit.

"What about the loose ends?"

Icy fingers gripped Vince's spine. "I'll personally alter the paperwork. No one will know anything is out of sorts."

"They better not. Just remember six years ago."

Vince's mind flashed back to the day the highway patrol officer knocked on the door with the news of Vince's best friends' deaths.

"Charles Clawson was a loose end." The threat in the shadow's voice left no doubt as to his intentions.

Two

Trevor drove to an office building a few blocks away. The stairway ended on the seventh floor, and he walked to a small office in the back. He fished a key from his pocket and fumbled with the lock. Upon entry, he flicked the light switch with his elbow as he kicked the door closed. A battered table and chair sat alone, and a single bare lightbulb illuminated the musty space.

He pulled a rag from the box in the corner and meticulously removed the thick layer of dust from the table. Then he placed the package from Coleman Industries on the surface and pulled out the prototype. "This has been in development for the last six years," he mumbled under his breath. "I doubt it's worth the tremendous price that was paid." His mind floated back to Charles and Eileen Clawson and the pictures of their accident. If only he'd had the chance to sound a warning. Trevor owed it to them to get to the bottom of this.

He carefully photographed the prototype from every angle before placing it back in the box. Positioning the tape precisely, he resealed the package so it looked undisturbed. Then he picked up his cell phone.

"I got the pictures," Trevor declared once the call connected. "I'm taking it over there right now."

He waited, listening, then replied, "No. It was brilliant to put the wrong address on the purchase order. No one suspects a thing. It went better than I hoped—even got a date with the Clawson girl. Call you later."

———

Staring at the picture of her parents, Jana jumped and almost dropped the frame when Trevor said her name.

Her hands flew to her face. "I . . . I'm sorry. I must have been on a different planet." She swiveled away from him and replaced the picture on the desk before patting under her eyes and taking a deep breath.

"Are you ready?" He held out his hand. "I figured with your boss out of town, you wouldn't have a lot of time, so I made reservations at The Terrace across the street."

Jana's eyebrow arched. The Terrace was usually booked up a month or two in advance, yet Trevor Willis managed to get a table with ninety minutes' notice.

She went to the coat rack in the corner and grabbed her sweater. Trevor took it from her. "Let me help you with that."

The restaurant was a study in elegant simplicity. Alternating cloths of white and burgundy covered the circular tables. In the center of each, candles and rose petals floated in a crystal bowl. The aroma of freshly baked bread teased Jana's taste buds.

The waiter seated her and Trevor immediately, presenting their menus with a flourish. Clearly the best in the house, their table was set apart from the others, with a magnificent view of the city. "Would you like to start with one of our wines, Mr. Willis?"

Trevor looked at Jana. "I normally don't drink, but feel free to have wine or whatever you'd like."

"Could I have water with lemon, please?" She smiled at the waiter.

"Same for me, Thomas."

"I'll be right back with that, Mr. Willis."

They perused the menus. "What would you like?" Trevor asked.

"I'm not sure. What do you recommend?"

"For lunch, their soups and salads are all outstanding. The quiche is also delicious." Trevor tapped his chin and then snapped his fingers. "I know. You'd like their chicken enchiladas. Not quite authentic, but a good Northwestern version."

She tilted her head and smiled at him. "It's interesting you mentioned that. I had a brief stint in the Enchilada Eating Club in high school."

"Oh, really?" Trevor cleared his throat and glanced at his menu.

The waiter returned with their water in beautifully etched crystal goblets, and set down a basket filled with a variety of piping hot rolls. "Have you made a decision yet?"

Trevor laid his menu down. "I'd like the seafood quiche."

"I—" Jana didn't have a chance to finish her sentence.

"And this beautiful lady—" he winked at her "—will have the chicken enchiladas."

"Excellent. I'll have it here shortly." The waiter bowed before retreating to the kitchen.

Jana fought to keep her jaw from dropping. "Yes, the Enchilada Eating Club was quite interesting."

Trevor flashed his brilliant smile and raised his glass of water toward her before taking a drink.

"They met at Pancho's Mexican Buffet the first Thursday of every month and ate all the Mexican food they could stuff into themselves. A friend convinced me to go. Once. After watching all those high school boys acting like pigs, I swore I'd never eat another enchilada again."

Trevor choked, spraying the water in his mouth over the table.

The waiter approached quickly. "Are you okay?"

"I'm fine." Trevor wiped his mouth with the cloth napkin. "It just went down the wrong pipe."

The wait staff cleared the table, including the cloth, within seconds, then replaced the items in an equally rapid manner.

"I apologize," Trevor said to Jana. "I assumed you would like enchiladas. Would you rather have something else?"

She gave a mischievous grin. "Don't worry. I rescinded that vow a couple of years ago."

Trevor held out the new basket. "One of the best things about this place is their bread. It's hard to beat."

"That's only because you haven't tasted my homemade rolls."

He leaned forward with his elbow on the table, his chin resting on his hand. "Is that an invitation?"

She laughed. "If you promise not to spray water all over the table, I might—"

"How about Friday?"

Her eyes narrowed. "You really don't waste any time, do you, Mr. Willis?"

He sat back in his chair and broke off a piece of bread. "Well, I don't let too many opportunities pass me by. Michael Jordan said it best—'Some people want it to happen, some wish it would happen, others make it happen.' I'm one of the latter. I make things happen."

She studied his smug expression, noting a vulnerability in his eyes before she heard herself say, "All right, Friday it is."

He slapped the table, causing the candles to bob up and down amid the rose petals. "I accept."

The waiter returned in a remarkably short time with their lunch. As they began their meal, Jana broached the subject foremost in her mind. "I'm curious. You said you normally don't drink alcohol. Why is that?"

"It impairs your judgment, and in business, I can't afford that. In my personal life, I choose not to."

She paused a moment, smiling slowly. "That's exactly what my father used to say."

"Is that why you don't drink?"

"Partly. I'm a Mormon—a Latter-day Saint—and because of what we call the Word of Wisdom, I don't drink alcoholic beverages."

"Very practical." Trevor sipped his water. "I want to hear all about you, Jana." He settled back in his chair and took a bite of his quiche, then glued his eyes on her.

"There's not a lot to tell. I really don't have family."

"What happened to your parents? "

"They were killed in a car accident a few years ago." She closed her eyes briefly as the events of that horrific day rose from her memory.

Something flashed across Trevor's features before he reached out and cradled her hand in his own, pulling her out of the past. "I'm so sorry. That must have been really tough."

Jana wiped a tear from her cheek and paused a moment. "It was. I don't know what I would have done without the Colemans." Seeing compassion in Trevor's eyes, she felt the weight of loneliness lessen its grip on her heart. *Could he comprehend a part of what I've experienced?*

A portly gentleman bumped into Jana's chair and startled her from her musings. She yanked her hand away from Trevor's and looked in the man's direction.

"Oh, I'm so sorry, miss. I must be getting clumsy in my old age." He bent down and picked up her napkin from the floor.

Trevor drew her attention back. "What on earth did you do?"

"Vince Coleman and my dad were best friends in college. He and Aunt Karen took me into their home."

"Is that when you started working for him?"

"No, I lived with them for a year and then went to BYU. I graduated a year ago. Uncle Vince gave me this job and helped me get settled into an apartment. That's my life in a nutshell." She shrugged, then picked up a fork and began eating her enchiladas.

"Where did you say he was?" Trevor looked a little nervous.

"He's in Texas, arranging a scholarship fund at the University of Houston."

"What kind of projects are you working on?" Trevor's gaze drifted over her shoulder.

"Is something wrong? You keep looking toward the door."

"No, nothing's wrong. I thought I saw someone I knew."

"Do I get to join in this twenty-questions game, or are you the only one who gets to ask?"

He laughed. "Well, I'm pretty boring."

"That's not what I've heard."

"You shouldn't always believe everything floating on the grapevine." A burst of steam escaped from a roll as he broke it open. "I went to Harvard, courtesy of a good friend and mentor, and I continued in the MBA program. I have one sister, Traci, who lives with her husband and three kids in Seattle. My parents live in Winchendon, Massachusetts, in the same white clapboard house I grew up in."

Jana's fork stopped halfway to her mouth. "You're from Toy Town?" *Maybe we are kindred spirits.*

His expression mirrored hers. "How'd you know about that?"

"I grew up in Keene, New Hampshire."

Trevor shook his head. "It really is a small world. So, why did we have to come three thousand miles to meet each other, when we grew up, what, twenty-five miles apart?"

"It might as well have been three thousand miles. By the time I graduated from high school, you were long out of college and already across the country."

He glanced at the door before he pulled his eyes back Jana. "I guess you're right. Although, I was visiting back home a few years ago, and I even went to the Pumpkin Fest in Keene."

"No way."

Trevor crossed his arms. "Yep. I did my duty and carved a pumpkin. It was Mike Wazowski from *Monster's Inc.* He was my nephew's favorite character. Since I'm a doting uncle and he is named after me, I couldn't resist his pleas."

Jana laughed. "My favorite was from Cheshire Medical Center's obstetrics department."

Trevor nodded his head. "I think I remember that one. Was it the pumpkin mom giving birth to a baby pumpkin?"

"Yes, that's it." She paused thoughtfully. "I wonder if we passed each other."

"I don't think so. I would have definitely remembered you." The intensity of his gaze startled her.

The man who had bumped into her chair approached and offered his right hand. "I just want to apologize once again."

"It was really nothing, sir," Jana replied without taking his hand.

Trevor's cell phone began buzzing, so he pulled it out of his pocket and pushed a button that stopped the noise. A few seconds later, the vibrations started again. The third time, he said to Jana, "It must be something important or they would just leave a message. Do you mind if I get this?"

"Go ahead."

He touched the display. "What is it, Brenda?" he asked with a touch of irritation. As he listened, his brows knit together. "All right, I'll be back in about ten minutes."

Jana looked at him with concern. "Is everything okay?"

"There's just a little problem, and unfortunately I'm the only one who can take care of it. Do you mind if we cut things short?"

"That's fine. I need to get back anyway."

He raised his hand to catch the waiter's attention. "Thomas, we'll be leaving now. Can you put this on my tab?"

"Of course, Mr. Willis."

Trevor signed the check and opened his wallet. "Everything was excellent, as usual."

"Thank you, sir."

He left a fifty-dollar bill on the table.

Jana glanced at the money. *With a tip like that, no wonder he was able to get the best seat in the house on such a short notice.*

A minute later, Trevor took her arm and safely maneuvered her across the street to her office building. He accompanied her on the elevator and escorted her to her desk, where an older woman with white hair waited.

"Trevor, I'd like you to meet Sue," Jana said. "Sue, this is Trevor Willis."

"I'm glad to meet you, Mr. Willis." She extended her hand.

Trevor clasped it between both of his. "Please, call me Trevor. Thanks for covering for Jana."

"No problem at all."

He turned to Jana and kissed her hand. "I'll see you on Friday."

"Goodbye."

When he left, Sue turned to Jana. "All right, spill the beans. Tell me all about it."

Jana smiled. "It was really nice."

"You have a date with Trevor Willis, Portland's most eligible bachelor, and all you can say is 'It was nice'?"

"I said *really* nice."

Sue rolled her eyes. "You're killing me here."

Jana laughed. "We went to The Terrace. It was a wonderful view. The food was excellent. You know what's funny?"

"What?"

"We grew up twenty-five miles apart."

"Wow!"

Jana nodded her head emphatically. "You're telling me."

"Do I have to pry everything out of you? What's going on Friday night?"

"Oh, that. I'm just making him supper at my apartment."

"Whoa! That one could charm the socks off a centipede. No wonder they wanted him on that TV show." She snapped her fingers a couple of times. "Now what was the name?"

"The Bachelor?"

"That's it!" Sue lapsed into mother mode. "Although, you know his reputation, don't you? Are you sure it's wise to have him at your apartment alone?"

"I'll be fine, Sue."

"Well, just be careful."

Sue left Jana staring at her computer screen. She smiled as she remembered Trevor's reaction to her enchilada comment. She shook her head, bringing her thoughts back to the present.

Later that afternoon, two boxes arrived at the office, one for Jana and the other for Sue. The labels read "Cacao's." It was the most exclusive chocolate shop in Portland. Sue's note thanked her for covering the front desk. Jana's note was a bit more detailed.

Thank you for lunch. The company was enchanting. Since we didn't have a chance to eat dessert, I'm sending you these toffee bars. They're my favorite. I'm looking forward to Friday night. T.W.

Sue's legs swung back and forth from her perch on the desk, where the open candy boxes sat between her and Jana. "I've heard these are to die for," Sue commented. They both took a bite and sighed as the confection melted in their mouths. "You can tell Mr. Willis if he keeps me supplied in chocolate like this, I'll cover for you anytime."

"I'll pass on the message." Jana pulled another candy from its paper cup. "Of course, what will your husband say if another man is sending you chocolate?"

"He'll say I better save some for him."

Trevor walked through the park, talking on his cell. "Lunch went off with only a minor glitch. Why wasn't it in the report that she only attended the Enchilada Eating Club one time? Fortunately, I was still able to finagle dinner on Friday, too."

After a short pause, he continued. "Hey, this is Trevor Willis you're talking to. I'll have her eating out of my hand in no time. She sure has changed since that time I saw her in Keene. Did they find anything in her purse? Oliver was sloppy. She almost caught him taking her handbag when he bumped into her. I had to distract her."

He listened. "And the cell phone?" He rubbed his forehead in a circular motion. "I have a feeling she'll check out as clean as her parents did. She doesn't even know where Coleman really is. She thinks he's in Houston."

The voice on the other end of the line droned on.

"I'll call again after Friday." Trevor tapped the screen, placed the phone in his pocket, and gazed off into the distance.

Three

On Friday night, Jana looked in the full-length mirror on the closet door. She sported her fourth outfit and third hairstyle. She inclined her head one way and then the other before wrinkling her nose and shaking her head. "What is wrong with you, girl? He might be the most eligible bachelor in town, but he's also the most eligible non-Mormon one. When he finds out you won't lower your standards, he'll be out of the picture in a flash."

The scolding must have worked, because after only two more outfits and one additional hairstyle, she decided to wear her hair down with the sides pulled back into a barrette. She chose black leggings with a long, shimmering blue sweater. Her grandmother's heart necklace and the delicate diamond earrings that had belonged to Jana's mother completed the outfit.

Sue knocked on the bedroom door. "Are you okay in there?"

Jana opened the door and turned around slowly. "What do you think?"

"You look prettier than a glob of butter melting on a stack of wheat cakes."

"Thank you—I think."

"Well, I'll hit the road now. He should be here soon."

"Thanks so much for bringing the whipping cream over. I could have sworn I had some. You're a lifesaver."

"Don't worry about it, dear. I was glad to help. Have fun." Sue patted Jana's shoulder before heading out the door and giving her a wave.

Jana crossed the living room and closed the bedroom door on several discarded outfits strewn on the bed and chair. As she thought of the mess, her thoughts raced. *I don't know what's wrong with me. I never leave a room like this. Get a grip, Jana.*

In a futile attempt to convince herself, she spoke out loud. "It's only a date. Everything doesn't have to be perfect." She strode with a purpose to her bedroom and hung up the rejected outfits.

Aunt Karen had tried to convince Jana to live with them, but she felt a need to be independent. The apartment was simple, but her mother's damask tablecloth and china made the table setting elegant. Jana added crystal candlesticks to complete the mood. She had just given the final touches to dinner when Trevor knocked. Panic threatened, and she forced herself to calm down. "Here goes nothing," she muttered under her breath.

Gathering her courage, she opened the door and smiled. Trevor held a bouquet of pink carnations and baby's breath in one hand. His other hand was hidden behind his back.

"Wow! You look great. These are for you."

"Thank you. I love carnations." She took the flowers and invited him to come in.

He closed the door behind him and followed her into the kitchen. "I have a confession to make. I asked Sue what your favorite flowers were." He produced a bottle from behind his back. "I also brought some sparkling cider for dinner tonight."

"That will go perfectly with the lasagna."

"Lasagna is one of my favorite foods."

"I'm glad." She rolled her eyes and shook her head as she turned toward the stove. *This guy knows how to flatter.* "I made pillow-soft rolls tonight. Next time I'll make the French ones."

His eyebrow lifted and his eyes lit up. "So there'll be a next time? I'll hold you to that." He looked around. "This is a really nice apartment." He walked over to the table and picked up a dinner plate. "These dishes are beautiful. Desert Rose, right?"

"How did you know that?"

"It's the same pattern my mom has. We used them every time we ate in the dining room. I know the pattern name because I needed to replace a couple of plates once." He held the dish in one hand, gently lifting it up and down as if checking the weight. "Do you want to see how well I juggle?"

Jana's eyes opened wide. "No!" She quickly reached out and confiscated the cherished plate. "Maybe we should keep it on the table. It's much safer that way." She replaced the dish, patting it with a sigh of relief.

Trevor laughed and winked at her. "Don't worry. I learned my lesson the first time. Now I just juggle with apples, balls, and plastic plates. I was banned from eggs, too. The chickens had to work overtime just to keep up with me."

Jana joined his laughter as she placed a trivet on the table. "Would you bring out the lasagna for me?"

"Sure."

He walked into the kitchen and returned carrying the hot Pyrex dish with Jana's floral oven mitts. "Everything smells fantastic. Beauty *and* the ability to cook—an irresistible combination."

A wave of warmth rose on her face. "Do you mind if I bless the food?"

"No, not at all. Go right ahead." He bowed his head as she prayed. Then, he stood, took her plate, and placed a piece of lasagna on it, expertly catching the trailing string of mozzarella and depositing it on the dish before serving himself. Jana passed the salad and the rolls. She held her breath and watched carefully as he closed his eyes and savored a bite of hot, buttered bread.

"Mmm. Forget The Terrace—you definitely win hands down, Jana. These are the best rolls I've ever tasted."

The breath she'd been holding escaped, and she beamed at his compliment. "Thanks. I was afraid this would be the one time they didn't turn out. It was my grandma's recipe."

"It's a definite keeper."

They chatted amicably over dinner. Trevor helped himself to two more servings of lasagna and several more rolls. As he and Jana put away the food, he offered to wash dishes. She grinned. "Maybe another time, when we have paper plates."

"It's funny, whenever I mention the juggling incident, I don't have to do the dishes. I can't figure it out." He winked at her again.

"You're definitely savvy—just like I've heard."

"Oh, and for the record, that's the second mention of a future time you'll cook for me. I'm keeping track of all the references. Each one is for a new meal. So far, we have a meal with French rolls and one with paper plates."

She shook her head. "Cunning too."

She served up slices of banana cream pie, and they carried the plates to the couch. Trevor had the first bite in his mouth before he sat down.

"Yum." He looked at his dessert. "By the way, what rumors have you been listening to?" The intensity of his eyes belied his casual manner.

Jana decided the best course was total honesty. "I've heard you're a ladies' man who has women lined up to cater to his every whim."

"Like I said, don't believe everything you hear. Most of those rumors are totally unfounded."

"You're saying you don't date much?"

He swallowed a bite of pie before responding. "No, I've dated quite a bit. But most of the women haven't had more than one date with me, so they spread the rumor that I'm a love-'em-and-leave-'em kind of guy. But it's not true."

Jana narrowed her eyes. "Really?"

"Scout's honor." Three fingers went up. "I'm a Boy Scout through and through—even made Eagle."

"That's impressive."

Trevor shrugged his shoulders. "I'm afraid I'm pretty old-fashioned for today's world. Coming from Keene, you know how it is—small-town New England values. I even believe people shouldn't sleep together before marriage." He looked a bit embarrassed as his gaze met the floor. "Most of the women I've dated didn't share that view."

Jana reached out and touched his arm. "I do."

He looked up and met her eyes. "You really feel that way?"

"Absolutely."

He shook his head with a wry grin. "Most women would burst out laughing if I were to actually tell them that."

"I admire you more for that than all your business success."

He put his plate on the coffee table and stood up, running his right hand through his hair before facing Jana. "I've never told anyone that before." He took a deep breath, then sat and captured Jana's hand in his. "What is it about you that makes me feel comfortable enough to share my innermost feelings with you? What makes you so different?"

Jana found herself speechless. He was definitely a different man than rumor made him out to be. His vulnerability only made him more attractive, and she was unable to look away from him.

Trevor broke the spell. "What did you do in high school? Any extracurricular activities?"

"I played volleyball and was on the debate team. Oh, and I already told you about the Enchilada Eating Club. What about you?"

"By the way, what is your favorite food? I know it's not enchiladas." He chuckled.

"Chinese food and cheesecake."

"That's an interesting combination." He finished his last bite of pie. "Are there seconds on this pie?"

"Of course." She took his plate to the kitchen and got him another piece of pie, then returned and handed it to him. "You changed the subject—I asked about you."

"Thanks." He took a small bite. "I do have another question. If you needed to get away from the rest of the world, where would you go?"

"That's easy. I'd head to the coast."

"Which one? West Coast? East Coast? Ivory Coast?"

She smiled at him. "Oregon, of course. What about you?"

"I have a cabin in the mountains. It's so quiet and peaceful—a small pond, tall pines, a cool breeze, and a large deck with a great view. I usually go there when I have major decisions to make."

At the end of the evening, Trevor stood in the doorway with leftovers in hand. He kissed the top of Jana's head. "Thanks for the wonderful evening. I'll call you." He stroked her cheek with his finger. "Good night."

"Good night, Trevor."

She closed the door and leaned against it with a silly grin on her face, then pushed herself away and headed to the kitchen. Her thoughts drifted as she began washing dishes. *He'll probably never even call—*

Her musings were interrupted by the ringing phone. She dried her hands on the dish towel before picking up the receiver.

"Hello?"

"Hello, beautiful."

"Trevor? It's only been ten minutes since you left."

"I know. I wanted to let you know I miss you."

She chuckled. "You're incorrigible."

"I know. Do you miss me? Even just a little?"

"Okay, Trevor, I miss you—a little."

"That's all I wanted to hear. Night.'"

"Good night, Trevor. Oh, I almost forgot. I heard from Uncle Vince. He'll be back on Monday."

"Thanks. I'll be in touch with him."

Trevor definitely didn't make a good first impression, but his second impression more than made up for it. She forced the thought away as her rational side exerted itself vocally for the second time that evening. "Be careful, Jana—he's not even a member." *But everything else seems perfect.*

———

Trevor disconnected the call before dialing the familiar number. "It's me. I just left her apartment."

"Is she beginning to trust you?"

"Yeah. I showed her my vulnerable side. It disarms them immediately." Trevor turned off his car engine.

"Keep close to her. See if you can get any information."

Trevor pulled away from the curb, his mind racing. He chuckled and thought back to this pint-sized girl standing up to him and realized she was more like her mother than he ever imagined. *Remember, this is just business,* he told himself.

Four

Trevor crashed into Jana's life like a tornado, shattering her well-ordered existence. From box seats to the Trail Blazers–Celtics basketball game, to an evening with the Portland Pops featuring the music of John Williams, or fresh bagels personally delivered to the office when she had to be there early, Jana was swept along by the current.

Whenever she was with him, she fell under his spell, and the loneliness for her family seemed to lessen. Away from him, she could think of nothing else, although lingering doubts plagued her mind. *Is there a chink in his armor? What about the explosive side he showed on our first meeting? Would he ever think of joining the Church? If not, would I ever consider marriage outside the temple?* The more time spent in his presence, the farther she forced this sensible side into the background.

A box of chocolates from Cacao's arrived Thursday afternoon just before closing time, accompanied by a pink carnation and a sealed envelope. She had known Trevor for a short time now, but his thoughtfulness and attention to detail never ceased to amaze her. *He actually remembered this was our three-month anniversary.* She carefully opened the note. In his confident scroll, he invited her to dinner at his apartment the following night.

Moments before Jana's scheduled arrival time, Trevor picked up his phone and checked the display. "Hello, Don."

"Trevor, I've been hearing some rumors about your objectiveness. Have you linked her to anything yet?"

"Nothing." Trevor tapped the speaker icon and placed the phone on the sink while he combed his hair.

"The boss still thinks there's a possibility. Maybe you should pull back a little—"

Trevor slammed his fist down on the counter, jarring the phone. "I don't work for him, and I don't work for you, either. I'm only doing this to repay an old debt. You'd do well to remember that."

"Okay. Let me get to the point. Traci says—"

"She's right." Trevor looked in the mirror in satisfaction. His shirt was a perfect complement to the freshly pressed suit.

"Now, don't go rushing into anything. This is too fast. You've only—"

"It's not too fast." He straightened his tie and smoothed down his hair, deliberately pulling a small lock out of place. "Besides, it's the best way to keep tabs on her. As long as there's any doubt, I'm staying right with her." The doorbell sounded. "She's here. Give my love to Traci and the kids. Gotta go." Without waiting for an answer, Trevor disconnected the call.

Jana waited outside his apartment. She wore a flowing, cream-colored dress with her hair pulled back into a clip, and curls cascading onto her neck. When he opened the door, Trevor's smile said more than words.

"You're an absolute vision, sweetheart."

He ushered her into the living room and retrieved a beautiful corsage of pink carnations and baby's breath. He removed it from the box. "May I?" She nodded, and he pinned the corsage to her shoulder.

"Thank you. It's beautiful."

"I hope you don't mind if we eat on the balcony."

"No. That sounds wonderful."

He led her out onto the deck, where a white-draped table set with fine silver and crystal waited. Candlelight cast shadows across the table and reflected off a bottle of sparkling cider encased in a silver ice bucket. He kissed her cheek before seating her, and then left to bring dinner out.

Jana looked around. She touched the chopsticks snuggled alongside the fork and smiled. *He never misses a detail.*

"This is the best Chinese food in Portland." Trevor appeared with a tray containing two bowls of egg-drop soup. He followed this with spring rolls, paper-wrapped beef, and wontons. The main course included cashew chicken and pork fried rice. Dessert was a heavenly strawberry cheesecake.

"You've sure gone all out for our three-month anniversary, Trevor."

He came around the table and captured her hand in his. "I'd planned on this night being more than our anniversary."

"What do you mean?" Her stomach felt like it was filled with lead. What did he expect?

He knelt down on one knee. "Jana, you're the woman I've waited my whole life to find. I love you and would like to ask you to become my wife." He produced a blue velvet box with his other hand and held it out to her.

Her smile froze on her face. *Did I miss something? Should I have known this was coming?* "I . . . I . . . don't know what to say."

When he opened the box, candlelight glistened off the most beautiful ring she had ever seen. As usual, it was perfect, as though he had plucked it right out of her dreams.

"Say yes."

The longer they had dated, the deeper Jana had fallen under his spell. It would be easy to imagine herself as his wife. "I, uh, I really . . . Oh, Trevor, I didn't expect this."

A trace of uncertainty entered his eyes. "Jana?"

Her hand reached out to smooth his hair. "It's just so sudden. I need more time." She walked to the railing and stared at the sweeping view without really seeing it. The little doubts inside her head began to wiggle toward the surface. *Am I ready to give up my dream of a temple marriage?*

Trevor stood behind her and wrapped his arms around her waist. He gently kissed the back of her neck and whispered in her ear, "How much time?"

She turned toward him and put her arms around his neck. "You're not making this easy, mister."

He laughed, his smile showing in his eyes. "That's the whole idea. It's supposed to be impossible to tell me no. You're supposed to melt at my touch. That's how you know you're as crazy for me as I am for you." He captured her left hand and slipped the ring onto her third finger. "Just see how this feels."

He slowly bent his head toward her. His kiss began gently but increased in intensity. Jana began to waver. *Just one word,* she thought. But it refused to come. "I care about you, Trevor, but please try to understand. There are some things I need to resolve first." She removed the ring and placed it in his palm.

He cocked his head, his fingers closing around the ring. "I'm trying to understand. Talk to me." He kissed her cheek.

Exasperated, she finally pushed him away. "Trevor! I can't think straight with you so close." He chuckled and tried to close the gap, but she held her ground. "There are a lot of things to consider here. I . . . I need time."

"You're repeating yourself, Jana." Once again, he placed the ring on her hand.

She watched the candlelight reflected in the stone. "It's just so sudden."

"I knew I wanted to marry you the first day we met, when you stood up to me. I decided right then I wanted you for my wife."

A haunted look crossed his face, along with something she had never seen in him before.

Her breath caught in her throat as realization hit. "What are you afraid of?" She watched as the urgency displayed in his features vanished with a deep breath.

His hands cradled her face, his eyes hypnotizing her. "I'm afraid of life without you. I don't see why we should wait any longer." Quiet desperation intertwined with his voice. "Please allow me to take care of you."

Every passing moment found Jana's doubts quieting. She felt drawn into his voice. Then she shook her head, breaking the spell. She handed the ring back to him and moved. "I need to get away and make my decision—without you so near to muddle my brain." She reached back and grabbed her purse. "I'll call you, okay?"

"Jana." He said it so softly, she wasn't sure she actually heard anything. She turned and saw an unidentified emotion etched in his face as he softly pleaded, "Marry me now. It's more important than you can imagine."

Jana stepped toward him, barely able to breathe. She reached up to smooth away the lines of worry on his face. "Please don't look at me that way. You're breaking my heart."

Without words, he pulled her toward him and held her tight. They stood like that for a few minutes before she gently pushed away, her hands on his shoulders. "This isn't goodbye, Trevor. I just need time to figure out how I feel." She looked into his eyes, hoping he would understand. "I love you and I'll call you tomorrow. All right?

"All right." He kissed her gently, then reluctantly let her leave.

Trevor sat on the white couch, elbows on his knees, his head supported by shaking hands. He took a deep breath. *Get control of yourself.* He stood and paced the floor, running his hand through his hair. His carriage straightened with sudden insight. *She'll be back. She has no one else to turn to.*

Five

Jana pushed the lighted button at Vince and Karen Coleman's home in Lake Oswego and heard the muffled chimes. Aunt Karen opened the door to a distraught Jana. She immediately reached for her niece, enfolding her in an embrace.

Mascara trailed down Jana's face, and more tears threatened. "Oh, I don't know what to do."

Vince entered the scene. "What happened?" As he came closer, his features darkened. "What has he done to you?"

"Oh, Uncle Vince—" Jana stopped when she saw his tightened jaw and the fire blazing in his eyes. "If looks could kill, I wouldn't want to be the person you're looking at." She noticed his fists opening and closing. Enfolding his hand in hers, she soothed. "Everything's okay. Trevor asked me to marry him tonight."

A sigh of relief escaped. "Jana, darlin', I don't think I'll ever understand women. Why are you crying, then?"

He led her by the hand through the professionally decorated living room to the comfortable country kitchen and pulled out a chair for her, then one for himself. Karen found their cookie mugs in the cupboard and appeared at the table with milk and Oreos. "Sorry they're not homemade, but you were always the one who baked them. My talents run more toward shopping."

"Yeah." Vince chuckled and patted his stomach. "I've really missed your baking. Now, darlin', tell us what's bothering you."

Aunt Karen placed a box of tissues in front of Jana. She pulled one out and wiped the remnants of her tears before grabbing another to blow her nose.

"I not sure what I'm feeling. You know how important my church is to me."

"Yes, we've always tried to support you." Vince patted her hand.

"Well, I think I love Trevor, but he's not Mormon, and whenever I mention the Church, he changes the subject. If we get married, it won't be in the temple."

Karen nodded her head. "If that's the only reason, I'm sure you two could work something out."

She looked at her aunt with a mixture of sadness and confusion. *I thought she understood.* "I've always dreamed about being married for eternity. That can only happen in the temple. Trevor acted kind of strange tonight, though. It was almost as if he was afraid something bad would happen if I didn't say yes."

"What do you mean?" Vince asked, his expression guarded.

"He tried to rush me into an answer. I think he wanted to get married right away—like in the next week. I told him I needed time."

"You did the right thing. Marriage isn't something you rush into, especially if there are some doubts."

Jana's cell phone rang, and she looked at the caller ID. "It's him." She looked at the ceiling and let out an audible sigh, then connected the call. "Hello, Trevor."

"Sweetheart. Where are you?"

"Over at Uncle Vince and Aunt Karen's."

She heard a sharp intake of breath. "If you need to talk, you can always come to me, Jana."

"I know."

"I thought about what you said—that you needed to get away."

She felt wary. "Yes?"

"I think it might be a good idea."

"You do?" She stood and walked around the table to put her cup in the sink.

"Yeah. I know how much you love the coast, so I talked to a friend of mine. He has a bed-and-breakfast in Seaside. I thought you might want to stay there. It's a great place—close to the beach."

Jana was quiet for a moment before answering. "Thank you, Trevor. I think I'd like that."

"Great!" He sounded relieved. "I made reservations. He's expecting you tomorrow evening."

"What? I wish you would have asked first."

"I'm sorry, sweetheart. He was about to fill the vacancy when I called. It was either book it right then or not at all. I can cancel if you want."

"No. I'll go." The draw of the coast was too great.

Vince had been pacing while Jana and Trevor talked on the phone. "Let me speak to him."

He grabbed the phone out of her hand and walked out onto the deck, then shut the sliding glass door behind him.

———

"Listen here, Willis. I want you to back off from my little girl."

"That's exactly what I'm doing. I'm giving her a chance to get away to the coast," Trevor barked. "You know quite well that's where she feels the most peace. She can make up her mind in a safe place."

Vince contemplated the words. "Okay," the older man said finally, all his bluster evaporated. "You might be right. It'll be a good idea for her to be away from here for a little while. Just make sure you give her the space she needs." He touched the phone screen to hang up before coming back into the house.

"Trevor promised to let you have time to make your decision. I assume he'll call you in the morning with the details."

Jana took the phone back and looked at her uncle. "Um, okay. If I'm going to get on the road tomorrow, I have to pack and then go into the office and prepare everything for Sue."

Aunt Karen hugged her as she left. "If you need to talk, just call me—even at 2:00 in the morning. You understand?"

"Thank you for always being there for me." She kissed her aunt's cheek.

"I'll see you in the morning. You take care." Vince embraced Jana briefly.

"Good night, Uncle Vince. I'll be in around 8:30."

Saturday morning, Jana sat at her desk, reviewing several accounts. On one product line, infrared detection devices, something seemed skewed. She reviewed invoicing and inventory along with the production records, before finally figuring out the discrepancy. The raw materials purchased and used accounted for more imagers than the stock on hand or items shipped. There had to be a miscount somewhere. She knocked on her uncle's office door and brought the paperwork to his attention.

Rubbing the back of his neck and bringing his hand around to his temples, Vince surveyed the documents. "What's wrong, darlin'?"

"The numbers don't match up at all." She pointed to the bottom figures. "See, with the materials used, there should be about fifteen more handheld infrared imagers."

"You're right." His face paled, and he gripped the edge of his chair. "Just leave these invoices here, and I'll take care of them on Monday. I can see why I can't run the company without you. Thanks for letting me know about this." He patted her hand.

Jana reluctantly left the documentation. "Just remember, since the technology is restricted, we have to account for each item. I can go down right now to see if they miscounted or missed a box."

"No, you're getting ready to go out of town. I'll have Jerry Smith take care of it on Monday. Nothing's going to disappear over the weekend."

She looked at Vince uncertainly. "If you're sure."

"Positive. Close up everything and get ready to go. Be sure to come by the house on the way out to say goodbye."

"I will. Thanks."

Before leaving, Jana called Sue to explain the situation and give last-minute instructions. "Oh, and there was a problem with the infrared imagers. Uncle Vince said he'd take care of it, but it wouldn't hurt to remind him."

"I understand. Don't worry—I'll take care of everything."

By Saturday evening, thoughts of restricted technology drifted into reflections on Trevor's proposal as Jana headed for the coast to hopefully get her answer.

Six

The weather did its best to prove the theory that the Pacific Northwest is a rainforest. Buckets of rain fell on the windshield, and the wipers struggled to clear the glass. As Jana watched the hypnotic swishing, her thoughts went back to her childhood.

She was sandwiched between her parents at the Portland airport as they made their way from the plane into the jetway. At the end of the tunnel, Uncle Vince and Aunt Karen waited. Nine-year-old Jana was swept up into Vince's embrace. He swung her around, secure in his strong arms, and kissed her cheek.

"How's my little pumpkin?"

"I missed you, Uncle Vince."

"I missed you too, darlin'."

From over his shoulder, Aunt Karen cleared her throat and spoke. "Aren't you forgetting something?"

He laughed and whispered in Jana's ear, "Maybe you'd better give Aunt Karen a hug and kiss too."

Jana hugged him one last hug before he put her down and gave her a slight push in his wife's direction. Once the luggage was loaded into the back of the car, they set off on their journey to the Colemans' cottage on the Oregon coast. Many summers were spent on the beach playing in the water and building sandcastles on the shore. They searched for seashells, went crabbing, and enjoyed bonfires at night.

Vince and Karen sold the cottage a few years ago, but the coast still represented safety and security to Jana. She fled to its refuge when her parents died, and now she came when problems hung heavy on her shoulders. It was a place to commune with her Heavenly Father—a place of peace. She was certain she'd receive her answer there.

Lightning illuminated the road, calling her back from the reverie and exposing a small brown rabbit in her path. To avoid the creature, Jana jammed on the brakes and swerved. As she pulled out of the swerve, she heard a popping noise. The car jerked violently to the left and went into a spin. Her head spun as well, until she felt like it was being lifted from her body. When the Camry slammed into a tree next to the mountainside, the impact jarred every inch of Jana's body. Upon looking out her window and seeing the severe drop on the other side of the highway, she managed to utter a short prayer.

The world dimmed as she began to lose consciousness. *I wish you were here, Trevor. You never would have lost control.* She blinked and spotted her purse. Using all her strength, she grasped the strap and pulled the purse toward her, then opened the pocket containing her cell phone. *I need to get help. Call Trevor . . .* Jana fought the force pulling her eyes closed. Suddenly, she felt the phone snatched from her grasp. "Who are you? My phone!"

Voices floated around her head while hands pulled her from the car. She cried out at the pain in her shoulder as she was strapped to a hard board. "Trevor?"

A man shined a flashlight in her eyes. "Can you hear me?"

"My shoulder . . ."

His hand probed from her neck, down her arm. Snatches of conversation fought their way through to her brain. "Eric . . . okay . . . to clinic . . . faster . . . "

Blackness crept its way into Jana's mind until she succumbed to the exhaustion.

A dark car lurking at the scene left as she was taken away in the ambulance.

———•———

Trevor stormed across the room and back as he talked to the innkeeper on speakerphone. "What do you mean she's not there? I sent her to you so you could keep an eye on her." He punched a pillow.

"Calm down, Willis. We can't watch her if she doesn't show up."

Trevor ran his fingers through his hair. "Call me when she arrives." He cursed cell phones. He would have preferred a good old-fashioned phone slam.

———•———

Vince awoke Sunday morning to a buzzing cell phone. "Coleman here."

Sleep fled from him as he heard the familiar voice utter chilling words. "Mr. Coleman, you have not tied up all of your loose ends. We had to take care of someone in your organization last night. She knew a little too much about unaltered paperwork."

There was no chance for a reply as the phone went dead.

"Karen." His voice sounded raspy.

"What is it, Vince?"

He tried to clear his throat. "Did Jana call last night when she got in?"

"No, but I assume she thought it was too late. What's wrong?"

"Nothing. Nothing." He tried to hide the worry in his voice. "I'm going to try to reach her right now."

Seven

Jana's next conscious moment found her in a soft bed with fresh white sheets. Gazing around the room, it felt like she had awakened in another era. Everything seemed old-fashioned, from the delicate lace curtains and floral wallpaper right down to the older woman sitting by her bed with her knitting needles softly clicking in her hands.

The woman smiled at her, put down her knitting, and walked to the door. "Eric, she's awake now." She turned back to Jana. "Why, hello. You've been asleep for quite some time. How are you feeling?"

Jana managed a whisper. "Who are you? Where am I?"

"I'm Emma Grant." She poured a glass of water and helped Jana sit up to drink it. "You're at the clinic where my son, Eric, is the doctor. He'll come in here to check on you in just a moment. I help him out every now and then—you know, answering phones, sitting with patients." Emma looked up when a knock sounded at the door. "Oh, here he is."

A man in a white lab coat came in, his attention captured by the medical chart he perused. With brown hair, gray eyes, dimples, and a square jaw, the thirty-something man looked like Dr. Kildare reincarnated. He was the kind of doctor every woman dreamed of. He looked up and smiled at Jana, who found herself staring at him. *Wow, talk about a smile that melts your heart.*

"How are you doing, young lady? I'm Dr. Grant. You hit your head pretty hard."

Jana rubbed a tender spot just behind her temple. "It hurts a little, but my arm feels like it's on fire whenever I move."

"You have a concussion and also dislocated your shoulder. You'll recover fairly quickly from the concussion. The shoulder will require some physical therapy. We put it back in place and have been icing it. You can start with our physical therapist tomorrow. It should take about six weeks to fully heal. Here, let me check it one more time."

As he handed the file folder to Mrs. Grant, Jana noticed his wedding band. He checked her shoulder for swelling, then manipulated the joint, causing her to wince.

"Sorry." He retrieved the folder from his mother and scribbled a few notes before addressing Jana. "The swelling has gone down a little bit. You should continue to alternate ice and heat on it for another day or so. Ibuprofen should help with the discomfort and inflammation. By the way, we couldn't find a number to notify your family. Would you like to use our phone?"

"I'll call my uncle."

"Is his name Trevor?"

She gave the doctor a quizzical look. "No, why would you think that? His name is Vince Coleman."

"You kept calling out to a Trevor when we brought you into the clinic."

"He's the man I've been dating." Jana bit her bottom lip and studied her hands. "I guess I should call him, too."

The doctor nodded. "Mom, could you bring the phone in here for Miss Clawson?"

"Of course." The older woman left the room.

Dr. Grant wrote a few more notes in the chart. "I'd like to keep you here one more night for observation. Since there's no hospital in town, we have a couple of patient rooms for situations like this. My mother will be here with you."

"Oh, I'd hate to put her out."

As if on cue, Emma entered the room with the phone. "It's no problem, it's part of my job description."

Jana thanked her and asked, "Do you know what happened to my phone?"

Emma's brows knit together. "I don't remember seeing it when they brought you in last night. They towed your car to the local mechanic. I'll give Al a call later and see if he can find the phone."

"Thanks. I'd appreciate that."

"Well, I'll leave you alone to make your calls. I'll check in on you later."

Jana lay there staring at the phone. The reason she'd come to the coast hadn't changed. She still needed time away to sort out her feelings. *As soon as Trevor finds out about the accident, he'll rush out here and whisk me back to Portland before I have a chance to object.*

Her nervous habit of talking out loud exhibited itself as she sat up in bed, gathering her courage. "You might as well get this over with, Jana." She took a deep breath, hoping the call would ring through to Trevor's voicemail so she could leave a message. She was unprepared for her mixed feelings when he answered the phone. Warmth flooded her body at the sound of his rich baritone voice, and she longed for him to wrap his arms around her. But once again her reasonable side began to surface.

"Hey, Trevor, it's Jana."

"Where have you been? I tried your cell phone, and I've been calling the inn since last night. They said you never got there. What's going on?"

She plunged ahead. "I was in a little accident. I'm okay, just a little bruised and slightly broken."

"What do you mean by slightly broken?"

"It's really nothing. Just a concussion and a dislocated shoulder. The doctor says I'll be fine."

"Where are you? I'll be there right away."

Jana heard a jangling sound and imagined him heading toward the door as he pulled his keys out of his pocket. Her heart started pounding. "No!" she said vehemently, then softened her tone a little. "I . . . I still need time to think. I'll let you know how I am. Please, Trevor, please don't try to find me."

A long pause ensued. "Okay, if that's what you want, but if you need me, I'm just a phone call away."

"I know. Thank you."

"Sweetheart?"

"Yes?"

"Can you tell me what's stopping you from saying yes to me right away?"

How could she ever convey what she felt? Part of her wanted to pledge her heart to him, but her cautious side kept poking at her. "Oh, Trevor, it's hard to put into words. It's just a niggling feeling. That's why I need this time alone to think."

"Take your time, honey. I'll be waiting for you. Remember, you can share any concerns with me, and we'll work them out, the same way we'll handle any problems after we're married."

"Thanks for being so patient. I'll talk to you later. Love ya."

"I love you too. Bye, sweetheart."

———•———

After Trevor ended the call, he paced the room like a caged animal. The word "accident" caused panic to well up in his chest. He recalled Jana's parents' so-called accident and couldn't stand the idea of not knowing how or where she was. *What did she mean by a niggling feeling?* He stopped in mid-stride, his brow furrowed. *Is "niggling" even a word?* He shook the thought and resumed his to-and-fro course. *I should've never allowed her to go on this trip alone. I should've delivered her to the inn myself.*

He ran his fingers through his hair. *I can keep her safe. She belongs with me—why can't she see that?*

———•·•———

Jana hung up the phone with a sigh, mumbling to herself. "That went a lot better than I thought it would. Now I better give Uncle Vince a call."

Vince picked up before the first ring finished. "Jana. Where are you? What's happened? Are you okay?"

"Calm down, Uncle Vince. My tire blew out and I had a little accident."

"Are you hurt? We'll come and get you right away."

"It's just a dislocated shoulder and a concussion. I'd like to stay here."

"I'm glad it's not serious, but why not stick with Dr. Mills? You've gone to him for years."

Jane sighed. "To be honest, I still need some space. And I trust Dr. Grant. He says I need a bit of physical therapy for my shoulder, and there's an excellent PT in town."

After a hesitation, Vince replied in his booming voice, "If that's what you really want, stay there and get the therapy you need. Don't worry about a thing. I'll take care of the cost. Just concentrate on getting better. Sue will cover for you at the office."

"Thanks, Uncle Vince. You're my lifeline."

"Have you talked to Trevor yet?"

"Yes, I just got off the phone with him. He was ready to drive over right away, but I was able to convince him to wait."

"That must have taken a lot of sweet talking. I'm surprised he's not halfway there right now."

"You're telling me. He actually took no for an answer."

"Well, maybe you're having a good influence on him after all. Just remember, if you change your mind, we'll drop everything and come get you."

"Thanks, Uncle Vince. I've decided to stay here till my car is fixed. It's good to know you're just a phone call away."

"Now, darlin', your aunt Karen is chomping at the bit to talk to you. She won't be satisfied till she hears your voice."

"I love you, Uncle Vince." Jana heard a crackle as the phone was passed.

"Jana, are you really okay?" Karen's voice trembled.

"Yes, Aunt Karen. I'm a little sore, but just fine." A longing for her mother and gratitude for her aunt and uncle brought tears to Jana's eyes.

"Are you sure you don't want us to come pick you up?"

"I'm sure. It's like an extra week or two of vacation—maybe I'll be able to sort things out in my mind. That's why I'm here. I feel this is where my answers will come."

"Okay. But remember we can be there in a jiffy if you decide that's what you'd like."

"Thanks. I'll call you later."

"Get plenty of rest, dear."

After Jana hung up, a sob broke through and she looked heavenward. "Oh, Father, help me make the right choice."

Eight

Early the next morning, Jared Carpenter stood at the reception desk at the clinic. Dr. Grant had called him the night before about a patient who had been in a car accident, and they were discussing her treatment.

"Thanks for making time for her this morning, Jared."

"Not a problem at all."

"I think she could use a friend to talk to. Mom will do what she can, but Jana might like someone closer to her own age."

"Of course, Doc. I'll try to lend a listening ear. I'll go wake her up right now, and you and I can talk about her physical therapy while she's getting ready."

"Thanks, Jared. I knew I could count on you."

Jana was pulled from her dream by a gentle hand touching her good shoulder. She pried her eyes open to see the blurry form of a man leaning over her.

"Good morning, Miss Clawson. I'm Jared Carpenter, your physical therapist. I know it's early, but the doc wanted to make sure we started today."

She closed her eyes and shook her head in an attempt to make him vanish. When she opened her eyes again, he was still there, but at least her vision had cleared. Jared was compactly built, and judging from his athletic frame, she assumed he worked out regularly. His dark brown hair had a slight wave to it, and his brown eyes held a hint of mischief. She tried to smooth her hair, positive the picture she presented was not a very good one. *How do all those actresses wake up perfectly groomed in the movies?*

As Jared reached out to help her sit up, she asked, "What will I need to get started?"

"I'll give you about twenty minutes to shower and get dressed—"

Jana looked upward and muttered under her breath, "Thank goodness."

Jared chuckled. "—while I go over your chart with Doc Eric. It'll give me a chance to formulate a treatment program. Then we'll start. Wear something loose and comfortable." He left the room.

It's not like I have much choice in clothing. Jana groaned as she put her feet over the side of the bed. She hurt all over, with aches in muscles she didn't know she had.

In college, whenever she or her roommates woke up with particularly messy hair, they always blamed "Larry the Nighttime Hairdresser." Limping to the adjoining bathroom, she dared a peek in the mirror. Flinching at her reflection, she realized Larry had indeed made his rounds, and had in fact spent an extra amount of time on her. She was quite a sight with her hair sticking out at weird angles. One thing for certain, Mr. Carpenter had seen her at her worst, a claim that few other people could make. She rushed her shower, wondering about the condition of her clothes after the accident.

When she exited the bathroom, Jana found some scrubs folded on the bed. "Thank you, Mrs. Grant."

Jana dressed with care and had barely finished running a comb through her damp hair and brushing her teeth when Mr.

Carpenter returned. She risked another glance in the mirror. Still not her best, but a major improvement.

They passed the reception desk and waved at Emma Grant. Jana took hold of the fabric of her outfit and jiggled it before mouthing a thank you. Emma winked in response.

Jared opened the front door of the clinic, gesturing for Jana to go first. "My office is just across the street." He paused a moment to allow a red Ford Taurus to pass before crossing the road. He looked closely at Jana and asked, "Do I know you? You look familiar."

"I don't think so."

"Well, no matter. Here we are."

Looking around as they entered the building, Jana decided the word "office" was misleading. Beyond the reception area was a small cubbyhole that housed a paper-strewn desk and rows of files. The obsessive-compulsive organizer inside of her cringed. In comparison, the therapy area was remarkably well ordered. It boasted various exercise machines—stationary bikes, treadmills, weight machines, rubber balls of various sizes, parallel bars, ramps, a small pool, a hot tub, and a few contraptions with the distinct look of medieval torture devices. Jana's shoulder began to throb at the thought of the coming session.

Jared had her lay face down on a padded table, then applied heated lotion to her shoulder. "The heat will relax your muscles so they'll be easier to work with. You know, in years past, an injury like yours would have resulted in several weeks of immobility before we even tried to work with you. Now we realize that if you don't use it, you lose it. We try to begin exercises within a couple of days. You'll recover more of a full range of motion that way."

He continued to massage the shoulder in a circular motion. "Just relax."

Jana closed her eyes. After a few painful minutes the massage and heat worked their magic, and she had no problem following the therapist's advice. Her thoughts drifted to Trevor and the decision she had to make. Her breathing deepened, dreams teasing at her brain. Jared had a gentle strength in his touch and before she knew it, he was trying to wake her for the second time that day.

He laughed. "I'm glad you can relax around me."

"I'm sorry, it just felt so good."

"I hope you hold onto that memory. I don't think you're going to find the rest of the session quite so relaxing." With that statement, he let out a mad-scientist laugh. "Muah, ha ha ha ha!"

She couldn't help smiling as Jared helped her down from the table. He ushered her into the room with mirrors and mats, where they worked on stretching exercises. "To limber you up and prepare for future torture sessions," he explained. "So, what do you do for a living?"

"I'm an executive assistant."

"That's really impressive, especially for someone as young as you."

"Thanks." Even though Uncle Vince was her boss, she worked hard to prove to him she could handle it. She was proud of the trust he placed in her. "I kind of had an 'in' with the boss."

"The 'in' might have gotten you the job, but to keep it, you have to be good at what you do."

"I am." She paused. "Does that sound conceited?"

"Not at all. It sounds like you have confidence. We're just about done. Do you have a swimsuit?"

"In my suitcase in the car. The mechanic is supposed to bring it over this afternoon."

"Great. If you bring it for your afternoon session, you can try out the hot tub after."

Jared escorted Jana across the street to the clinic. "So, do you plan on staying in town for treatment, or will you head home?"

"Doctor Grant mentioned a small guest house behind his parents' home. Emma said they'd be willing to rent to me for a reasonable price. I figured I might stay there for a little while—at least until my car is fixed, maybe longer."

Jared nodded. "That's a nice little place and only a couple of blocks from the beach. Doc Eric and Andie lived there when they first got married. I think you'll like it."

"I hope so. I'll be heading there this afternoon."

"Why don't I pick you up for your afternoon session around 3:00, and then I'll take you over there."

Jana shook her head. "That's sweet of you, but I don't want to be a bother."

Jared opened the door to the clinic and smiled at her. "You're my last patient today, so it won't be a problem at all. Besides, I have a proposition for you." He turned toward the door, calling over his shoulder, "Bye now."

Jana stared at his retreating form with her mouth open. *What could he possibly mean by a proposition?*

She visited with Emma and received a tour of the entire clinic. Pride showed in Emma's eyes as she led Jana through the remodeled 1910 Victorian mansion. They ended the tour at Jana's room, and she imagined herself curled up in one of the soft chairs standing sentinel in front of the bay window. The antique table between them held several inviting magazines. It looked like the perfect escape from troubled thoughts.

"Whoever designed this really knew what they were doing. It's beautiful."

Emma took a small bow and smiled at her. "Thank you very much!"

"Wow! I'm really impressed. Remind me to call you when I need to decorate."

A tall, white-haired gentleman quietly approached Emma from behind and kissed her loudly on the cheek. "Hello, my love. Are you ready to go?"

"Almost, dear. Jana, this is my husband, Karl. Karl, this is one of Eric's patients, Jana Clawson."

He held out his hand. "I understand you'll be staying in our guest house. It'll be nice to have someone there, even if it's only for a little while." He squeezed his wife's hand. "I'll wait out in the lobby for you."

Jana looked at her watch. "I better make a couple of phone calls. Can I use your phone again? I'll be glad to get my cell phone back this afternoon."

"It's in the hall right outside your door. Go ahead and use it anytime. I'm off to get the cottage ready."

"Thanks again for staying the night here with me, and especially for the scrubs this morning."

"It was no problem at all." Emma gave a small wave as she left the room.

Jana settled into one of the comfortable chairs overlooking the yard and watched the Grants walk down the street arm in arm. *That's the kind of marriage I want. It reminds me of my parents.* She checked in with Uncle Vince before daring another call to Trevor.

"What do you mean you won't tell me where you are?" he barked about ten seconds into the call. "I'm not a stalker. I'm the man who just asked you to marry him."

"Please, Trevor. Don't raise your voice." Jana rubbed her temple where a headache was starting. "The reason I set off on this trip was to put some distance between us so I could think clearly."

"Jana, please reconsider," he said in a softer voice. "I'm going crazy here. I need to see for myself that you're okay."

A wave of guilt swept over her as she heard the quiver in his voice. He was a lot of bluster on the outside. He was arrogant, loud, and good at what he did. He knew what he wanted, and he went after it. But Jana was privy to this sensitive, vulnerable side of him.

On their two-week anniversary, Trevor had charmed Mrs. Cummings, the building manager, convincing her to let him inside Jana's apartment in order to scatter Hershey's hugs and kisses all around. He had been amused when Mrs. Cummings wouldn't allow him anywhere other than the kitchen and living room, but agreed to personally place the candy in the bedroom and closet for him. Jana found them in her kitchen drawers, the cabinets, all over her bed, on her nightstand, in her jewelry box, and under pillows on the couch. To this day, she was still finding little foil-wrapped candies in odd spots around her home—in fact, she'd found several in her suitcase when she was packing to go out to the coast.

Her heart softened at the memories. "Trevor, really, I'm okay. I've already had my first physical therapy session. Mr. Carpenter says I'm doing well. I leave the clinic this afternoon. See, I'm fine."

"No!" She heard a slam against something wooden. "I don't see. That's the problem. Please tell me where you are."

"Not yet. When I'm ready, I'll call you."

She cringed when Trevor hung up without saying another word. In three months of dating him, the only other time she'd seen him exhibit any kind of temper was the first day they met.

———•◦•———

Trevor was angry with Jana, and angry with himself for allowing her to bring out his anger. He seldom let his temper get the best of him. He prided himself on being in charge of his emotions at all times. He needed to get this situation under control or things would become unmanageable.

Why is she so stubborn? Why won't she tell me where she is? Doesn't she know I'm going crazy? He sighed and shook his head. *She won't tell me because she knows I'd head out there as soon as I learned where she was. She has no idea how important it is for me to know her location.* Those thoughts ran through his head as he picked up the phone and dialed a number he was thoroughly familiar with.

"Agent Townsend's office. May I help you?"

"Carole, this is Trevor Willis. Is Don in?"

"Just a moment."

Don's voice sounded on the speaker. "Trevor, how are things going?"

"They could be better. How are my sister and the kids?"

"Doing good. Your namesake just learned to ride a two-wheeler. But enough of the small talk—tell me what's wrong."

"Jana never made it to Seaside."

Trevor's brother-in-law sobered at once. "What?"

"She was in an accident, but she won't tell me where she is. She says she's trying to sort out her feelings and can't do that with me around."

Don let out a breath roughly. "So, she's okay?"

"Yeah. The accident seems genuine, but I need to know for certain."

"We all do. What do you want me to do?"

"Can you send someone to check things out? Find out where she is?" He ran his hand through his hair again. "And Don, have someone watch her."

"Weren't they going to do that at the inn?"

Trevor shook his head with an exasperated sigh. "If she was staying there, I wouldn't be nervous and would know where she was. Let me know when you find her."

"Sure, just let me get some details."

Nine

During the afternoon therapy session, Jared made his proposition. "As you can tell, paperwork and organization is not quite my thing." He gave Jana a lopsided grin.

"You can say that again," she mumbled.

He looked intently at her. "Did you say something?"

"Oh, uh, I just said I needed a pen." She smiled sweetly.

He reached into his shirt pocket and handed her one, along with a small notepad. His expression turned quizzical. "Can you write during therapy?"

She shrugged and handed back the items. "I guess not."

"Anyway, I was hoping you might be sticking around, and we could work out a deal where you would set up a system for me to track everything and get my files in order in exchange for your physical therapy." He stretched Jana's arm a little farther than was comfortable.

She gasped. "Ow!"

"Sorry. What do you think?"

"Well, it sounds interesting. What kind of hours are you talking about?"

"Maybe a couple per day—I might even throw in a few sightseeing tours if you want."

Jana told him she would think about it that night and let him know in the morning.

Fifteen minutes later, she soaked in the hot tub while Jared prepared to close the building. He drove her to the Bonnie Bee, the town's small grocery store, to pick up a few things, and then took her to the guest house.

After unloading her groceries, he went back to the car for her suitcase. "I must admit you pack pretty light," he commented as he brought it inside.

"I was only supposed to be gone for a week. How long will I need physical therapy?"

"We should have you ready to do cartwheels in about three weeks. After that, you'll be able to do some exercises at home till your shoulder is fully healed. What do you think?"

She smiled. "With your torture sessions, it sounds like an eternity. I'll just have to live with it."

He made to leave but turned to face her again. "Do you like Chinese?"

"Chinese what?" she asked mischievously. "Dragons? Jump rope? Checkers?"

Jared chuckled and shook his head. "Everyone's a comedian. I meant food."

"Actually, it's my favorite."

"We have a great Chinese place here in town. If you'd like, I'll get some takeout and bring it back for dinner. Consider it a bribe to get you to say yes to my files."

Jana thought about it, then made a conscious decision to encourage this friendship. "I'd like that."

"Great, it'll take about twenty minutes. You should ice your shoulder while I'm gone. See ya."

She watched the door close before calling the Colemans. "Aunt Karen, how are you? I moved into a little cottage, and I just wanted to let you know where I am." She paced the floor and tried to put away groceries while she visited. When she cradled the phone between her ear and good shoulder, she couldn't lift anything with her other hand. One attempt at cradling it on her injured side was enough to stop her in her tracks.

"Are you sure you don't want me to come over there and help you out?" Karen asked.

"No. I'm doing well. The doctor's parents are renting this place out to me for a great price. Emma's very nice. You'd like her."

"Okay. Vince says I need to let you have your space. But if you need anything, I can clear my schedule and be there in a flash."

"Thanks, Aunt Karen. You're awesome. I'll call you later. Love ya."

"I love you too, dear."

Jana faced her groceries and began to organize them. She folded the last bag as Jared knocked on the door.

He returned with several takeout cartons in tow. "I got a variety of stuff. We have egg drop soup, sweet and sour pork, beef with broccoli, orange chicken, and of course, pork fried rice, egg rolls, and fortune cookies."

Her eyes opened wide as she looked at the numerous containers in his hands. "I think you bought enough for an army."

He shrugged sheepishly. "It's my favorite food, too."

"I was just thinking about my friend Sue. She says her little mother-in-law from China can't believe what we Americans call Chinese food."

Jared dished out a generous portion of fried rice. "Well, whatever it is, I love it."

Once they finished dinner, Jared presented the fortune cookies to Jana and said, "They gave us an extra one."

"They probably thought all of this food was for a lot more people than two."

"You choose one, then I will, and we'll share the last one."

"All right," Jana replied.

"You read yours first."

She carefully broke open the cookie and pulled out the small slip of paper. "'You are about to make a new friend.' I like that one."

"Me too. Okay, here goes." He crushed his cookie and pulled the slip of paper out of wreckage. "'No man is without enemies.'" Jared pretended to shiver. "That's rather ominous."

"Wow. If you like the next one better, you can keep it instead."

"It's a deal."

They each took an end of the final cookie and broke it apart like a wishbone, then held the paper between them and read it together. "Help! I'm being held prisoner in a Chinese bakery!"

Stunned silence followed before they simultaneously broke out in peals of laughter.

Jared wiped tears from his eyes as he stopped laughing long enough to comment. "That's the weirdest fortune cookie I've ever had."

"You can say that again."

"I better go and let you get your rest. Try to load up on calcium and vitamin D—plenty of dairy products and sunshine." He opened the door and looked at the threatening sky, holding his palm out as if testing for rain. "At least, as much sunshine as you can get here. Oh, don't forget protein, too. It'll help strengthen your muscles and get you ready for the inquisition the next few weeks."

"Good night. Thanks for everything."

"Do you need me to pick you up in the morning?"

"No. I think it's supposed to be a nice day, so I'll walk on over. Hopefully I'll get the sun exposure I need."

"Okay." Jared looked skeptically at the heavy clouds. "Do you have a cell phone?"

"Yes."

"Why don't I input my number and you can call if you change your mind."

Jana retrieved the phone from her purse. "I just got it back from the mechanic when he brought my suitcase by the clinic. It must have fallen out of my purse during the accident. Funny thing, though, he said it was in the back seat." She opened it and pushed a few buttons before handing it to Jared. "I'll even put you on speed dial. You're number 9."

He keyed in his number and returned her phone. "See ya tomorrow."

The next morning, Jana woke up tired and sore. She had a hard time getting comfortable and ended up tossing and turning. She couldn't stop thinking about Trevor and how hurt he had sounded. *Why can't he understand I need time away from him so I can make a decision?* At 3:03 AM, she had covered her head with her pillow, letting out a frustrated scream, before she finally got up and settled into the comfortable, cocoa-colored suede recliner with some milk and cookies, ultimately falling asleep watching infomercials on TV. This prompted dreams about growing herbs on a Trevor chia head, dicing them with the Quick Chopper, and sealing the chopped spices in a Space Bag before freezing them.

Six thirty came a lot sooner than she expected. After a minor struggle, she finally won the battle with the footrest and pulled herself out of the chair. A hot shower did much to ease the aches and pains, and Jana spent the final few minutes under an invigorating spray of cold water in an attempt to wake up.

She looked at the clock and dressed in her swimsuit with sweats and a T-shirt over it. She didn't bother drying her hair or putting on makeup, since she'd probably end up in the hot tub after her session. It was only a five-minute walk to the physical therapy building, and she arrived at her appointment with seconds to spare.

Jared looked up from the file in his hand. "Good morning. How are you feeling?"

"Do you want the truth?"

"Always." He closed the file, giving her his full attention.

She groaned. "I'm tired and sore."

He ushered her to the padded table. "Well, I'll try to do something about the sore. I don't know about the tired."

"Another one of those massages might do the trick." Jana grinned hopefully.

Smiling, he shook his head. "Remember, today is inquisition day. You ready to be even sorer?" He cocked his head to one side. "Is 'sorer' a word? No matter. Let me help you onto the table."

She complied and closed her eyes as he began the heated massage again.

"Have you thought about my proposal?" he asked after a few minutes. "I could really use your help."

"I did," she replied groggily. "I've decided to stay here for therapy, so I'll go ahead and help you out."

"Great! When can you begin?"

"Today?"

Jared gave her a little bow. "Thank you, thank you, thank you! I really don't know where or how to start."

"After we finish the session, I'll go home and eat breakfast, then try to rest for a bit. I'll be back here around ten."

"Fantastic. Now, come over here by the wall. This is an exercise you can do at home. Stand about ten inches from the wall." He scooted her over a bit.

At his touch, a tingly feeling spread through her. "Is it warm in here?" she said with a frown. "I know I'm too young, but I feel like I've just had a hot flash."

He put his hand on her forehead. "Are you okay? Did you need some water?" He pulled up a chair for her, then went to the water cooler and returned with a small, cone-shaped cup of cold water. "Here, drink this."

Jana took the water. "Thanks. It seems to have passed now."

"Has this ever happened before?" With her wrist in his hand, Jared found her pulse and counted while he looked at his watch.

"Never, but I'm fine now." She stood up.

He looked at her skeptically. "This sort of thing can happen with exercise, especially after a head injury. If it happens again, make sure you sit down immediately. No fainting on my watch." Checking her position, Jared supported her arm. "Good. Good. Now let your fingers climb the wall."

"Is this a case of letting my fingers do the walking?"

"If you can joke about it, you must not be in too much pain."

Jana looked over her shoulder at him as her fingers continued their ascent up the wall. "Where did you go to school?"

"Checking my credentials?"

"Maybe," she teased.

"I got my bachelor's in exercise science at BYU, then my masters in physical therapy from University of Utah."

Her eyebrows arched, and she stopped in mid-motion to face him, momentarily forgetting the exercise. "You're LDS?"

Jared smiled back at her. "Guilty as charged. Do you want to check my horns?" He leaned toward her and rubbed the top of his head.

"Want to check mine?" she replied with a chuckle.

"Really? You're LDS too? Awesome." He readjusted her position. "There's a Young Adult activity this Friday—a dance and hayride. Would you like to go?"

She thought a moment. "I'm not sure. I don't really know if I'll be up to dancing."

He coaxed. "It's a free dinner, and the company's great."

"Well . . ." She looked at his expectant expression and didn't have the heart to refuse. "All right. I'll come."

"Fantastic. I'll work your shoulder extra hard to prepare for the evening."

She rolled her eyes. "Oh, great."

Jared left her in the hot tub as another patient came in. The swirling jets seemed to erase Jana's tension, and by the time she left, her shoulder really did feel better.

After breakfast with Emma, Jana returned to the clinic and sat down in Jared's office. She started looking at the files. *Everyone has a method of organization. Now, if I can just figure out Jared's.* She sorted through the papers on the desk, reading all the little yellow sticky notes on them. She tried comparing the appointment book with the names on the files.

"Bingo!" she called to no one in particular.

"Want me to verify your card?"

Jana jumped and turned to see Jared casually leaning against the doorjamb with his arms folded across his chest.

She laughed. "Are you trying to give me a heart attack? I think I've decoded part of your so called 'system.'"

"You're even better than I thought."

"Why, thank you." She rose to file some papers and directed a curtsy toward him. "I aim to please."

"Did you get some rest?" he asked.

"I slept about an hour."

"That's good." He nodded toward the rows of medical charts. "Any suggestions?"

"A secretary?"

Jared raised his eyebrows. "Are you applying for the job?"

"I don't think I could handle the emotional stress of keeping you organized—it's much more relaxing to help keep a multimillion-dollar business running. Back to the task at hand, do I have a budget for supplies?"

"Just get whatever you need. See Marty at Casey's Office Supply. He'll answer any questions and arrange to have it delivered. I'll get the bill later."

"Okay, I'll try to not put you into bankruptcy."

"That's nice of you."

She walked to the office supply store and found Marty at the front register. "Jared Carpenter sent me over here to get some office supplies. He said to talk to you."

"Sure thing, ma'am. Let me get a cart."

Jana smiled as he rounded the corner with an oversized cart reminiscent of Costco or Home Depot.

"Jared's a great guy," he remarked, "the kind who would give you the shirt off his back, but I've seen his office."

Marty followed her around making useful suggestions while grabbing file folders, pens, pencils, a whiteboard, dry-erase markers, and stacking trays. An hour or so later, Jana walked back into the therapy office.

Jared looked up from some paperwork. "I was about to send out a posse. Did you find everything?"

"Mostly. Marty said he'd load up the big truck and deliver it in the morning. I think I stopped short of bankrupting you. Actually, I was afraid to ask how much it cost, but my best guesstimate is somewhere under a thousand dollars."

Jared pretended to stumble backward in shock. "You sure know how to spend a guy's money. I was going to offer to buy lunch, but now it looks like you'll have to treat me."

"Of course." She smiled and reached for her purse. "It's my turn anyway."

He offered his arm and ushered her outside. "Not on your life. There's no way I'd let a beautiful woman buy my lunch."

"Are you a chauvinist?"

"No, just a gentleman. Plus I'm extremely grateful for what you're doing. Let's go get a sandwich."

Jana didn't notice the nondescript car parked across the street and the man behind the wheel, snapping pictures of her and Jared.

As they walked to the café, an older man in jeans and a plaid flannel shirt stopped raking his yard and called out, "Hey, Jared. How's it going?"

"Great, Herb. How's the new grandson?"

"Growing like a weed."

A few houses later, a woman hanging white sheets on her clothesline greeted him. "Hi, Jared!"

"Hello, Mrs. Schuler."

A voice hailed him from above. "Good morning, Jared."

Jana spotted a man on a ladder painting the trim on the house.

"Hi, Fred," Jared replied. "Nice day."

Fred waved back with his paintbrush. "Sure is."

Jana turned to Jared, chuckling. "I feel like we're in a Subway commercial and everyone's saying hi to Jared."

He laughed heartily. "We're a regular Mayberry. Sometimes I expect to see Andy Taylor walking down the street." They approached a building with a green-and-white awning with the words "Gardner's Garden Deli" in large white lettering.

A set of bells jingled when Jared opened the door, bringing a stout, middle-aged woman to the front counter. Her apron was stained with mustard, and wisps of gray escaped the bobby pins holding her hair back into a bun. She was a plain woman until her smile erupted, transforming that plainness into beauty.

"Good morning, Jared, or should I say afternoon?"

He looked at his watch. "I think afternoon is more accurate. I'd like you to meet Jana Clawson. Jana, this is Mrs. Gardner. She makes one mean sandwich."

Jana smiled. "It's nice to meet you."

"What can I get for you?" She wiped her hands on her apron.

Jana looked over the numerous offering on the menu before addressing Mrs. Gardner. "What do you recommend?"

"My personal favorite is chicken salad on a ciabatta roll."

"That sounds delicious. I'll try it."

Mrs. Gardner reached for the fresh bread and sliced it with a sharp knife. "Mustard or mayo?"

"Mustard, please."

She slathered on the mustard with practiced ease before adding a generous scoop of homemade chicken salad. "Do you want bacon, lettuce, tomato, alfalfa sprouts, and onion?"

"Everything but onion."

"I just made some fresh strawberry lemonade. Would you like some?'

"Yes, please."

"The usual, Jared?"

"Yes, and I'll have some lemonade too."

Mrs. Gardner handed Jared the glasses and straws. "Go on and sit down, and I'll get your food right out."

"Thanks."

They found a small table in the corner with a view of the street. A red gingham tablecloth graced the table, with a single daisy in a vase. A painted flower garden with a white picket fence filled an entire wall. Jared placed the drinks on the table, pulled out the white wrought-iron chair for Jana, and sat opposite her.

"So, what brings you out here?" he asked her.

"I was heading to Seaside for a vacation. On the way I swerved to avoid hitting a rabbit, and you know the rest."

"So why were you on vacation by yourself?" He twisted the end of the paper sleeve on the straw. "If I'm too nosey, just tell me." He blew on the straw, sending the wrapper toward her.

"Hey! Just remember, Mr. Carpenter, I don't get mad, I get even."

Jana brushed the wrapper off her arm onto the table. She looked into his eyes and felt nothing but kindness. In that moment, a ping of recognition nudged her soul. *Where have I seen those eyes before?* Her heart whispered that anything she told him was safe.

She picked up the straw wrapper and held it between her fingers before she tossed it toward him. "After this wrapper fight, I kind of feel like you're the brother I never had. So, I guess from a brother, it's not too nosey."

He leaned forward, giving her his complete attention. "Go ahead, Sis."

She took a deep breath. "I came because I received a marriage proposal, and I needed to get away to figure out how I feel."

Jared picked up the discarded wrapper and rolled it into a ball. "You know, it's really none of my business, but if I asked a girl to marry me and instead of jumping into my arms she took off for a week to decide, I might be worried."

She nodded. "He doesn't know where I am, and he's pretty upset that I won't tell him."

Jared threw the paper wad, which bounced off Jana's forehead. "Would it help if you talked about it? I'm told I'm a good listener."

They were interrupted by Mrs. Gardner delivering their sandwiches. "Here you go—enjoy. Let me know if you need anything else."

"Thank you. It looks wonderful." Jana picked up the crumpled wrapper and tossed it back at Jared, missing him completely. "Now what was I saying?"

"You were about to tell me about the guy who proposed to you."

"Right. I'll try." She closed her eyes and rubbed her temple before looking at Jared again. "Trevor Willis is a very successful businessman. I met him when he came into the office." She looked down, absently playing with a potato chip on her plate while a smile found its way to her face. "Dating Trevor is like dating a tornado. He swept me off my feet. I really like him, and it's been rather flattering, but he's not a member of the Church."

"Oh." Jared gave her a knowing look. "I see."

"He doesn't mind if I go to church, but he always has an excuse not to go with me. That's part of what bothers me." Jana took a bite of her sandwich. "Mmm. This really is good!"

Jared laughed. "I told you, this is the best place around."

"I didn't realize you meant *this* good. The bread is to die for. I wonder if I could package Mrs. Gardner up and bring her back to Portland with me."

"You might have to fight Mr. Gardner for her." Jared speared a cherry tomato with his fork. "Back to the subject at hand. If Trevor was a member, would you have said yes right away?"

Jana took another bite of sandwich and thought as she chewed. "I don't know. There's just something about him that scares me a little."

Jared frowned. "What do you mean? Has he ever hurt you?"

"No, of course not! He's always been a perfect gentleman, except the first time I met him. No, I take that back. He's always been a perfect gentleman. It's just . . . well, I've seen some of his business dealings. He seems to feel that the end always justifies the means."

"And sometimes the means are not quite as kosher as you'd like."

"Yeah. That's the other thing. He says it's just business."

"Well, I don't want to sway you one way or the other," Jared said solemnly, "but just remember, sometimes the professional spills over to the personal."

"I know. I just need to make sure of how I feel. I care about him very much, and I don't want to hurt him." Jana sighed. "Every time I'm around him, all the doubts disappear, and I think, 'Yes, I could spend my life with this man.' Then, I go home and those pesky little concerns come flooding back."

"Ahh. Hence the reason for the solitary vacation. Wow, you've got a lot to consider. I don't envy you. You're welcome to use me as a sounding board any time you want." Jared looked at his watch. "I have a patient coming in fifteen minutes, so we better get back to the office."

He stood and began to clear their plates from the table, then bent down to grab the wrapper from the floor. When he helped her out of her seat, she impulsively kissed him on the cheek.

"Thanks, Jared."

He laughed. "I'd be glad to listen anytime—especially if I get that kind of response. Did you want anything else?"

She gazed toward the counter with an impish grin. "I think one of those chocolate chip cookies is calling to me."

Jared called out to the shopkeeper in the back room. "Mrs. Gardner, could we have a couple of cookies to go?"

"Sure, Jared." She picked the two largest cookies, placed them in a small white paper bag, and handed it to him with a wink. "No charge."

"Thanks." He turned toward Jana and guided her out the door. "Let's head back to the office."

The moment was digitally captured by the man in the inconspicuous dark car.

Ten

Trevor pressed his forehead against the cool glass. Like a brain freeze after ice cream, pain shot through his head. "What more can I do, Jana? How can I convince you to let me take care of you?"

He paced the floor. *Maybe I underestimated how much her church means to her. I've told her I'd never stop her from going. Maybe I should—*

The buzzer interrupted his thoughts. "Mr. Willis, Mr. Townsend is on the phone."

"Thanks, Brenda, put him through."

"Yes, sir. Line two."

"Don. What did you find out?"

"We located her late last night. She's in a small town on the coast where a Dr. Eric Grant runs a clinic. She was brought there after the accident. When she was discharged, she rented a guest house from the doctor's parents. She goes twice daily to physical therapy. There should be an envelope being delivered any time now with—"

A knock sounded at the door. "Mr. Willis, this just came for you from Mr. Townsend. I thought you'd want it right away."

Trevor covered the mouthpiece as he spoke to his secretary. "You're right. Thanks, Brenda." She closed the door behind her. "It just got here, Don."

Trevor opened the envelope and glanced through the pictures. He gripped the phone with white knuckles, trying to control the anger surging through him. "Who is he?"

Don laughed. "I guess I don't need to ask who you're talking about. His name is Jared Carpenter. He's the physical therapist. Seems like a good guy. Everyone in town speaks highly of him. He graduated from Brigham Young University and has a master's from the University of Utah—"

"So, he's Mormon," Trevor interrupted. "Is he married?"

"No, he's single, twenty-eight years old. He served a mission for the Mormon Church in England. He's a third-degree black belt and even had a top-secret clearance in the military—which is a bit odd since he was only on active duty for a couple of years. He checks out clean. So do the doctor and his parents."

"Are you sure? No significant cash deposits or debts that could be used to turn him?"

"Do you think I can't do my job? I know what to look for." Irritation seeped into Don's voice.

"What about that guy you took in for questioning—the one hanging around Coleman Industries?" Trevor tapped his pen on the desk.

"There was a perfectly innocent explanation."

Trevor made a dismissive gesture with his hand. "Like what?"

"He's Sue Williams's husband."

"Oh. Well, I just don't like her so out in the open. Any more insight into her accident?"

"We're looking into it. Lasky arrived this morning. He's one of my best. With his team, she'll be covered 24/7."

"Okay. Thanks, Don."

"If you asked my advice, I'd tell you to give her the space she needs. She's safe. Don't go rushing in like a bull in a china shop."

"I'm not asking," a tired Trevor replied. "Give Traci and the kids my love."

He hung up the phone and finished flipping through the pictures, his jealousy increasing with every photo of Jared and Jana. He got to the last one, which showed Carpenter taking her by the elbow as if he owned her. Trevor tore the picture in half, then crumpled Jared's image and tossed it in the trashcan. "Clean or not, this guy could be trouble," Trevor said in a tone so menacing it would've sent shivers down a person's spine. He punched the intercom button. "Brenda, could you step in here?"

"What do you need, sir?"

"I want a complete financial and personal work-up on Jared Carpenter. Don't involve Don Townsend." Trevor fished through the report. "Here's Carpenter's address. This is top priority."

"Yes, sir." Brenda headed toward the door.

"Oh . . ." Trevor began.

She turned back to her boss.

"Clear my schedule for the next couple of days. I'll be heading out of town on personal business."

"Okay, will do, sir."

The door closed, and Trevor looked at another picture of Jared. "We'll see about you, Mr. Carpenter. I think I'll check you out personally." He slammed his fist down on the remaining pictures.

———•———

Jana spent her days doing physical therapy and trying to set up a filing system for Jared. When she wasn't at the therapy building, she spent a lot of time wandering the beach and reading. A couple of times Emma invited her, along with Jared, over for dinner. Friday night found Jana excited for the Young Adult activity. She hadn't realized how much she missed associating with Church members since she'd started dating Trevor.

She couldn't stop thinking about her last conversation with him. It had ended all right, but some things he mentioned had set off warning bells in her head.

"I'm doing pretty well. Therapy is helping. I can move my arm up a few more inches than when I started. Jared says I'm improving."

"I'm glad." Trevor's voice was full of forced nonchalance. "Who's Jared?"

"He's my physical therapist. I'm doing some work for him in exchange for the therapy. He's a bit, well, more than a bit, disorganized, and I'm setting up a sys—"

"You don't have to do that!"

Jana flinched at Trevor's intensity. "What is wrong?"

He exhaled. "All I meant was that you don't have to worry about the cost. I'll take care of everything. You just use this time to rest and recuperate."

"Trevor, it's no big deal. It's just a couple of hours a day. It helps to pass the time. Jared's been really kind to me, so it's the least I can do to thank him."

"Oh, I see," Trevor said, and Jana pictured his eyes narrowing. "And how 'really kind' has he been to you?"

Jana's annoyance turned to indignation. "And just what are you insinuating? Jared is a perfect gentleman, and he's been a good friend to me."

She heard Trevor inhale a deep breath. "I'm sorry, Jana, I didn't mean to sound that way, and I certainly didn't mean to insinuate anything."

"It's okay." A tear escaped her eye.

"Jana, before you go, I have something to tell you."

"I'm listening."

"I've been thinking about us. I think it's important for a husband and wife to have the same goals and values system, so I've decided to try to learn about your church—see if I can believe it."

"That's great! But you have to do it for yourself, not for me."

"I know. It would never work otherwise. Why don't you tell me where you are, and I'll come down on Saturday and we can discuss it. It's been a week now."

"Trevor, no. I still need to find an answer for myself. When you're here, I can't think straight."

He laughed, and for the first time in the conversation he sounded like the pre-proposal Trevor. "I know. That's what I'm counting on—to woo you with my charm!"

"You're incorrigible." She shook her head.

"I know, but you have to love me, right?"

"Goodbye, Trevor," she said with a chuckle.

A knock on the door interrupted her thoughts. She opened it and found Jared waiting. He smiled. "Hi! Are you ready to go?"

"Yes, just let me grab a sweater."

"You look great. How's the arm feeling? I tried to go easy on you today."

Jana rubbed her shoulder. "Thanks for the compliment and for going easy on me. You look nice too. I like that shirt."

"Thanks. My mom has pretty good taste. So, we'll be picking up a couple more people on the way. There are only a few young adults in town, and we try to carpool as much as possible." He helped her with the sweater.

"Great. I've really been looking forward to tonight."

He closed her car door and then climbed into the driver's side. As he backed out of the driveway, he said, "You seem like something's weighing on your mind."

"I talked to Trevor. He said he wanted to learn more about the Church."

"That's wonderful." Jared paused. "Has he ever mentioned it before?"

"No. He's always said it was fine for me, but he wasn't interested."

"Well, I'm glad he's thinking about it."

Jana stared at her hands. "What if this is the end justifying the means?"

"Ahh. You mean he'd join the Church if the end result was marrying you?"

"That's exactly what I mean."

"Tread carefully, Jana. I'd hate to see you hurt." Jared squeezed her hand just before they pulled in front of a small home. "This is Caitlyn's place. She's a lot of fun—you'll love her. Zack's around the corner. He comes to town every few months and helps his uncle for a month or two, then leaves again."

"What does he do that lets him get off work so often?"

Jared shrugged his shoulders. "I have no idea, but he just got back in town on Tuesday. I think he's sweet on Caitlyn. You'll discover he's one of a kind."

"One of a kind? What do you mean?"

Jared grinned mysteriously. "You'll see."

A cute redhead bounded down the driveway, her short curls bouncing. Jared jumped out of the car to open the back door on the driver's side.

"Hi! I'm Caitlyn. You must be Jana." Caitlyn's smile lit up her green eyes as she climbed into the car. "It's nice to have another girl on these outings."

Jared put the car in gear. "Well, we better get going. Zack isn't always the most patient person."

After they pulled up to his uncle's house, Zack plopped down next to Caitlyn in the back seat. He nodded his head toward Jana. "Hey there." While buckling his seatbelt, he asked, "Why did the chicken cross the playground?"

"I don't know. Why did the chicken cross the playground?" Jana chuckled.

"To get to the other slide."

A chorus of groans erupted in the car, and Jared said, "Already, Zack?"

"Why did the gum cross the road?"

"We're afraid to ask." Caitlyn put her head in her hands.

"It was stuck to the chicken's foot!" Zack erupted in laughter. "How about this one? Yo momma's so fat that when they went to the ocean, a whale started singing 'We are family . . .'"

"Boo, hiss," Jared exclaimed. But under all the jeering, everyone laughed as hard as Zack, which was a good thing, because his stream of corny jokes lasted the entire thirty-minute drive.

The singles activity was held in a red barn decorated with Chinese lanterns, crepe paper, and bales of straw. A large green John Deere tractor attached to a hay-covered trailer sat by the side of the barn. After the opening prayer, the partygoers ate a dinner of hamburgers, potato chips, and oversweet fruit punch.

A man stood up and took the microphone. "May I have your attention? We'd like to thank the singles ward elders for the wonderful meal of grilled charcoal—er, hamburgers. For the next activity, the Relief Society is in charge of the food." Laughter and applause erupted in the group. "We'd like to thank the Pattersons for letting us use their barn, and especially Brother Patterson for volunteering to take us on a hayride." He pointed to a tall redheaded man in overalls, who blushed and raised his hand as the crowd cheered for him. "Now, if we can get everyone over to the trailer by the barn, we'll get started."

The foursome headed over with the crowd. Jana was about to climb onto the trailer when Jared surprised her by scooping her up in his arms and gently placing her on the hay-cushioned surface. He winked at her. "We can't have you re-injuring your shoulder. If you hurt it again, who would I get to do my paperwork?"

She answered with a grin and settled comfortably with her back against a bale of hay. Zack lifted Caitlyn onto the wagon before sandwiching Jana between himself and Jared to protect her from too much movement. Caitlyn sat on the other side of

Zack. Jana had forgotten how nice it was to be with a group of friends who shared her beliefs and cared about one another.

Following the hayride, Jana sat on the sideline watching the square dancing. Placing her hands in her sweater pocket, she was surprised to feel a few small lumps inside. Pulling them out, she smiled at the small, foil-wrapped Hershey's Kisses. *I guess it's been awhile since I've worn this sweater.* She enjoyed a chocolate while watching her companions.

Jared and Caitlyn were pretty good. Zack was a crackup, and Jana wondered where some of his moves came from. As Jana tossed the final piece of chocolate up in the air several times, her mind wandered away from the festivities.

Trevor pulled up to a modest home with tulips and daffodils overflowing the flower beds. Jana's nervousness increased while she waited for him to open her door. This was her first meeting with anyone in his family, and to meet his sister was especially unnerving. Traci and Trevor were as close as peanut butter and jelly—after all his stories, it was hard to think of one without the other.

He reached for Jana's hand and helped her out of his classic Mustang, giving her a squeeze. "Don't worry, sweetheart. You're going to love Traci." He kissed her forehead. "And she won't be able to help loving you. Trust me."

"But what if she doesn't? I know how much her opinion means to you."

"Honey." He faced Jana and placed his hands on her shoulders. "She'll love you, because I love you."

Panic welled up in her chest, and she fought the urge to flee. Her chance slipped away when Traci Townsend opened the door and embraced her.

"Jana, it's so good to finally meet you. I can see why Trevor is so enchanted." After giving Trevor a kiss on the cheek, she took Jana's arm and led her out to the patio.

Traci introduced Jana to her husband, Don, who was grilling chicken.

He clasped her hand. "So, you're the girl that finally turned Trevor's head."

Her gaze lingered on the floor. "I . . ."

Trevor rescued her. "Come on, Don. Don't embarrass her. Remember, this is the one I don't want you to scare away."

Jana and Traci sat at the picnic table watching Emy, Little Trevor, and Scott play with their golden retriever puppy. Trevor and Don talked by the grill.

"I'm trying to work a deal with Jim Avery," Trevor said to his brother-in-law.

Don held a piece of chicken above the grill and stared at Trevor. "Really?" He finished turning it.

"I need to find out what makes him tick."

"He's a hard one to crack. From what I've heard of him, he has no vices—a real family man."

Trevor slapped Don on the back. "I'm sure you'll find something. You're the best."

Jana looked at Traci. "What does Don do?"

She reached down to pick up her toddler. "He's a spe—"

"He's a specialist in finding missing persons. A private investigator." Trevor touched his sister's shoulder, giving her a strange look.

Traci glanced between her husband and brother. "Um, yes. He's a P.I."

Jana shifted her gaze from Trevor to his sister. In the intense silence, the faint sound of a neighbor's piano drifted on the breeze. The children giggled and danced in a circle.

Trevor's smile erupted, and he pulled Jana into his arms. "Dance with me."

She snapped back to the present. "What?"

"Jana. Would you like to dance?" Jared held his hand out.

Forgetting the candy still in her grasp, she accepted.

"Is that for me?"

Jana laughed. "I found it in my pocket. Are you sure you want it?"

"I never pass up chocolate." He unwrapped the slightly melted Kiss and popped it into his mouth. "Thanks!"

She danced a few times with Jared and once with Zack. Zack polka'd when he should have waltzed, and added a few quick steps and turns. She jumped back when he kicked above her head with a lanky leg, completing the move with a karate chop or two. Yes, one dance with Zack was more than enough.

On the way home, they stopped at Baskin Robbins. Jana took a lick of her nutty coconut ice cream cone. "You're a pretty good dancer, Jared. Where did you learn?"

"I was on the ballroom dance team at BYU. It was a lot of fun."

"What about me?" Zack asked. "Have you ever seen anyone dance like me?"

"Why Zack, I . . . um . . . I can honestly say I've never seen anything like it before."

Zack feigned hurt feelings but couldn't contain his laughter.

"You have an extremely unique style of dancing," Caitlyn assured him. "There's only one of you." She squeezed his arm. "Zack and I were talking about visiting Mount. St. Helens tomorrow. Would you guys like to come with us?"

Zack grinned. "Actually, Jared's car is the only reliable one, and we thought he might like to drive."

"I don't have any therapy sessions tomorrow, so I can do that. What do you think, Jana, would you like to go?"

"Does it entail much hiking or use of my shoulder?"

"No, there shouldn't be a problem. You can actually drive within five miles of the crater, to the Johnston Observatory."

"I'd like that."

"Great!" Jared slapped the steering wheel. "You can count Jana and me in."

They stopped at Caitlyn's house. Zack exited the car with Caitlyn. "Jared, I think I'll see Caitlyn to the door. Thanks for the ride."

Jared called through Jana's open window, "We'll see you guys around 8:00 tomorrow morning."

"Bye. It was nice to meet you both." Jana waved.

The car door closed, and Jared's headlights illuminated Zack as he casually draped his arm around Caitlyn's shoulder.

Jared laughed as the two headed toward the house. "I hope you had a good time tonight, Jana, even though you didn't get much of a chance to dance."

"I had a blast. It was great to be with everyone. Thanks so much for inviting me."

He stopped in front of her house and walked around the car to help her out. He placed his hand on her back and gently guided her to the door. "Well, thanks for coming with us. I'll see you in the morning."

"Thanks again, Jared."

He headed for his car but turned back. "I almost forgot. Be sure to bring a jacket. It might be cold on the mountain. See ya."

Once again, no attention was paid to the dark car across the street. Only this time, there were two men inside, and one of them fumed as he watched Jared escort Jana to the door.

———•———

Jana woke with a start in the middle of the night. She sat straight up in bed, her heart pounding wildly.

"Is someone there? Trevor?"

She shook her head. *Why in the world would I think he was here?* Attempting to convince herself, she whispered, "It must have been a dream—those charcoal burgers talking back to me." She shivered as she rubbed her goosebump-covered arms. "It was just so real."

She went into the kitchen to get a drink of water. After she left the bedroom, a silent figure quickly stepped out of the shadows and through the sliding glass door into the dark night.

———•—•———

Back at his hotel, Trevor unlocked the door. He collapsed in the chair, still feeling unnerved by Jana's near discovery. *How could she know I was there? That was definitely too close for comfort.*

"This has got to stop," he said aloud. "In the morning, I'll go to her, and we'll talk. She'll have to come home with me."

Sprawled out on the bed fully clothed, he closed his eyes, but nightmares soon disturbed his sleep. One of his dreams was especially vivid. In it, he asked Jana to marry him and kissed her. As he stepped back from her, she turned into a bird. He tried to hold her, but she flew just out of his reach. He got a net and snagged her, but her wing was injured. She flew crookedly to Jared Carpenter, looking at Trevor accusingly. Sweat poured off his face as he woke up in the blackness calling, "Jana! Come back!" After that, sleep came in snatches.

Eleven

Jana jumped at every noise she heard, eventually falling asleep in the wee hours of the morning. She woke in time to take a shower, put a little makeup on, and pull her wet hair into a ponytail before Jared arrived.

A knock called her to the front door. "Good morning, sunshine." He smiled. "How did you sleep last night?"

"Pretty good till about 1:00 when I woke up from a strange dream." She shivered.

Concern clouded his expression. "Hey, are you okay? Do you want to tell me about it?"

Jana filled him in as they headed to his car. "I dreamed Trevor was in the room watching me. It was so strange. I woke up with a start—you know how it is when you're sleeping and feel someone watching you?"

"Yeah, I've felt that before." Jared chuckled. "Usually, that someone was my mom, and I knew I was in real trouble."

"Well, when I woke up, it just seemed like Trevor had been there."

"Dreams can be pretty strange sometimes," Jared said lightly.

They drove to Caitlyn's house, where Caitlyn and Zack were out front waiting for them. Jared rolled down the window. "Going our way?"

Caitlyn scooted across the back seat. A white bag crackled as she moved, sending the aroma of fresh bread drifting up to the front seat. Jared took a deep breath. "Whatever's in the bag sure smells good. I hope you're planning on sharing."

Caitlyn opened the Gardner's Garden Deli bag. "Good morning to you too. I decided that this early, we could all use some breakfast, so I brought bagels and orange juice."

"Oh, Caitlyn, you're heaven sent," Jana exclaimed. "Jared came too early for me to eat anything, and I'm starved."

"Hey guys, what do you get when you blow a hair dryer down a rabbit hole?"

"Nooo, Zack! It's too early for that." Jared groaned.

"You get hot, cross bunnies!" Zack laughed uproariously at his own joke and was bombarded with crumpled-up napkins.

Jared glanced in the rearview mirror. "What kind of bagels do you have, Cait? I didn't have much time to eat either."

"I've got cinnamon, sesame seed, whole-wheat honey, and everything. For cream cheese, I have plain, honey-nut, and blueberry."

"You always bring the best refreshments. You should have been in charge last night," Jared said. "Let's see, can you spread a whole wheat with blueberry for me?"

"Sure. What about you Jana?"

"I'll have sesame seed with honey-nut."

Caitlyn passed the bagels up front, along with two small cartons of orange juice. Jared balanced his bagel on his lap while securing his juice in a cup holder.

"Hey, beautiful, don't I get one too?" Zack gave Caitlyn a cheesy grin.

"Sure, if you refrain from bad jokes during breakfast."

"Agreed." He grinned mischievously. "I think cinnamon with blueberry tickles my funny bone."

"I warned you, Zack," Caitlyn said, a smile threatening to break free.

"That was just a statement, not a joke." He grinned.

Jana changed the subject. "How long does it take to get there, Jared?"

"About an hour and a half to the first visitor's center, then the closest observation point to the volcano is about fifty or sixty miles beyond that."

"Jana," Caitlyn managed between bites of bagel, "I forgot to mention that when Jared drives he also assumes the role of tour-bus guide."

Keeping his eyes on the road, Jared tilted his head toward Jana. "What she didn't tell you is that I assume the role to keep Zack from telling jokes the entire trip."

"Why won't elephants use a computer?" Zack piped up.

"Noooooooooo!"

"Because they're afraid of the mouse."

"Should I start the commentary now?" Jared asked.

Jana and Caitlyn answered instantly, "Please!"

"Do you want to hear the Indian legend about Mount St. Helens?"

"Sounds better than the jokes!" Jana chuckled.

"Long ago, there were two brothers who both fought over their father's land. The Great Spirit took them to a new land separated by a large river. He had them shoot their arrows in opposite directions, and where their arrows landed would be their territory. One shot—"

"What did that sign say?" Jana had been gazing out the window while listening to the story when her head snapped back to get a better view.

Jared looked at her as though she had just landed from Mars. "What sign?"

"That billboard. Did it just advertise seventeen toilets at that truck stop?"

The jokester called from the back seat, "The concussion must have affected her vision, Jared."

"No, it didn't. I could swear that's what the sign said."

"I'm sure it must have," Caitlyn put in. "They advertise a lot of strange things out here."

Jared laughed. "Do you want me to turn around and check it out?"

"No, it's not necessary." Jana took a final backward glance at the fading sign. "Go on with your story."

"Okay, where was I?"

"The chiefs were shooting arrows," Jana said.

"Oh yeah. The first brother shot his arrow south into the Willamette River valley and became the chief of the Multnomah people. The other one shot his arrow north and became the chief of the Klickitat people. The Great Spirit built the Bridge of the Gods as a sign of peace."

Caitlyn laughed. "If I shot an arrow, I'd get to go three feet from where I started."

"With my shoulder, it would fall right at my feet," Jana declared.

"I'm afraid I wouldn't get to go a whole lot farther," Jared continued. "Anyway, after awhile people began to be selfish and fight again. The Great Spirit took fire from them. They began to repent."

Zack interjected, "Wow, Book of Mormon déjà vù!"

Jared shook his head and continued his tale. "The Great Spirit had compassion and went to an old woman who still had some fire in her lodge. He would grant her one wish if she would share her fire. She wished for youth and beauty. The Great Spirit granted her wish, and she took her fire to the middle of the bridge and shared it with everyone."

"It's just like now—the Lord uses other people to bless us," Caitlyn observed.

Jared nodded his head. "The two chiefs both fell in love with her and began to fight. The Great Spirit was angry and broke up the Bridge of the Gods. The two chiefs were changed into Mount Hood and Mount Adams, who still throw rocks and flames at each other. The woman, Loo-Wit, who kept her youth and beauty, was changed into Mount St. Helens."

"Wow! That's quite a story," Jana remarked. "Where did you learn it?"

"I grew up in Washington around the Cascades and heard all kinds of stories and legends."

"I have a question for you, Jared," Zack said without a hint of a smile.

"Shoot."

"What did Loo-Wit wear when she went out on the town?"

"Not again," cried the unanimous chorus in the car.

"She wears her lava lava! Get it? lava lava? She's a volcano."

He was answered by moans and groans.

Jared looked in the rearview mirror. "Caitlyn, can you knock him out or something?"

"I'll try, but he's pretty hard headed."

Laughter, friendly banter, and a few more bad jokes filled the car as they made their way to Mount St. Helens. The visitor's center at Silver Lake offered two movies and several exhibits. One was about the actual eruption of Mount St. Helens, and the other about the Fire Mountains of the West.

As the four young people walked out of the small theater, Jana said, "I never knew I was living so close to so many volcanoes. It's overwhelming and a bit scary."

"The one you really have to watch out for is Rainier. If it blows, everyone in Seattle better beware. It has more snow and glacial ice than all the other Cascade volcanoes combined."

"I had no idea that the most damage when St. Helens blew was done by mud flows and avalanches," Caitlyn commented. She looked around for Zack and found him snapping pictures of all the exhibits.

"If you guys think this is amazing, wait till you catch your first glimpse of St. Helens close up."

As if on cue, Zack started again. "What did the dad volcano say to the mom volcano? Give up? Okay. He said, 'Do you lava me like I lava you?'" Zack guffawed loudly.

The people around him rolled their eyes. Caitlyn, Jared, and Jana quickly walked away, pretending they didn't know him.

"Hey! Wait for me." Zack took a few more pictures and caught up with them in the parking lot as Jared was explaining the rest of their itinerary.

"Jana, your shoulder will be pretty sore by the end of the day, so I thought we might just want to take in the Johnston observatory on the other end. It's the one that's closest to the volcano and the most spectacular."

Her stomach growled. "I think this morning's bagel is wearing off. Is there anywhere to eat on the way?"

"Well, there's 19 Mile House," Jared replied. "They have pretty good burgers, and they're famous for their cobblers."

Zack turned an interesting shade of green. "I'm not sure I'm up to hamburgers after last night."

Jared laughed. "These are actually good, and there's a deck with a view of the river valley."

Hunger finally won out, and they stopped at the restaurant. Jared was right about the view, and the food was decent. They all had to try the "world-famous" cobbler à la mode. Everyone ordered a different kind and shared it with the others. Zack couldn't resist buying a T-shirt that read, "Mount St. Helens— she really blew her top!"

When they reached the reforested areas, Jana took off her sunglasses. "Jared, why does it look like all these trees are out of focus? I keep trying to clean my glasses or the windshield."

Caitlyn strained to look through the windshield. "She's right. They look like blurs."

Jared rubbed his chin. "I'm not really sure, but my theory is that they were all planted at the same time and are pretty much identical. They don't have the usual variations that you would have in an old-growth forest. It kind of makes the lines blur together."

The occupants of the car fell silent as they rounded the bend and caught their first glimpse of St. Helens. As Jared rounded each curve in the road, Jana craned her neck to view the mountain. When they reached the Johnston observatory, she was grateful Jared had told her to bring a jacket. A brisk wind blew through the mountains, since the volcanic eruption had destroyed or flattened all the trees that would have provided a wind break.

The four friends looked at the volcano and the surrounding areas ravaged by nature's fury. The whole scene reminded Jana of a moonscape. Many of the other areas had begun the process of rebirth, but everything immediately surrounding the volcano remained stark and barren. More than thirty years since St. Helen's violent eruption, only a miniscule amount of scraggly vegetation poked its head through the desolate landscape.

One of the rangers talked about the volcano. Behind him, steam vented from the most recent lava dome. The sightseers enjoyed a rare clear day with a magnificent view of the interior of the crater, and they had trouble tearing their attention away.

Some tourists from China were snapping photos, so Zack offered to take a picture of their group. He double-checked the image before bowing to the photographer and returning the camera with a few words in Cantonese.

Jana and her friends soaked up all the information about volcanoes and the eruption before finally calling it a day and heading home. The trip home was more subdued, and she wondered if the others felt the same reverence she had for the things they'd observed. It had been a long day, though, and Caitlyn was the first casualty, falling asleep on Zack's shoulder. Zack followed shortly thereafter.

Jared looked in the rearview mirror. "Looks like those two have bit the dust. Are you feeling sleepy at all?"

Jana sighed. "A little, but I think I'd like to talk awhile."

"Sure. Is there anything on your mind?"

"Actually, I feel like I always do the talking. You've listened to all my problems, but I haven't been a very good listener. Tell me about yourself."

"Sure, what do you want to know?"

"Well, I already know you grew up in Seattle. How did you end up here?"

"When I returned from my mission, I went up to BYU. As luck would have it, I roomed with Eric Grant. He was a few years older than me, but we really hit it off. He was in his last year of pre-med, and I was just beginning my bachelor's degree in exercise science. He told me about his dream to open a clinic in his hometown."

"He seems very caring."

"Definitely. Eric said the area needed a good physical therapist, and we always planned to open up shop close to each other. When he and Andie came back to town after he completed his residency, they opened the clinic."

"Who's Andie?" Jana asked. "You mentioned her before."

"The doc's wife. She was one of our home evening sisters. Anyway, after finishing my PT degree and my time in the military, Eric invited me to open up shop in town. It seemed like the perfect opportunity, so here I am."

"Do you plan on staying?"

"For a few years, at least. Possibly permanently."

Jana stifled a yawn. "I'm sorry." She shook her head. "I didn't get much sleep last night. Have you always wanted to be a physical therapist?"

"I'd thought about it for awhile. My dad was in an accident, and I watched the therapist work wonders with him. That really cemented my decision. I wanted to be able to help people the way they helped Dad."

"You've helped me, Jared. Both with therapy and with your friendship."

He smiled at her and touched her hand. "Glad to be there for you."

She adjusted her air vent. "You said 'possibly permanent.' What would pull you away?"

"I'm trying to expand the therapy practice to include some time for open gym, so I can help people learn about exercise and nutrition. I may even throw in a few karate or self-defense classes. If that doesn't work out, I might move to a larger area where I could make it happen."

"Karate?"

"Yeah, I'm a black belt."

"Wow. Pretty impressive." Jana took deep breaths, attempting to keep the yawns away. "I hope it works out here for you. This is such a wonderful town."

"Yeah, it is. I loved growing up in Seattle, but I think I prefer the small-town lifestyle."

Finally, unable to stop herself, Jana succumbed to sleep. But just before she drifted off, she felt Jared reach out to touch her hair and heard him whisper, "If only . . ."

Twelve

Familiar landmarks appeared, and Jared called to the resting passengers, "Wake up, all you sleeping beauties. You too, Zack. We're almost home. Who wants to bribe me to not tell the others they snore?" He was greeted with yawns and stretches.

He stopped at Caitlyn's house and dropped off both back-seat passengers. This time Jana noticed Zack took Caitlyn's hand as he walked her to the door.

Jared's stomach growled, and he turned to Jana. "Would you like to grab some Chinese food for dinner?"

"That would be nice." As they rounded the corner, Jana gasped, "Oh no!"

"What's wrong?" Jared asked right before he noticed a sleek red Shelby GT 500 parked in the driveway of the guest house.

"It's Trevor. My guess is he's been waiting here for a while and won't be in a good mood. I told him not to try to find me."

I wonder how he did, Jared thought, but kept his voice light as he said, "Maybe he'd like to come with us for Chinese."

Jana shook her head. "I somehow think he'd prefer not to."

"Well, I'll walk you to the door and get a chance to meet him. We can offer, anyway. The worst he can do is say no. Right?"

"Actually, the worst he can do is punch you in the nose."

Jared pulled into the driveway, and before he was able to get out of the car, Trevor had already helped Jana to her feet. The air buzzed with tension.

"This is a surprise, Trevor. Dare I ask how you found me?"

"Just my internal radar. It automatically points me to your side. Where have you been?" His smile seemed forced.

"We went to Mount St. Helens with a couple of friends from church. Trevor, I'd like you to meet Jared Carpenter. He's my physical therapist *and* my friend. Jared, this is Trevor Willis."

Jared extended his hand toward Trevor and caught an unmistakable malevolent flash in his eyes. "It's good to meet you, Trevor. Jana's told me a lot about you. I feel like I already know you."

Trevor ignored Jared's gesture, putting his arm around Jana's waist instead. "I'm afraid I'm at a disadvantage. She hasn't told me anything about you."

"Maybe we can get to know each other. Jana and I thought we might go get a bite to eat. Would you like to join us?"

"No thanks. Before I return home, I hoped to have some time alone with the girl I'm planning to marry. I'm sure you understand." Trevor began to pull Jana away.

"Of course, no problem. Would you like me to pick you up for church tomorrow, Jana?"

"What time do you meet?"

"Singles ward is at 1:00. Over in Astoria."

"Why don't you give me a call in the morning? I'll let you know then. Thanks for everything, Jared. I really enjoyed the day."

Jared took her hand and looked directly into her eyes. "Bye. Call if you need anything, Okay?"

"Okay. Thanks."

Jared backed out of the driveway as Trevor took the key from Jana's hand. "Here, let me get that for that for you." He opened the door and stepped back for her to enter. After flicking on the light switch, he maneuvered Jana in front of him and took her in his arms. "Oh, lady, I've missed you so much." Before he could kiss her, she stepped away.

"Trevor, how did you find me?"

"I . . ." He looked down. "I had Don help me." When Jana eluded his kiss again, he slammed his hand down on the mantle. He breathed deeply, exhaling through his teeth.

She faced away from him. "Why, Trevor? Why a P.I.?"

"I love you and couldn't stand the thought of you being hurt." He turned her around and looked directly into her eyes. "Don't you know how much I love you? I had to know you were all right."

"But a detective agency, Trevor?"

"Honey, don't look at me like that."

"Don't you trust me?"

"It wasn't a matter of trust. I was so worried about you." He took her by the shoulders to lead her to the couch, but quickly dropped his hand when she winced.

"Come and sit down. Please? I brought something for you—it's in the car." He ran out the door and soon returned with a gift-wrapped box and a bouquet of pink roses. "Here, I noticed you were missing this." He handed the box to her.

She inclined her head and smiled. "What is it?"

"Open it and find out."

"Okay." With great care, she undid the package to find a water pitcher matching her mother's china. "Oh, Trevor, it's beautiful." She wiped away a tear. "The one from my mother's set was broken in the move from New Hampshire."

"And these are to put in it." He presented her with the flowers. "They match the desert roses on the pitcher." He took the pitcher from her, filled it with water, and placed the flowers in it. He set them on the table before joining Jana on the couch. With her head on his shoulder and his arm around her, they sat in silence.

After a few minutes Trevor kissed the top of her head. "I love you more than life itself. Please say you'll marry me."

She traced a button on his shirt. "Part of me wants to say yes, but I'm still not sure. Especially after I specifically asked you not to try and find me."

"Come home and we'll work it out. I promise you."

He tilted her head up and brushed her lips softly with his own. Jana found herself under his spell, once again melting against his shoulder. *It would be easy to give in and tell him yes . . .*

"No!" She pushed him away and stood up. "That's why I needed to put some distance between us. My brain turns to mush when you're near."

His face lit up as he laughed. Capturing her hand, he pulled her toward him. "Why do you think I wanted to see you in person? You're thinking too hard. Just let the mush take over."

This was the Trevor she had come to love, but she had to be firm. "I've committed to stay here for another two weeks. My car won't even be fixed for another six or seven days, and I told Jared I would help him until my therapy was done."

"You can drive the Classic for now, and I can have your car delivered when it's finished. I'm sure Jared would understand if you came home with me." Trevor stood. "Go on, get your things packed. We can be home by nine or ten tonight."

"No! This is my home for the next two weeks, and I'm staying." Jana faced the window and stepped away from him.

Trevor reached out and grabbed her roughly, then whirled her around and stood between her and the window. He pulled her onto her tiptoes and ignored her gasp of pain, then spoke inches from her face. "Listen here, lady. Your home is with me." He turned his head, and his eyes seemed to focus for a brief moment on something outside the window. "Not in this Podunk town, not with Jared Carpenter, but with me." His full attention returned to Jana. "Now get your things packed. We're leaving in five minutes."

Pain shot through her shoulder, bringing a gasp. "You're hurting me, Trevor. Please let go."

He released his grip and stepped back as Jana looked at him in anguish. When he found his voice, he reached out to her. "I . . . I'm so sorry. Please forgive me." He drew her into his arms and held her tight, but she couldn't relax. As soon as he severed the contact, she backed away, terrified.

He stepped toward her as she continued to back up. In shock, she reached the wall and slid to the floor.

"Are you hurt?"

Jana held her injured shoulder and shook her head no, refusing to look directly at him.

"I love you, Jana." He took another step toward her.

"Please just leave." She began to tremble.

"All right, I'll go." He spoke calmly, moving away from her. "I'll be back in the morning and we'll talk. I'll even go to church with you and Jared. Nothing like this will happen again. I promise."

She turned her head, averting her gaze. "Just go."

———•———

Trevor walked out the door and closed it quietly, then got in his car and drove away. When he reached the inn, he entered his room and slumped to the floor. *I really thought I saw something in the window. How could I have been so stupid? I need to get her away from here.*

———•———

Jana continued to stare at the door, too numb for tears. She had no concept of how much time passed before she finally reached for her cell phone and pushed number 9. The phone rang once on the other end.

"Hello?" a male voice said.

All she could manage was one whispered word. "Jared."

———•———

"I'll be right there." Jared grabbed his jacket as he headed out the door. In his haste, ingredients for a shake, including ice cream and milk, remained forgotten on the counter. Fear gripped his heart as he sped through the town with every imaginable scenario playing through his mind. *I should've never left her alone with him! I was afraid something might happen.*

Jared pulled into the driveway with his tires shrieking and threw the car into park. He turned off the engine, then jumped out of the vehicle and ran to the house. He burst through the unlocked door and scanned the room to find Jana sitting in the corner with her knees pulled up to her chest, holding her injured shoulder. She stared straight ahead with the phone still in her left hand. As Jared rushed to her, she seemed to snap out of it. Tears started down her cheeks, and she reached for him. He sat next to her, holding her and speaking calmly in her ear.

"Jana." The tears continued as she clung to him. "Jana," he repeated more firmly, "look at me." He absently wiped at her tears with his thumb, her face cradled in his hands. "Jana, did he hurt you?"

"No. Not really. He . . . he grabbed my shoulders roughly. Oh, Jared, nothing like this has ever happened before. I was so afraid." She looked down. He picked her up, careful to avoid her injury, and set her gently on the couch.

"Let me see." Jana turned away as he cautiously probed her injured shoulder. Fury hit him hard at sight of the ugly purple discoloration. He quietly whispered, "How could a man do that to a woman he claims to love?"

She faced him again. "What did you say?"

"I think it's all right," Jared said in a calmer tone. "We might want to get Doc Eric over here and have him check it out." He paused a moment to draw a breath. "You might want to talk to the sheriff, too."

Her head snapped up. "No!"

"What if he comes back tonight?"

Wringing her hands as she spoke, she wouldn't look directly at Jared. "No. He won't. He was really upset. He said nothing like this would happen again."

Jared frowned. "Jana, I know he doesn't think he will, but—"

Her eyes reached out to his, pleading. "He said he'll be back in the morning and will go to church with us. He said we can talk in the morning."

"Okay, okay. But I'll be here when he comes."

Blinking, she fought back the tears that threatened again. "It might make him angry."

"I'll take that chance. I'm calling the doc now. And Jana, I'll be staying here tonight."

She looked up at Jared through her tears. "Thank you."

He left Jana on the couch as he dialed Eric's number. After speaking in hushed tones for a few moments, Jared hung up the phone. "He'll be right over. Would you like me to call Emma, or maybe Caitlyn?"

"Not just yet. I don't think I can face either one."

Jared nodded. "I understand."

———•———

By the time the doctor arrived with his wife, Jana's hands no longer shook, and her voice was steady. She smiled and exchanged pleasantries when Doc Eric introduced Andie to her.

The doctor stepped closer. "Let's check out your shoulder. How far can you move your arm?" Jana brought it up a few inches. "Good. Jared, how does that compare to yesterday?"

"I think the range of motion may have decreased a bit."

Doc Eric turned back to Jana. "Is the pain worse?"

"Yes, but that may be from the bruise."

He probed her shoulder again. "There's some swelling, but any additional damage is minimal. It may have set therapy back a day or two, but I think you'll be fine. Make sure you ice it tonight and take ibuprofen to reduce the inflammation." He turned to his wife. "Andie, maybe you can help Jana get ready for bed."

The doctor's wife smiled at her. "Sure." Jared helped Jana to stand, and Andie put an arm around her to walk her into the bedroom.

"My pajamas are under the pillow," Jana explained.

"Any robe?"

"Yes, it's hanging in the closet."

"Let me help you with that shirt." Andie placed the pajamas next to Jana on the bed.

"I think I can get it just fine. I've had a lot of practice over the last week." She gingerly slipped her arm out of the sleeve.

Andie gazed around the room, running her hand along the worn dresser. "Eric and I have a lot of happy memories attached to this home. Did you know that we lived here when we were first married?"

"Yes, Jared mentioned it."

"I hated to move out, but as you can see, it's really not big enough for a family. I miss not having Emma right next door. I really lucked out with my in-laws."

"I'd have to agree with you on that one." Jana looked at the top in her hands.

"You know, Emma's a really good listener. Would you like me to give her a call when we leave? I'm sure she'd stay with you tonight."

"Jared said he'd stay here." Jana looked toward the bathroom. "I think a shower will do me good."

"That sounds like a great idea. I'll be right outside the door if you need anything." Andie paused before leaving the room. "Think about having Emma come, okay?"

Jana smiled. "I'll think about it." She hesitated a moment. "Andie?"

She turned back into the room. "Yes?"

"I appreciate you and your husband coming out right away."

"It's no problem." Andie chuckled. "We'll consider it our date for the week. Would you like Jared and Eric to give you a blessing?"

"Yes, I would."

———•———

After the women went into the bedroom, Eric leaned against the couch, folded his arms, and turned to his friend. "Okay, Jared, what's going on here?"

"Her boyfriend found out where she was and came out to talk to her. He got a little rough."

"Have you called the sheriff?"

Jared paced the room. "No, she won't let me." He stopped and turned to Eric. "But I do plan on staying here the entire night—just in case he returns."

"Have you met this guy?"

"Only tonight. I don't really know much about him," Jared admitted. "What I do know makes me more than a little nervous."

"It might not hurt to alert the sheriff. Maybe I'll give him a call to let him know what's going on—unofficially."

Conversation stopped when Andie walked through the door and stood by her husband. He put his arm around her. "How's she doing?"

"Holding out pretty well, but a bit shaken up. She's taking a shower and would like a blessing when she gets out."

"That's a good idea," Eric replied. "Did she say anything else about what happened?"

"No. I tried to convince her to let Emma come over, but she's pretty independent."

Ten minutes later, Jana came out of the bedroom, combing her towel-dried hair. She smiled at Jared. "I feel so much better. I'm ready for a blessing now."

In the priesthood blessing, where Eric was the voice, she was promised comfort and safety and blessed with wisdom in making decisions about her future. Eric and Andie left shortly afterward.

Jared asked Jana if she'd eaten, and she said she hadn't had a chance. "Would you like me to cook you something? I make a pretty mean omelet." Jared began to look through the cabinets for a pan.

"Maybe just a small one. I swear there's a knot in my stomach." Her voice was louder, and he turned to see her standing in the doorway of the kitchen.

"I understand. What would you like in your omelet?" He rummaged through the refrigerator for ingredients. "There's some cheese, and mushrooms, and tomatoes—um . . ." He moved a few items. "Oh, I found an avocado, too."

"That's fine." She paused. "Jared?"

"Yes?"

"This was totally out of character for Trevor. What makes a man act the way he did tonight?"

"I'm not sure. Can you tell me what happened?"

"Well, he tried to convince me to go home with him tonight. I stood my ground and told him this was my home for the next two weeks and I was going to stay here. That's when he went crazy." Jana stared at the ceiling, reliving the evening in her mind. "He grabbed me and yelled, 'Your home is with me, not

in this Podunk town, not with Jared Carpenter, but with me!'
Then he told me were leaving right away. When he realized
what he'd done, he started to cry and tried to apologize."

Tears fell in torrents now. Jared flipped the omelet onto a
plate, then took Jana in his arms. He carefully guided her to the
table as though she would break if he released her. He held the
chair for her and set the savory omelet before her. "Try to eat as
much as you can. You've had a shock, and protein will help you
regain your strength. Would you like something to drink?"

"Yes. I think there's some orange juice in there—behind
the milk."

He placed a small glass in front of her, and she said a
blessing on the food and took a forkful of omelet. She stared
at it as if trying to determine if she really wanted to eat it, then
finally put it in her mouth. "Mmm, this is really good. I didn't
realize I was so hungry."

Jared laughed. "Don't be so surprised, I'm a pretty good
cook—at least with omelets!" He paused, then continued where
the conversation had left off. "I think he's afraid—afraid he'll
lose you, and afraid of his life without you." Sadly, Jared was
familiar with such thoughts.

After Jana ate another bite of omelet, she said, "I think
you're right. He acts all tough, but there's a vulnerable little
boy underneath it all."

Jared turned away under the guise of cleaning up the
dishes. Numerous emotions ran through his heart—anger,
worry, loneliness. He attacked the frying pan fiercely and
muttered under his breath, "Maybe Willis needs a dirty frying
pan whenever he gets frustrated."

He jumped when Jana spoke right behind him. "If you keep
scrubbing so hard, you'll wear a hole in the pan." She handed
him her plate. "It was delicious, Jared. Try to be gentler with
the plate." She quickly kissed his cheek. "Thanks for being my
friend."

"Did you want to watch some TV when I'm done here?"

"I guess. I'll go brush my teeth first, in case I fall asleep."

"Good idea. Can I borrow some toothpaste?" Jared held up his index finger. "I'll use my finger like when I was a kid." He gave her a lopsided grin.

"I am so sorry. You came over here without even a toothbrush. Maybe you should go home and grab a few things."

He stepped close to tenderly grasp her face and look into her eyes. "With Trevor out there, I am *not* leaving you alone."

She laid her head on Jared's chest, and he wrapped his arms around her waist. He closed his eyes as he savored the moment.

"I feel so safe with you, Jared. It reminds me of when I was a kid after a bad dream. My dad would hold onto me, and I felt like all the monsters in the world didn't have a chance with him protecting me."

Jared released her and bowed gallantly. "I would slay the fiercest dragon for you, Milady Jana."

A smile lit her face, flooding the room with sunshine. The burden weighing down on her visibly lightened. She curtsied. "Thank you, Sir Jared. You are my knight extraordinaire."

After she retreated to the bathroom, Jared settled on the couch with a large bowl of popcorn. He picked up the remote and began flipping through the channels. "Let's see what's on TV. Reality, reality, reality. No, no, no." Finally finding a movie, he called out to the other room. "Oh, here's something—*While You Were Sleeping.*"

Jana poked her head out the door, wiping her face with a towel. "That's one of my favorites."

"Then that's it. Come on and take a load off your feet." He patted the seat next to him.

"I'll be right there."

She hung up the towel and joined him on the couch. When he put his arm around her, she leaned on his shoulder and sighed. "I always feels so warm when you're next to me."

He smiled and tightened his hold. They laughed together at the antics of Sandra Bullock and Bill Pullman till they cried. Pretty soon, Jared noticed he laughed alone. Sleep had overtaken Jana. He stroked her hair and whispered, "If only . . ."

———•———

Collapsed against the wall in his hotel room, Trevor was pulled him from his misery by his ringing cell phone. He looked briefly at the number, tempted not to answer, but he finally gave in. "Yeah, what is it?"

"They took the Colemans in for questioning tonight, under the guise of a weekend getaway. They're going to offer them a deal."

Trevor sat upright. "What about Jana?"

"She should be fine. The pictures from St. Helens showed no known suspects."

"Are you sure?"

After an eternal pause, Don answered, "Officially, yes."

"But unofficially . . ."

"If it was me, I would temporarily transfer her to a safe location."

"So I can finally tell her? I thought I saw something outside her window tonight and yanked her out of the way. I covered my tracks by acting like I was angry at her for staying here." *At least I think I was acting.* "It may have blown any chance I had with her."

"That's a negative, brother. Remember, moving her is still unofficial."

"Just how am I supposed to get her to come with me if I can't tell her why?" Trevor's voice rose in pitch.

"Hey, you're Trevor Willis. You'll think of something."

"Don, you don't understand. This is the girl I want to marry. I can't risk alienating her any further."

"You know it's a bad idea to get personally involved. You're a professional. Act like one."

After a grunt of disgust, Trevor acquiesced. "Okay. You know where I'll be."

He removed all trace of his residency in the room and headed out the door, flipping the light off as he left.

Thirteen

A scream rose to her throat as a hand covered her mouth.

"Shh, shh. It's just me, sweetheart. Do you promise to be quiet? I don't want anyone to get hurt, especially if Jared came bursting in here and misunderstood the situation."

Jana looked at Trevor in wide-eyed terror, debating whether or not to scream. *What does he mean by anyone getting hurt? Jared?* Her heart lurched in her chest. *I couldn't live with myself if something happened to him because of me.*

With his hand still clapped over her mouth, Trevor said, "Honey, do you promise not to scream?"

She nodded her head. He removed his hand. "What are you doing here?" she asked angrily. "How did you get in?"

"Hush!" He put his finger to his lips. "Please don't be afraid. I just want to talk to you alone."

She tried to think clearly. "I'm listening."

"Not here. We'll go to my cabin. It's only a couple of hours away. I'll have you back for therapy on Monday morning."

"I . . . I don't know. Jared will worry." She prayed in her heart. *Please help me, Father.*

"You can write him a note." Trevor stroked her cheek. "Isn't what we have worth trying to save? Please come with me."

"You're frightening me, Trevor." An involuntary shiver ran through her body.

He flinched, and she saw the hurt in his eyes. "I'm sorry, Jana," he said gently. "Please give us this chance." He looked over his shoulder. "This is more important than you realize."

She thought of Jared in the other room. *All I have to do is call out to him.* She prepared to scream, drawing air into her lungs, only to let it out in a sigh. She pictured Jared's face and imagined the possibilities. *What if he was hurt in a fight with Trevor?* "You promise I'll be back for therapy on Monday morning?"

"Cross my heart." He made an *X* across his chest with his index finger.

"And I can write a note?"

"Yes." Trevor looked out the sliding glass door. "Just do it quickly."

Believing there was no other way to protect Jared, she made her decision. "Okay, I'll go."

"Just grab some clothes and shoes. I have everything else you'll need." He handed her a small duffel bag.

Jana took the bag and went into the bathroom to grab her cosmetic case. "Should I get dressed?"

"There isn't time." Trevor looked around nervously.

She opened the dresser drawer and grabbed a couple of T-shirts and two pair of jeans, plus a few other necessities. At the last second, she grabbed the worn-out towel given to her by the stranger on the beach after her parents died. It had helped comfort her over the years, and she certainly needed that now. She reached into the nightstand to find a pen and paper, then knelt by the bed. With the pen paused in midair, she carefully formulated her words.

She felt Trevor move to stand close behind her. "Make sure Jared knows you're going willingly," he said over her shoulder.

Jana nodded and began the note with shaky hands. "Trevor? Can you get my white sneakers out of the closet?"

When he turned around to open the closet door, she grabbed her cell phone off the end table and hid it under the pillow with a small corner protruding. She placed the paper over it, hoping Jared would notice it when he picked up the note. Trevor stood next to her and reviewed the note. He took her arm, and they quietly stepped out the sliding door. He helped her into the car and locked the door, then went around to the driver's side.

"I have a pillow and blanket if you'd like to sleep while I drive. Why don't you take your shoes off and make yourself comfortable?"

She took the offered items, turning away from Trevor as he threw her shoes in the back. With the pillow against the window and cocooned in the blanket, she feigned sleep. Tears silently coursed down her face, and her fear grew with each passing mile. *What have I done? Jared would have protected me—but at what cost? Please help me, Heavenly Father, please.*

———•———

Jared woke with a start. "Jana?" He threw off the blanket that covered him and rushed into the bedroom. "Jana!" The urgent whisper escaped his mouth. There was no response. The rumpled bed was empty, with only a piece of paper to answer his unasked questions.

Jared,
Trevor came and I chose to go with him. It will be safer for us both. He said he just wants to talk and promised to have me back in time for therapy on Monday. Please don't worry. I'll see you Monday morning.
Jana

Crushing the note in a shaking hand, Jared fell to his knees. "Father, please help me find her. Help me know she is safe."

He opened his eyes and saw Jana's cell phone. Maybe

he could talk to her! He grabbed the phone and opened the contact list. His eyes were drawn immediately to Trevor's name and he touched number 1, holding his breath while the call connected.

———•———

The ringtone of Trevor's cell startled Jana from her thoughts. He chuckled. "It seems that you're calling me, Jana. Should I answer it?"

"Yes, please!" She turned away from the car window, wiping her tears with the back of her hand.

He connected the call. "Trevor Willis here." After a brief pause, he gave a derisive laugh. "She's right here. She came with me willingly." Another quick pause, and Trevor held the phone out to her "Your friend wants to talk to you."

Jana grabbed the phone like a lifeline. "Jared."

"Are you okay?"

She sniffed. "Yes. It's good to hear your voice."

"Did he force you to go with him?"

"No, I went willingly. I thought it would be safe—" Trevor gave her a withering look. "I mean, I thought it would be better for both of us if I came. He promised I would be safe."

"Do you want me to come for you?" When she didn't respond, Jared urged, "Jana?"

"No," she answered quietly.

"I'm calling the sheriff right now," Jared said.

"No! Please don't. I'll see you on Monday." She glanced sideways at the man she thought she knew. "You can call Trevor's phone anytime you want to reach me." She forced herself to sound normal. "Can you bring my swimsuit and sweats to the therapy building? They're in my top drawer."

"Sure. You'll be there by 7:00 AM?"

"That's what Trevor said. May . . . maybe you can call after sacrament meeting and tell me about the talks."

"I'll do that. You're sure you're all right?" Jared asked, his voice full of doubt.

"Yes, we're both safe." *You are safe. That's the important thing.*

"I'll talk to you tomorrow."

Jana ended the call with a sob. *Will I ever see him again?*

Trevor reached over and squeezed her hand. "Sweetheart, please don't be frightened. I only want to show you that I meant what I said. You'll never have to be afraid of me. I'll keep my word. Try to rest. We'll be there soon."

She turned and stared out the window again, a lone tear slowly making its way down her cheek.

Jared punched the pillow in frustration, then paced the floor, talking to himself and growing more agitated as the minutes passed. "She says she's okay, but she didn't sound okay. And what did she mean it would be safer for her to go with Trevor. Did he threaten her?" Jared stopped. "No. She wouldn't have gone because of that. All she had to do was call out to me." Suddenly, he knew. "He didn't threaten her. He threatened me." His shoulders fell. "Oh, Jana." He held his head in his hands.

Trevor pulled up to a mountain cabin just as the new day was dawning. "Honey, we're here."

Exhaustion had finally won out about forty-five minutes earlier when Jana fell asleep. Now she yawned and stretched. "What time is it?"

"Just after 5:00." Trevor came around to the passenger side

of the car and opened her door. "Your shoes are somewhere in the back. I'll carry you to the cabin so you can get settled in."

She looked at the ground. Sharp gravel covered the driveway, and the area surrounding the cabin was littered with wood chips and debris. Partially covered roots hid among the shards, making the route treacherous.

Trevor picked her up, then carried her over and deposited her on the large front porch. "Don't try to go outside without your shoes. Your feet could really get cut up out here." He unlocked the door and held it open, allowing her to enter first.

When he'd mentioned his cabin, Jana had envisioned a small, one-room log structure with a wood-burning stove for cooking. She was unprepared for this grand home, although knowing Trevor, she should have expected it. The entire rear wall of the living room opened to a majestic view of a pond encircled by pines, with a meadow of tall grass and flowers bending gently in the breeze. The kitchen was worthy of a grand chef. Jana wasn't quite sure how many doors exited onto the balcony overlooking the great room, but she imagined at least five.

He led her up the stairs toward the front of the house. You're bedroom's right over here." He put his hand on the small of her back to guide her into a large master suite. "The bathroom is right through that door. My room is just over there." He pointed down the hallway. "I'll get your things."

"Thank you." She surveyed the bedroom. *Definitely masculine and definitely professionally decorated.* For lack of anything better to do, she curled up in the comfortable overstuffed chair and looked out the window at the sunrise. That was where Trevor found her a few minutes later as he entered the room with her things.

"There are spare toothbrushes and probably anything else you need in the drawer. Would you like to try to sleep some more, or did you want me to make you some breakfast?"

Without looking at him, Jana answered, "I'd like to sleep more." She wiped a tear away.

He put her bag on the bench in front of the rustic bed. "I'll see you in a couple of hours, honey." He left the room and closed the door behind him.

———————

She's never going to forgive me this time. Trevor's shoulders sagged as he leaned into the soft brown leather couch and closed his eyes. *Oh, Jana. I didn't mean to hurt you.* He was raised with small-town New England values, and his parents taught him to treat women with respect. But he was so afraid something would happen to Jana. *Lasky's been watching you, but if we were married, I could keep you safe and you wouldn't be frightened.*

He picked up his cell phone and dialed. "Yeah, it's me. We're here."

Trevor looked into space as his brother-in-law said, "You're the one with the inside data. I need you in the background, feeding me information."

Trevor shook his head. "Can't do it, Don. In case you don't remember, I'm on protection duty, and I won't neglect that."

"It may fall apart without you, and then what position would that put her in?"

He sighed, knowing Don was right. "I want to tell her."

"The answer is no on that one. The boss is still unsure about her."

Trevor barked, "Well, I'm sure about her."

"Come on, old buddy," Don said. "Remember, officially she is not considered at risk. What happened to the man who never let emotions interfere? If you want Jana to be safe, it's imperative that man returns."

Trevor punched a pillow. "I'll have to figure out how to leave."

"Is she asleep right now?"

"Yeah. Why?"

"And you have your men surrounding the house?"

"Yes." Trevor definitely didn't like where this was heading.

"I gave you some of that new drug. There are no side effects, and she'll sleep like a baby. Just slip it to her, lock up, and you'll be back in four or five hours. She should be safe and will wake up feeling rested. She'll never know what really happened."

Trevor's agreement came with a hiss of exhaled air. "I'll be there this afternoon."

Fourteen

Trevor knocked on the bedroom door around 9:00.

A quiet voice answered, "Come in."

Jana hadn't moved since he left her earlier. Her head leaned on the back of the chair, and her legs were tucked underneath her. Trevor walked up to her and touched her arm.

Her instinctive reaction was to pull away, but she knew if she wanted to get back to Jared, she had to cooperate. She took a deep breath before smiling at Trevor. "Good morning."

"Can I get you some breakfast?"

With her stomach tied in a hundred knots, she didn't think she could eat a thing. *Remember—back to Jared.* "Yes, I'm kind of hungry."

"Let's go down to the kitchen. Would you like an omelet, pancakes, or muffins?"

Tears sprang to her eyes as she thought of Jared's omelet last night. *He must be worried sick about me.* "Maybe just a muffin and milk. I'll get dressed and meet you down there."

"Sure, honey, whatever you want," Trevor said.

When Jana walked into the extensive kitchen, he held a tray with blueberry muffins and two glasses of milk. He inclined his head toward the living room. "Let's eat out on the deck. It overlooks a pond, and there are usually some ducks this time of year."

Jana opened the sliding glass door and breathed in the scent of pine. "It's a beautiful view. Did you have the cabin built?"

"No, I bought it a couple of years ago. All the trees reminded me of Massachusetts and home."

"You're right. It reminds me of New England. It's peaceful, too."

They leaned against the railing. He held her hand, rubbing it absently. "Jana, I wanted to bring you here because it is peaceful. I wanted to get away from the city and away from other influences so we could just enjoy each other's company. This is where you should have come to think. I feel close to nature and close to God."

"Just taking a breath up here is like praying."

"Jana, have I destroyed any chance for a future together?"

She bit her lip and looked down. *Is he in his right mind? Can I tell the truth? No, keep it neutral.* "Maybe. I keep thinking about last night."

She paused, and her mask of neutrality shattered. She filled her lungs with air and her heart with courage. "If you hurt me like that when we are just dating, what would you do if we were married?" She touched Trevor's face and asked in a softer tone, "Would I have to walk on eggshells just to keep you from blowing up?"

Walking a few steps along the railing, Jana continued. "I've heard about abused women who keep going back to the men who abuse them. There were always signs they ignored." She faced him head on. "I won't be one of those women. I won't stand for any kind of abuse."

"Hon, I know. I took a good look at myself. I didn't like what I saw. I plan to get some kind of help as soon as I can. Is there still a chance for us?"

"There's a part of me that is scared to death of you. That part says to run as fast and as far as I can, but there's another part. The one that sees the good in you and thinks you can change."

"Kind of like the proverbial angel and devil on each shoulder?" His lopsided grin melted a little piece of her heart.

She gave him a small smile. "Exactly."

"Are you willing to give it another try?"

Tears threatened to fall again. "I just don't know."

Trevor breached the few steps between them and held her. "It's all right, Jana. It's all right. I'm right here for you. I'll always be here for you, no matter what. I love you." He stood there stroking her hair. "You know, one of the reasons I fell in love with you was your honesty. You tell everything exactly as it is. I'm a better person by being around you. Your goodness rubs off." He lifted her chin and kissed her tentatively. "Let's eat."

He ushered her to a bistro table near the edge of the deck. Morning mist hung low over the pond, and a small rowboat bobbed near a wooden pier.

"This is the perfect place for a warm summer day," Jana commented. "Can you swim in the pond?"

Trevor laughed. "I don't know. It's a bit too muddy and slimy for my taste. There's good fishing, though. Would you like me to row you around it?"

"Yes, I'd like that when we're done eating."

She nibbled at her muffin, not able to eat much. Finally, she pushed the plate away. "I'm done."

Trevor looked at her muffin, sadness filling his eyes. "I'll go get your shoes. I brought them in from the car." He walked into the house and returned with the shoes a minute later. "Let me help you."

"I feel like Cinderella." Jana lifted a foot.

He shod her feet with the white sneakers and then tied the frilly laces.

"If you're Cinderella, does that make me Prince Charming?"

She grinned impishly. "No, one of the mice, I'd say."

His laugh filled the mountain air, and he grabbed her hand. "Well, don't expect me to start singing anytime soon. Let's go."

He helped her into the boat, then jumped in as he pushed off the dock. He rowed the craft smoothly across the water's surface, leaving barely a ripple. The soft swishing of the oars hypnotized Jana with a rhythmic cadence.

"I wish we could go on like this forever," Trevor said after a while.

"It would get boring after a while, especially for a man like you. You need excitement in your life, not tranquility."

She saw the wheels turning in his head as he contemplated her words, but he changed the subject. "How are you feeling? How's your shoulder?"

"Okay. The doctor looked at it last night after . . ." She lowered her eyes.

The oars went still in their mounts, and Trevor lifted her chin and said in a hushed voice, "I'm sorry, Jana."

"I know." She looked away. "Anyway, Doc Eric said that other than a bruise, there wasn't too much damage. It might have set physical therapy back a few days." She paused a moment, seeing Trevor's confident mask fall away and fear flash through his eyes. "Why did you really bring me here, Trevor?"

"Maybe we should go back." Looking determined, he rowed toward the dock. The silence continued as he knotted the rope to anchor the rowboat to the wooden structure. After he hopped onto the weathered beams, his hands encircled her waist and he lifted her onto the dock. He strode to the house, with Jana barely able to keep up with his steps.

"Would you like to lie down for a while?" he asked her.

Slightly out of breath, she replied, "Yes. Can I call Jared first? He's really worried and was ready to call the sheriff when I talked to him. I'm still not sure he didn't."

"Go ahead. You might want to talk on the deck. There's more privacy." Trevor placed the cell phone in her hand, casually pushing a lock of her hair behind her ear. She watched a mask fall into place as he turned away.

"Thank you." *What is happening? He's acting so strange.*

He called over his shoulder. "I'm going to lie down, so just leave the phone on the coffee table. I'll get it when I wake up."

"Okay." She stared at him, then at the cell phone in her hand.

Trevor watched her close the sliding glass door before he retreated to the kitchen. He grabbed a milk jug from the refrigerator and poured some in a glass. Then he opened a bag, took out two chocolate chip cookies, and placed them on a plate. From his pocket, he removed a vial of clear liquid. *I'm so sorry, Jana. I hope you'll forgive me for this.* After stirring the substance into the milk, he left the spoon in the sink and climbed the stairs. He entered her room and set the milk and cookies on the nightstand. Then he walked down the hall to his room to wait for her to fall asleep.

Jana didn't know Jared's number by heart, so she hoped he still had her cell phone with him. She took a chance and placed the call. He answered before the first ring finished.

"Jana?"

"Yes."

He let out a breath all at once. "I've been so worried."

"I know. That's why I called."

"Are you okay? Has he hurt you?"

"I'm fine, and I'm not very frightened anymore."

"Is he listening?"

"No. In fact, he suggested I come out on the deck so I could speak with you privately. But don't worry—he went to lie down."

"What possessed you to go with him, Jana? Did he threaten you?"

"No. He didn't threaten me."

"Did he threaten me?" Jared asked quietly.

Jana hesitated before answering him. "Indirectly." She sighed. "Oh, Jared, I couldn't take the chance of you being hurt because of me."

"I can take care of myself. I'm much more worried about you. What if he cracks and gets violent again? Next time will probably be more than a bruise."

"I don't think there will be a next time. I think he really means it." She remembered his personality change this morning. *Do I really believe that? Will there really be no more episodes?*

Footsteps sounded, and she pictured Jared pacing the room. "Jana, where are you?"

"I don't know. We're at his cabin. It was dark, and I fell asleep on the way up here. I think we headed north, though. We got here around 5:00."

Jared paused a moment. "That probably puts you in Washington. Can you see any of the mountains, like Rainier or St. Helen's?"

"No. It's kind of a case of not being able to see the forest for the trees. There is a pond out back."

"I'll do what I can to figure out where you are."

"Thanks, Jared. I'll see you in the morning."

"Not one minute later than 7:00?"

"Not one minute later." She closed her eyes and thought of how good it would feel to be safe in his arms. "I'm really tired, so I think I'll go lie down."

"That's a good idea. Sleep well." He started to hang up. "And Jana—"

"Yes?"

"Does your bedroom door have a lock on it?"

She thought a moment. "I think so."

"Use it."

"I will."

Jana opened the door and started to enter the cabin until she looked down at her muddy sneakers. A white rug stood between the deck and the stairs, so she removed her shoes. Leaving them by the door, she set the phone on the coffee table and headed up the steps in her white sports socks.

After locking the bedroom door behind her, she noticed the milk and cookies. *Leave it to Trevor to get the best of everything.* She slid under the covers. She felt like a kid, dunking her cookies in the milk and eating them in bed. *Sometimes it's scary how well he knows me.* Jana drank the remainder of the milk as a mind-numbing weariness descended over her. With a fleece blanket tucked under her chin, she felt her troubled thoughts dissipate into dreamless sleep.

———•———

By the time Jana woke, the sun had begun its downward journey west. She gasped when she looked at her watch and saw it was past 4:00. *I can't believe I slept so long.* She went in the bathroom and brushed her hair and washed her face. After unlocking the bedroom door, she stepped onto the interior balcony overlooking the living room. Trevor was nowhere to be seen. She descended the stairs and looked in the kitchen. Her first thought was to call Jared, so she ambled into the great room to retrieve Trevor's cell phone. In its place was a note.

Sweetheart,

I had to leave for a little while. The fridge is stocked, so help yourself. There is a variety of books and DVDs on the shelves near the TV. Enjoy the peace—it's conducive to decision making. Just remember, things are not always as they seem. I love you.
T.W.

Jana sat on the couch holding the note. *"Things are not always as they seem." What does he mean by that?* Warmth erupted from her heart and filled her body, and her heart felt lighter. The feeling didn't last long.

"Maybe I'll take a walk around the pond," she said out loud. She ran to the bedroom and grabbed a sweater then went to the back door, but her shoes were gone. "I know I left them here." Fear once again clutched her heart. *Without my shoes, I can't leave the house.* Frowning, she tried the door to the deck. It was locked. She sprinted to the front door. There was no key in the deadbolt, and it wouldn't budge. She went to see if there was a key in Trevor's room, but his door was locked. She hurried up to her room. The only open portal to the outside exited from her room to the front deck, twelve feet above the ground. The realization hit her. *I'm a prisoner!*

***

Jana paced the length of the living room, her agitation growing. *What gives Trevor the right to keep me locked up here?* Crossing her arms and drumming her fingers on her sleeve, she turned sharply to cross the floor again. *If he thought I was upset before, wait till he gets back.* The far edge of the room-sized rug met her feet. No matter how elegant or beautiful, a cage was still a cage. She stood with her fists to her sides, stomped her foot, and screamed in frustration.

In an attempt to calm down, she reclined in a deck chair outside her room, reading an ancient copy of *Madam, Will You Talk,* by Mary Stewart. A glass of water and a bowl of Peanut Butter M&M's occupied the small table next to the lounge. Two hours later, Jana heard Trevor's car crunching on the gravel driveway.

Carrying plastic shopping bags while trying to manipulate his key for the front door, he attempted to wave at her. She smiled innocently at him from the railing.

Trevor looked up. "Hello, sweet—"

He was doused with a pitcher of ice water. "What are—"

M&M's rained down on him, followed by the Tupperware bowl for good measure.

"Ouch!" He rubbed his head and mumbled, water dripping from his hair. He glanced up at Jana again. "Your aim definitely improves with anger!"

She turned on her heel and entered the house, slamming the door behind her.

A few minutes later she heard a gentle knock on the master-bedroom door. "Jana, honey, can I come in?"

"Go away!"

"Sweetheart, I have something for you."

"Go away."

He knocked louder. "Do I have to break down the door?"

"It's your house. You can do what you want to it."

"Please?"

She sighed and turned the lock. He entered the room wearing a sheepish expression. "Jana, I'm sorry. I didn't expect to be gone so long."

She glared at him. "That's supposed to make me feel better about being left locked in a house with no way out—and if there was a way out, no shoes to take it?"

"What are you talking about?"

She stormed up to him and poked him in the chest with her finger. "Don't even try to play innocent, Mr. Willis. The doors were deadbolted with no key in sight, and my shoes were not where I left them. That spells prisoner to me."

"Oh, honey, I'm so sorry. It's not as bad as it sounds. You were asleep, so I locked up."

She raised her hands in front of her chest, palms up. "Hello! And what about my shoes?"

"They were muddy, so I threw them in the washer. In fact, the keys are behind the door in the laundry room."

Arms crossed over her chest, she turned away from him and gave a derisive snort. "Yeah, right!" Her right foot kept up a steady tapping.

Trevor walked up behind her, wrapped his arms around her, and whispered in her ear. "I love you, Jana. I would never keep you prisoner."

She whirled to face him. "You wouldn't? Then why am I here? Why would you even own a house where someone could be locked in?"

"Oh, honey, I wish you'd believe me." Anguish showed on his face. "Things aren't always as they seem."

As soon as the words were uttered, Jana felt the Spirit confirm their truth. "You . . . you're trying to muddle my brain again," she said to Trevor, then drew in a deep breath. *Why do I feel this way? How could this possibly be all right?*

"No, but I would appreciate it if you would come downstairs with me." He reached out to her. "I can show you where your shoes and the keys are."

Her anger began to dissipate as she looked into his eyes. "Okay." Still, she refused to take his hand.

After she moved her shoes from the washer to the dryer and grabbed the key hanging on the hook next to the door, Trevor led her to the living room. On the coffee table sat a slightly damp Doubleday edition of the Book of Mormon. "I thought you might want to have this to read while you were here."

How could he know how much I longed for the scriptures today? "Thank you," she said in a subdued tone.

"I thought you might be able to tell me a little about your church and why it is so important to you."

Jana frowned. "Let me get this straight. You kidnapped me just so I could tell you about my church?"

"No, I asked you to come with me so we could rebuild our relationship. The first step is to find out what makes you tick.

Why are you the person you are? I never realized how much your church is an integral part of you."

"Okay." Holding the Book of Mormon on her lap, she flipped through the pages until she reached Alma 32 and read, "'Now, as I said concerning faith—that it was not a perfect knowledge—even so, it is with my words . . .'"

Time flew by as Jana and Trevor talked of the gospel, and both of them jumped when his cell phone rang.

"Is it Jared?" she asked hopefully.

"No, it's Don. I'll take it in the kitchen."

Jana used Trevor's key to unlock the door to the deck. She walked out into the cool night air, rubbing her arms against the chill. *I don't know what to do. Trevor seems genuinely interested in the Church. Can I forget what's happened the last few days? Would marriage to him be paradise or prison?*

She recoiled as he came up behind her and took her arm. "I didn't hear you come out."

"It's hard to hear something on Earth when you're visiting Mars."

She chuckled. "No, Mars is *your* home planet. Remember, men are from Mars, women are from Venus. Is everything all right?"

Trevor made a dismissive gesture with his hand. "Something is just taking longer than I wanted it to. Nothing I can't handle." He cradled her face in his hands and bent his head toward hers, her name on his lips barely a whisper.

The blaring of his cell phone interrupted the moment. He looked at the screen and handed the phone to her. "I'll be in the kitchen getting supper ready."

Jana answered the call. "Jared?"

"Are you all right?"

"Hearing your voice, I'm more than all right."

"How is Trevor?"

She paused, weighing whether or not to mention being locked in the cabin.

"Jana, what happened?"

"Nothing happened." After a slight hesitation, she continued. "He brought me some scriptures, and we spent the last hour talking about the gospel."

"What aren't you telling me?"

"Please, Jared, don't ask anymore." She tried to still the tremor in her voice. "I'll tell you everything tomorrow. If you're nice, I'll even tell you about the ice water and M&M's. I just want to hear your voice right now."

"Okay, but I wish you'd tell me what's going on."

"Why don't you tell me about the talks at sacrament meeting?"

"Well, since Zack is back in town, they asked him to speak. He started out by reading some actual letters sent to the family history department. They were pretty funny."

"Sounds like Zack. Do you remember any of them?"

Jared paused a moment. "Yeah. One said, 'I am mailing you my aunt and uncle and three of their children.' And there was one that said something like 'We are sending you five children in a separate envelope.' Oh, and this is my favorite." Jared gave a little chuckle. "'We lost our grandmother. Will you please send us a copy?'"

"It's amazing what some people will say without realizing it!" Jana giggled, her spirits rising from just listening to him.

"What was really amazing is the talk Zack gave on genealogy. He can be pretty sharp if he's not clowning around."

They continued to discuss the topic from sacrament meeting, and before long, Trevor came outside to announce dinner.

"I better go, Jared. Thanks for calling."

"I'll see you at 7:00 AM—sharp."

"Bye." She held her breath, not wanting to sever the connection. "I'll be there at 7:00 on the dot."

Fifteen

Jared looked at the clock—6:59. He paced the floor in the physical therapy building. Jana wasn't there yet, and she'd promised not to be even a minute late. He went to the weight machines and did a few butterfly curls while waiting. He pushed himself harder. "I'll give her till 7:30 before I call the sheriff." He got on the treadmill at 7:17.

Suddenly the door opened and Jana walked in. Jared hurried over to embrace her. "I was so worried! Are you okay?"

She clung to him. "I am now."

He looked up as Trevor entered with her overnight bag. Jared pushed her gently away. "Jana, your stuff is in the bathroom." He gestured with his head down the hall. "Go change."

Jared maneuvered her behind his back, urging her toward the rear of the building. "Jared, please," she exclaimed as he stared at Trevor.

"Don't worry. I won't do anything I'll regret." Jared strode over to Trevor and grabbed hold of his jacket. "If you ever pull a stunt like this again, I'll call the sheriff faster—"

Trevor stepped back with his hands in the air. "Calm down, Carpenter. She came willing—"

Jared's fist shot out, connecting with Trevor's jaw. Jana screamed as Trevor fell back against the glass door, holding his bleeding lip.

Jared raised a cautioning hand. "Stay back, Jana." He pointed at Trevor. "And don't ever try to tell me she went willingly again. Now, get out of here and stay away from Jana."

Trevor dabbed at his lip with a handkerchief. "You're messing with the wrong man, Carpenter." He straightened his jacket and walked out of the clinic.

Once in his car, Trevor pulled out his cell and called his brother-in-law. "She's back with the therapist," Trevor said before Don could utter a hello.

"Is she safe with him?

"I have every reason to believe she'll be safe with him while I make the rendezvous. Is Lasky still watching?"

"Yeah," Don replied. "He's got a few leads to check out, but he should be around Jana when she's not with Carpenter. I'll also have a few other guys rotating shifts to keep an eye on her."

"Just remember, my patience is running pretty thin right now." Trevor ran his hand through his hair. "I won't wait much longer to tell her."

"Not more than a week or so. I promise."

"Yeah, well, it's that 'or so' that worries me," Trevor said before he severed the connection.

Jana stood in the hallway watching the exchange. When Trevor left, she ran to Jared's side. "Are you all right?"

He rubbed his knuckles. "Just fine. Like I told you, I didn't do anything I regret. In fact, I should have hit him harder." He embraced her and kissed the top of her head, and she felt him relax a little. "When I realized you were missing, I thought my heart would stop beating."

"I am so sorry to have put you through all of that, but if anything had happened to you because of me, I couldn't have lived with it. You do understand, don't you?"

"Of course I do. But tell me what happened, and what he said to convince you to go with him."

Jana closed her eyes a moment. "Can we start my therapy first, please? I think that will help us both calm down."

"Sure, let's get you back to the grindstone." He nudged her toward the bathroom. "Go change."

Once she was dressed in her workout clothes, he examined her shoulder. "Well, you've got quite a bit of swelling, but we'll do a few stretches and then ice the shoulder really well. Let's try the butterfly."

"Do I flap my arms and flit around the room?"

He chuckled. "We'll start with an exercise band and then move to one-pound weights when you're stronger. He handed her a wide yellow band with handles attached to either end. "Step on the middle and hold the handles to the inside." He touched her arm to help position her correctly. "Now, slowly bring your arms up. Don't worry if you can't go very far at first."

She looked into his eyes and saw kindness and strength in their depths—and something else she couldn't place. Her heart did a little flip-flop.

After a few reps with the band, she began talking about her experience that weekend. Anger smoldered on Jared's face when she told him about being locked in the house with no way to contact anyone. "How long did you say you slept?"

"I'm not quite sure," Jana replied. "It must have been at least five or six hours. When I realized he'd left me there alone with no way out, I stopped being afraid and got really mad. I was on the deck outside my room when Trevor returned." She bit her bottom lip. "He waved at me, and someone else took over my body. I dumped an entire pitcher of ice water on top of him."

Jared was laughing. "Way to go."

"That wasn't all." She looked up at him sheepishly. "I was so mad that I dumped the M&M's on him, too, and threw the plastic bowl at his head for good measure."

Jared took the band from Jana and moved her to an unusual-looking machine.

"I wish I could have seen that. Sit right here." He had her turning a wheel, almost like pedaling a bike with her arms. He adjusted the tension. "How does that feel?"

"Okay."

"We'll have you turn forward for about a minute. Let me know if it's too hard."

Jana nodded her head and watched the hand grips as she pushed them around in circles. "Jared, I know I was tired and under stress, but does it seem odd to you that I slept so long?"

Jared inhaled sharply. "Yes, it does. It sounds very suspicious."

She stopped in mid-motion, her tears falling freely. "I was so afraid. Trevor acted strange. His mood kept changing, and I almost didn't know who I was with."

Jared gathered her in his arms and smoothed her hair. "It's okay now. It's okay."

"What should I do?"

He led her to a chair and crouched in front of her. "Jana, we need to think about pressing charges."

She shook her head. "I went with him willingly. The threat to you was implied, but never really spoken." Her eyes filled with tears again.

"It's going to be okay. Let's start by talking to the Grants about securing the sliding glass door." Jared handed Jana a box of tissues. "I'll see if the sheriff will make a few extra passes by your place every night."

"Thank you."

"Now we're going to get you home so you can rest. Emma said she'd check in on you today. Do you think you'll be up for home evening tonight? It might be the distraction you need."

"Sure, I'm in. What are we doing?"

"We're playing miniature golf. There's a little Fun Center in Seaside—only a dollar to play ten holes. They have bumper cars and a tilt-a-wheel for only $1.25. It should be fun. If you thought Zack's dancing style was unique, wait till you see him play miniature golf."

Jana rolled her eyes and smiled. "What time?"

"We need to be in there by 6:00, so maybe twenty minutes before."

"Do you think my shoulder is ready?"

"Your shoulder should be fine. It's your stomach I'd worry about." Jared grimaced.

Jana stopped the exercise and looked at him quizzically. "My stomach?"

"Did I mention we were going to eat at Pronto Pup before golfing? 'Looks like a corn dog, but it's better.' It's all part of the experience."

"You're joking, aren't you?" she said hopefully.

"You're mixing me up with Zack."

"You're serious? That's really their motto?"

"Yep."

She shook her head with a chuckle. "This will be interesting."

———•———

At 5:35 the front bell rang. Jana held the phone to her ear as she opened the door and put a finger up to signal "just a minute" to Jared. She motioned him into the living room, then walked back to the bedroom. "You're right, Sue. I would never have thought Trevor was capable of that." Jana ran a brush through her hair. "Yes, I'll be careful. Any other questions?"

With sweater in hand, she came out of the bedroom. "I have to go. Let me know if you need me."

She ended her call and said, "No fair, Jared, you're early."

He smiled. "Zack's driving today, so I told him we'd meet him here. He threatens to leave if everyone isn't ready when he is. Of course, that would mean he wouldn't have anyone to listen to his jokes, so I don't think he'd actually do it."

"I think you're right, but I'm ready for him." She wiggled her eyebrows.

"What do you mean?"

"Oh . . . I just might have a few jokes of my own." She winked at him over her shoulder as she grabbed her purse.

"What did you do today?" Jared asked.

"I might have done a little research in the art of corny jokes." *So I can keep my friends from asking about last weekend.*

Under his breath, Jared muttered, "This should be good." A long honk followed by a couple of short beeps shattered the evening's peace. "That's Zack. We better get out there. I don't want to miss a possible joke war." Jared helped Jana into the back seat of Zack's ancient green Mercury Capri, spreading his denim jacket on the seat before she sat down.

"Hey, I cleaned it out this afternoon," Zack protested from the driver's seat.

Jana wrinkled her nose. "Um, thank you." She turned to Jared and whispered in his ear, "I'm afraid to ask what it looked like before. I can see why they wanted you to drive the Corolla to Mount St. Helens."

"The junk is what's holding this heap together," he whispered back. "If he gets rid of too much, it will fall apart. But don't worry—it's Caitlyn's turn to drive next. Her car is old, but it's clean."

Zack looked back at Jana and Jared. "This is a no-secrets car. No whispering. By the way, I have a question for you."

"Oh no! How long is the drive, Jared?" Jana laughed.

"Fortunately, only ten or fifteen minutes."

Caitlyn put her hand on Zack's arm. "Can't you even wait for them to put their seatbelts on?"

"Hey, I've been looking forward to this all day. I have a lot of jokes to tell, and I can't wait to start."

"I have one for you, Zack," Jana started. "Why did the golfer bring two pairs of pants?" She waited expectantly. "In case he got a hole in one."

Zack guffawed. "Good one, Jana! You know, I've heard that this is a pretty small course, so instead of yelling 'fore' you only have to yell 'three and a half.'"

"Jana," Caitlyn called from the front seat. "You're encouraging him."

"Answer me this," Zack said as he looked in the rearview mirror. "What is the difference between driving in golf and driving a car?"

"I give up. What's the difference?"

"When you drive a car, you don't want to hit anything."

"So, with you, there's no difference?"

"You're funny, Jared. Would you like to get out and walk?"

"No problem, since we're here."

They climbed out of the car to join the rest of the ward young adults gathered at Pronto Pup. Jana's three friends perused the menu, and she read from the large whiteboard, "'Pronto Pup. Looks like a corn dog, but it's better.'" She stared at the motto for a moment and then burst out laughing. "You really were serious. I thought you were pulling my leg."

"Your shoulder maybe, but never your leg." Jared stood next to her and casually draped an arm around her. "Are you ready to order? The 'Pup Deal' includes chips and drink."

"I'll have that with lemonade, although" —she winked— "the free cup of water with purchase sounds inviting."

He leaned forward to speak through the glass and placed their order. "I'll have two Pup Deals with lemonade and one free cup of water with purchase. Jana, what kind of chips do you want?"

"Why, Ruffles with ridges, of course," she replied, rolling her *R*'s dramatically.

Jared chuckled and relayed the order. When it was ready he brought the tray to an empty table. After he and Jana sat down, he tapped her on her good shoulder and pointed at Zack and Caitlyn as they waited for their food with clasped hands. "Looks like things are progressing well with those two."

"It sure does. Do you think she could stand his jokes for the rest of eternity?"

Jared opened her chips, snitching one as he placed the bag on the tray in front of her. "I have a feeling he's a lot quieter alone with Caitlyn than he is in a group setting. Anyway, I think he's a pretty slow mover. I wouldn't expect anything too soon."

"You're probably right. Here they come."

Zack approached the table, holding up his pronto pup. "Why is a corn dog the noblest of all dogs?"

Jared glanced at Caitlyn. "What if we just ignore him?"

"Because it feeds the hand that bites it," Zack finished.

Caitlyn feigned a whisper to Jared and Jana. "It doesn't work."

Jana chuckled. "Oh, that was bad. But I can do better. What kind of dog is covered in water?"

Jared took the bait. "I don't know, Jana. What kind of dog is covered in water?"

"A wet one."

Zack laughed so hard that tears formed in his eyes. "Finally, someone who appreciates the fine art of corny joke telling." He winked at Jared. "You might not want to let this one go."

Jared looked down at his hands, while Jana blushed and bit her bottom lip.

Caitlyn kicked her boyfriend under the table. "Zack, shh!"

He put his hands up and shrugged. "What did I do?"

They finished their meal and cleared away their trash. Jared escorted Jana toward the miniature golf course. "Let's get our stuff to play. The course is just through this door."

Jared and Zack stood in line to get the clubs and balls, while Jana and Caitlyn talked.

"Oh, Jana, I'm so glad you're back and everything's okay."

"Did Jared tell you about it?"

"Yes. He was so worried. I've known him a few years, and I've never seen him upset like this."

"It was scary at first, but by the time I left, I wasn't frightened anymore," Jana said as lightly as she could.

"I'd be glad to stay with you tonight or for as long as you need me to."

"Thank you so much, Caitlyn. I think I'll be okay. I need to stay on my own sometime—I might as well start tonight."

"Well, just call if you change your mind."

The guys returned with clubs and balls in hand. Jared nodded toward the course. "Let's get started."

Zack commented over his shoulder, "Ah! I just love to play miniature golf. I get to hit the ball more than anybody else."

Groans erupted from everyone around and Jana spoke up. "What is the only thing you can break when you say its name?"

"I give up."

"Silence."

"Get the hint, Zack?" Jared elbowed him in the ribs.

His reply of "What hint?" won him a punch on the arm from Caitlyn.

Jared sailed through the course, never needing more than two or occasionally three shots. Caitlyn's and Jana's scores were respectable, and Zack came in last. He tried driving from behind his back, through his legs, pool-cue style, and finally, on the sixth try on every hole, a basketball slam dunk. He had their group laughing, and the group behind them cursing. Fortunately, Zack kept inviting the other parties to play through.

Next, the four friends tested their skills at the bumper cars. Jared ran protective interference around Jana, attempting to make sure she didn't get jarred too forcefully. Zack drove like a maniac. All the cars parted like the Red Sea when the drivers saw him approaching.

As they walked out of the ride, Jana whispered to Jared, "I'm glad he drives better in the real world."

Jared nodded. "Let's get some ice cream. My treat."

Zack grabbed Caitlyn's hand and headed for the Pronto Pup stand. "You know I never pass up free food. Come on, Cait!"

"What would you like, Jana?"

She looked over the ice cream options. "I'll take an ice cream sandwich on a chocolate chip cookie."

"What about you, Caitlyn?"

"Um, I'll have a small chocolate cone."

"Zack?"

"A root beer float with chocolate ice cream."

Jared placed their order and shuddered when he saw Zack's float. "The idea of root beer and chocolate ice cream definitely goes against the grain."

"You're just jealous because you don't share my sense of adventure when it comes to food." Zack looked at Jared's choice with mock disdain. "Can you get any more boring than a vanilla ice cream cone?"

"Probably not, but at least it doesn't assault my taste buds."

They piled into the rolling trash an for the ride home. When Zack dropped Jana and Jared off at the guest house, Jana leaned back into the car and said, "I was wondering, Zack. If the former ruler of Russia was the Czar, and his wife was the Czarina, what were their kids called?"

He rubbed his chin. "Grand Duke and Grand Duchess?"

"No. They're Czardines!" Jana laughed as she and Jared made a mad dash to the house. At the door, they turned to take one last look at Zack's stunned expression.

Sixteen

Jared and Jana closed the door before Zack could retaliate with another corny joke. They slid down against the door and laughed so hard that tears started to flow. When they finally stopped laughing and caught their breath, Jared helped her up.

"I brought a couple of movies and some microwave popcorn if you're interested.

"I'd like that. I really don't want to be alone right now." She looked intently at her hands.

"You okay?" Jared leaned back, trying to look in her eyes.

"Yeah, I'm fine. I'd just like some company."

"Glad to oblige. I brought *National Treasure* and *Seven Brides for Seven Brothers.*"

"Either is fine, as long as there's popcorn." Their conversation was interrupted by the ringing of Jana's cell phone. She looked at the screen and announced with trepidation, "It's Trevor."

"I could go get gas and be back in about fifteen minutes, or do you want me to stay?"

Taking a deep breath, she looked up. "Go ahead. I'll be fine." She connected the call as Jared closed the door. "Hello, Trevor."

"Jana! How are you doing?"

"I'm all right." She sat on the edge of the couch and crossed her ankles.

"I've been doing a lot of soul searching."

"That's good. Have you found anything?"

Trevor laughed. "There were things I didn't like, but I did find a couple of redeeming qualities. Is Jared there right now?"

"No. When you called he went to fill his car with gas. He'll be back soon."

"Can I ask you a question?"

"Sure. I can't guarantee an answer, but I'll try."

"I just had the LDS missionaries over. At the cabin, you said you knew we lived with God before we were born. How do you know?"

"You had the missionaries over?"

"Yeah. Now, how do you know?"

"Through study and prayer." She stood up, and with one hand on her hip and the other holding the phone to her ear, she paced in front of the coffee table.

"But how do you know you've received an answer?" Trevor pleaded. "How does it feel?"

"I can tell you how I feel the Spirit, but it might be different for you."

"Go ahead."

Jana took another deep breath, searching for the correct words. "It feels warm and glowing. It starts in my chest and just kind of explodes from there. I feel it when I pray, and that's usually how an answer comes."

"I think I'm starting to feel that. Is this why you feel so strongly about your church?"

"Yes. At times I just get an impression to do something, and I've learned to act on it. Does that help you at all?"

"I've always acted on my hunches. Do you think it could have been the Spirit telling me what to do?"

"Yes, it could very well be. I believe a lot of what people call intuition is actually the Spirit talking to us."

"Wow! I can hardly wait for the missionaries to come back tomorrow."

"They're coming back tomorrow?" Jana couldn't hide her surprise. *I guess when Trevor wants to know something, he doesn't waste any time finding out.*

"Yes. I told them I'd feed them. They seemed pretty happy about that."

"I can imagine." A smile played on her lips. "Dinner and a discussion—just what the mission president ordered."

"How was therapy?"

"Good. Jared thinks I should be back to the same point as last week by tomorrow or Wednesday. I'm feeling stronger, anyway. Tonight we played miniature golf, and I held my own. Caitlyn and I tied. Jared won, and Zack was . . . Zack. We finally had to stop him after six strokes per hole so other people could play."

Trevor's deep laugh filled the air space. "Was it just the four of you?"

"It was home evening—all the young adults from the area were there."

"Sweetheart, I wanted to let you know that I am so sorry for what happened."

Jana paced the floor before she finally curled up in the comfortable recliner. "I know."

"I wish you were home again."

"I'll be here a couple more weeks." She looked toward the door, hoping Jared would return quickly.

"Would you and your friends like to do something this weekend?"

"I . . . I don't know." Panic welled up inside of her. "I'm not ready to see you again right now."

She heard a sharp intake of breath before Trevor said, "Let me know."

Jana jumped when a knock sounded at the door. "Jared's back."

"I'll let you go. I love you, Jana."

"Bye."

After a slight pause, he said in a subdued tone, "Night, sweetheart."

Jana touched the phone and wiped a tear from her eye before opening the door for Jared.

"Is everything all right?"

"I guess. Hold me?"

Jared complied, and she relaxed into his shoulder.

"I feel so safe with you."

He stroked her hair. "What did Trevor want?"

Jana pulled away and hugged her arms to herself, turning to the window. "He asked me how the Spirit felt. The missionaries were there tonight. They're coming back tomorrow."

"Maybe he's serious about changing." Jared approached her from behind and put his hands on her shoulders.

"Maybe." She faced him.

"You sure you're okay?" She nodded her response, and Jared asked, "So, do you feel like an adventure or a musical?"

"I think I'm in the mood for adventure. Why don't you get it ready while I pop the popcorn?"

After unwrapping the package, she placed it in the microwave and pushed some buttons. She pulled a bowl out of the cupboard, along with a couple of glasses. *Trevor is investigating the Church.* Jana looked at Jared crouched in front of the DVD player in the living room. *Why don't I feel happier?*

"The movie's ready to go when you are," he called into the kitchen.

An hour and a half later as the final credits began playing on the screen, Jana stood up to take the popcorn bowl to the kitchen. "I just love Riley. He's so funny."

"Yeah. I wish that they would make more movies like that." Jared picked up their glasses and followed her into the kitchen. "Well, it's getting late, so I should probably go. Did Karl bring the dowel for the door?"

"Yes, he did."

"Good. Will you be okay alone?"

"I'll be fine." At the door, Jana embraced him and kissed his cheek. "Thanks for everything."

"See ya tomorrow." Jared touched his cheek as he headed toward his car, whistling the theme from *National Treasure.*

Jana leaned against the doorjamb and watched him get in his car. He gave one last wave, and she smiled as he drove away.

Solitude suspended time for Trevor. The thick darkness hung around him as he knelt by his bed and attempted his first solo prayer, trying to follow the steps the missionaries had outlined.

After several minutes, he leaned back onto his feet. "Whoa!" His body felt shaky and weak, yet his spirit soared. His eyes turned heavenward. "Thank you."

Jared walked into his office cubby. "Wow. You can have a job here anytime. I can't believe how much you've accomplished."

"Ah yes, just call me the miracle worker." Wagging her finger, Jana admonished in her best motherly voice, "Of course, it won't do any good if you don't keep it up."

He stood up straight and saluted her. "Yes, ma'am! Are you about ready to leave?"

She twirled around in the new office chair, pushing with her feet toward the file cabinets. "Just a few more things to file, then I'll straighten up the desk and I'm out of here."

"Got a big night planned?"

"Maybe." She drew out the word. "There's this guy who's been a good friend to me, and I thought I would ask him to have dinner at my place tonight, as a kind of a thank you."

"Oh. Would that be Marty at the office supply store? You might want to invite his wife and four kids over."

"Seriously. I wanted to thank you for everything. Do you want to come over for dinner?"

"Just like chocolate, I never turn down an offer for a home-cooked meal. What time?"

She tapped her chin with her forefinger. "That depends. Do you want homemade rolls or store-bought French bread?"

He reached across her and grabbed a handful of M&M's from a candy dish on the desk. "Given a choice, I'd go for homemade rolls." He popped a couple of candies into his mouth.

"That means you have to come over early and knead the dough for me. I'm still pretty much one handed when it comes—" His mortified expression stopped her in mid-sentence. "Have you ever kneaded dough before?"

"My mom had me try it once." He gave a wry smile. "You may want to have a backup loaf of bread, just in case."

"Oh, I think we can manage to put your muscle where your mouth is," she teased. "Be there at 5:00 sharp." She slung her purse over her right shoulder.

"Yes, ma'am."

"I'll see you later. I have to grab a few things for tonight."

"Did you want me to drive you? I don't want you carrying anything too heavy."

"I'm starting to enjoy walking everywhere. Although you could come by the Bonnie Bee in twenty minutes or so to transport me and the groceries home."

He threw an M&M up in the air and caught it in his mouth. "I'll be there."

Jana got to the door and turned around. "By the way, what's your favorite dessert?"

"I love anything with peaches."

"Okay, peaches it is."

"There's a great farm stand not too far out of town," Jared called, stopping her. "They usually have killer fruit this time of year. Would you like to go after we put your groceries away?"

"That sounds terrific. See you soon." Jana started toward the door again but turned back. "Oh, one more thing. My recipe makes a large casserole. Could you call Zack and Caitlyn to see if they want to come?"

"Sure. Anything else?"

"No, that's really it. See ya." She heard him chuckle as she left the building.

———••———

Trevor gazed out the office window without seeing the sweeping Portland skyline. *Jana claims he's like a brother to her. She's over there with him, when she should be home with me.* He rubbed his tender jaw. On his desk, a folder held his chance to destroy the dream of Jared Carpenter. All Trevor had to do was call in a favor—just one phone call. Jared would never know it was Trevor who made it impossible for him to procure a loan to cover the balloon payment. Jared's therapy practice would be doomed. If he was facing financial ruin, it would be harder for him to pursue Jana.

Suddenly, Trevor remembered his feelings after his prayer the previous night. *Do I really want to stoop to that level? Maybe I'll make a phone call just to find out the status of his loan applications. That's something a friend might do.*

He picked up the phone and dialed. "Tom, Trevor Willis here."

"It's good to hear from you. How are things going?"

"Fine, fine. I need an unofficial favor. Jared Carpenter has a loan application in with you. Can you check the status of it?"

"Sure. I think I remember that one." The sound of shuffling papers carried over the line. "Yes, here it is. That's a lot of money for such a small town. I was ready to put it in the rejection pile. You want me to add a good word from you?"

"No, not just yet, but why don't you hold onto it for a few days."

Trevor thanked Tom and hung up. He wouldn't have to do anything, since Jared wasn't going to get the loan. Of course, one good word might help the guy. *Do I really want to be a better person or not?* Trevor closed the folder and pushed it away.

With his eyes closed, he took a deep breath, trying to relax. The door banging open jarred him out of his reverie. Vince Coleman stood framed in the doorway.

Vince stood taller than Trevor by an inch or two and outweighed him by forty pounds. With Vince's generally jovial demeanor, it took a lot to make him angry, and that anger only manifested itself on rare occasions. Apparently, this was one of them. Fire blazed in his eyes, and his large hands clenched into fists.

Trevor's secretary followed Vince into the office. "I'm sorry, Mr. Willis. I couldn't stop him."

"It's okay, Brenda." Trevor extended his hand to the older man. "Vince, how are you doing? Can I get you a soda?"

"I just talked to my niece." Vince's eyes held malice.

Trevor ran his hand through his hair. "I can't tell you how sorry I am. I assure you it will never happen again."

Like lightning, Vince's hammer of a fist connected loudly with Trevor's jaw. He staggered back with the force of the impact, tumbling head over heels as he tripped over the glass coffee table. Trevor's secretary screamed and ran out of the office.

"If you ever lay another hand on my little girl again, you'll wish you'd never been born."

"You better look at the state of your own house before you start throwing stones." Trevor rubbed his jaw. "Or punches."

"What are you talking about, Willis?"

Two burly security guards rushed in, followed by Brenda. They took hold of Vince and began to escort him out.

The secretary ran to Trevor and helped him to his feet. "Are you okay?"

"I'm fine. Tony, Bruce, let him go. He won't cause any more trouble." Trevor straightened his tie.

Tony looked skeptical. "You sure, Mr. Willis? I can call the police if you want."

"No, I'm sure. It was a personal matter." Trevor extended his hand to Vince. "Once again, I apologize for my actions and promise you that it will never happen again."

The older man turned on his heel and stormed from the office.

Trevor watched Vince Coleman exit before answering his cell phone. "How much longer, Don?"

"A week or two—a month at the most. I think Coleman is leaning our way. Our deal should sound much better to him than a long prison term for developing and smuggling restricted technology out of the country."

"It better be soon. I just got punched for the second time in two days—this time by Coleman. We're lucky I don't have a glass jaw."

"All for your country, brother."

"I thought I had quit."

"You were our best agent. We couldn't have come this far without you."

"I may have lost the woman I love because of this. I'm really beginning to question the cost."

"Trevor, I'm sorry. After this is all behind us, I'll do what I can to smooth things over with Jana."

"Yeah, I know. I know. Keep me informed."

Upon his return to the office, Vince also made a phone call.

"It's me. I want a favor."

"What?"

"I don't like how Trevor Willis is treating my niece. I want you to give him a warning, but remember, I want him scared, not dead."

"I understand. Is everything ready?"

Vince paused a moment. If he cooperated with the government, would they really be able to keep his family safe? What would happen to his business? Would he be able to keep up appearances until the FBI broke up the smuggling ring? "It should be done within the month." He hung up, his shoulders sagging.

Seventeen

Jared arrived at the Bonnie Bee as Jana came out the door with two bags of groceries in her cart. "Perfect timing," she said when he got out of the car.

He bowed gallantly. "Your chariot awaits." He took the bags and peeked at the contents. "I can hardly wait for dinner." He moved a few items in the larger bag and then looked at her. "Did you pick up bread just in case I don't come through on the rolls?"

"No, I'm putting my faith in you. Was it Cortez who burned the ships when he arrived in the New World? There's no going back—either come through, or no bread."

A broad smile erupted on Jared's face, and he bowed once more. "I'll do everything in my power to be worthy of that trust, milady." After setting the groceries on the back seat, he quickly returned the cart and helped Jana into the car.

"Now, on to the produce stand." As they drove out of the parking lot, she marveled at how relaxed she felt around Jared. *Why do my troubles always seem to revolve around Trevor?*

Jana carefully tossed a peach in the air before placing it in her basket. "Mr. Carpenter, I have to admit that you definitely know what you're talking about. These peaches look and smell heavenly. Have you ever made a pie crust, or would you prefer a cobbler?"

"Why don't we get enough peaches to do both, and we can have the other later in the week. Or"—Jared smiled sheepishly— "I could freeze as much as you're willing to make. That way I'll still have some when you're gone and I don't have anyone to make such delicious desserts for me."

Jana grinned. "I'd love to make some peach desserts for your food storage. How long do you think they'll have to last?"

"Oh, I figure about a day or two. But maybe not even that long."

They continued through the rows of fresh vegetables and fruits, picking a variety and deciding to try a few new things. Jana examined a basket of blackberries. "Do you like Marion berries?"

"Almost as much as peaches," Jared replied.

"Great. I'll get some." She handed the berries to him, and he realized he must look like a pack mule.

When they finally reached Jana's little guest house, they began to construct supper.

Jared looked at the assembled ingredients for the rolls with a measure of panic. "Zack and Caitlyn had other plans tonight so they can't make it. I know Eric has a meeting tonight, but I wonder if Emma and Karl would like to come over."

"What a good idea." Jana's hands were messy from the lasagna filling, and she held them up toward Jared, threatening to share the mess. "Maybe you should call them. It should be ready by 6:30."

"Fine." He tried to shield himself with a kitchen towel. "Anything, just stay back." He retreated to pull out his cell phone and make a call. "Emma, this is Jared Carpenter. Would you and Karl like to come over to the guest house for dinner tonight? Jana's making lasagna, and I'm supposed to attempt rolls because the kneading is too hard on her shoulder."

"We'd love to," Emma said, "but why don't you let me make the rolls?"

"No, I couldn't let you do that," Jared replied hopefully.

"I insist."

"Are you sure?"

"Yes, it's no problem at all."

"That will be a lot better than what would have come from my hands! Jana said around 6:30."

"We'll see you then."

"Bye."

He turned to find Jana right there, reaching out to touch his face with the ricotta-cheese-covered hands. "Now, Jana, you wouldn't dare."

"Wouldn't I? You thought you'd get away scot-free and have Emma do the rolls?"

"She offered." Jared continued his backward retreat, bumping into the table and nearly upsetting a chair, fumbling with it till it was upright. "In fact, she insisted."

Jana tried to touch the tip of his nose, so he grabbed her wrist to stop her. His face was only a few inches from hers, and without meaning to, he closed the distance and kissed her. He stepped back, his eyes locked with hers. "I'm . . . I'm sorry, Jana. I really didn't mean for that to happen." He dropped her wrist.

Heat rose in her cheeks as she looked down. "That's okay," she said quietly before she reached out and dabbed some of the ricotta filling on his cheek. "Gotcha!"

She fled to the kitchen as he laughed and declared, "I may never wash my face again!"

"Okay, mister, you got out of the bread, but that means you'll have to roll out the pie crust."

"Yes, ma'am."

At precisely 6:30, Emma and Karl knocked on the door. As they walked in, the aroma of freshly baked bread wafted in with them.

"Oh, Emma, that smells wonderful." Jana hugged her and whispered something. They both laughed as she took the napkin-lined basket from Emma.

Jared walked to Jana's side, offering his hand to the white-haired gentleman next to Emma. "Hello, Karl. Any idea what they're laughing and whispering about?"

Karl laughed heartily. "Darned if I know! If I understood that kind of thing, I could write a book and make a whole lotta money."

"Well, maybe someday we'll figure out women," Jared conceded. "Right now I think it's enough to be able to eat their cooking instead of our own. What do you think?"

"I think you're becoming a mighty smart young man." Karl slapped Jared on the back. "Now let's hurry to the table before they decide not to feed us."

"Wise words from a wise man."

After Karl offered the blessing, talk turned to the older couple's courtship. "We met at the BYU just after my mission," he explained. "She was a vision, and it seemed like every young man on campus vied for her attention. She wore her hair in a ponytail most times, but once in a while, she wore it loose around her shoulders. I wooed her with my charm and stole her away from another fella. I've been filled with wonder ever since."

"What he didn't realize was that he chased me till I caught him." Emma leaned forward and patted his arm.

"I've never been so happy to be caught." He gave his bride of forty years a kiss on the cheek.

When everyone finished eating, Jared rose and began to clear the table. "Karl, since Emma and Jana did the cooking, maybe you and I should clean up."

Karl stood. "I'd say that meal was definitely worth it. Why don't you two go sit down and visit while I teach this young whippersnapper a thing or two about cleaning a kitchen."

"If I'd known I didn't have to clean up, I would've made a bigger mess." Giving Jared a pointed look, Jana rubbed her cheek.

As she walked into the kitchen, he chased her with the snap of a wet dish towel. He reached her side, rubbed his cheek, and whispered in her ear. "Vengeance is mine, saith Jared Carpenter!" He snapped the rag one more time for good measure.

Jana grinned. She turned off the oven and put the pie inside to keep it warm, then joined Emma on the couch.

Once the last dish found its way back into the cabinet, Karl came up behind Emma, wrapped his arms around her shoulders, and gave her a loud kiss on the cheek. "What do you think, dear? Are you up to a rousing game of Uno?"

She looked at him sweetly. "Only if you're ready to lose."

He helped her off the couch and gave her a wink. "The usual bet?"

"Of course." She returned the gesture.

Laughing at the interchange, Jared said, "Do we dare ask what the usual bet is?"

Emma's musical laughter filled the air. "Whoever wins gets control of the remote for the next evening."

"That's why I never lose," Karl returned.

"No, dear. That's why *I* never lose."

"This could really get rough," Jana added as she handed the deck to Jared.

He took the cards and began to shuffle them. "How would you like to make this interesting?"

"What do you mean?" Jana eyed him suspiciously.

"We'll put in a few house rules."

"What kind of house rules?" Emma asked.

Jared grinned. "If someone plays a '0,' everyone passes their hand to the left. If you play a '7,' then you have to trade your hand with someone else of your choosing."

"Sounds tricky." Emma rubbed her hands together. "Just my kind of game."

The game moved quickly, with fairly even scores. When they came to the last hand, Jared had only two cards, while everyone else held at least eight or nine. He could smell victory when his turn came around. The card on the deck was yellow, and he set down his card with a flourish and called out, "Uno! Like I said, 'Vengeance is mine,' Miss Clawson!" With a smug look on his face, he sat back in his chair, hugging his single card to his chest.

Jana smiled innocently and put out her hand to him. "Hand over your card, Mr. Carpenter—you put down a '0.' And you might want to pick your jaw up off the floor while you're at it." She laughed at his stunned expression. Then she handed her cards to Emma, grabbed the single card from Jared, and put it on the discard pile. "I win!"

Emma and Karl laughed while Jared stared at the pile of cards Karl placed in front of him.

"Whoa, Jared. That's an awful lot of points." Jana clicked her tongue and began mentally tallying them.

Jared finally joined in the laughter. "I guess you know what they say, 'Pride goeth before the fall.' It's sure true in my case. Would you like some peach pie before you leave?"

"I think having to share the pie with us sounds like an appropriate penalty for pride. By the way, Jana, I have forty-two." Karl called out as he tossed his cards on the table.

Emma finished totaling hers. "Thirty-seven."

Jana busily added the scores. "How bad was the damage, Jared?"

He threw his hand on the pile. "Ugh—154."

"Okay, here's the final score. Jared—632, Jana—481, and . . . I don't believe it! Emma and Karl are tied at 522."

"I guess we have to share the remote, Karl."

"Just so I get my own piece of pie, love."

Jana pulled the pie out of the oven while Jared reached for dessert plates. "Does anyone want ice cream with their pie?"

A chorus of yeses echoed through the room. Jared procured the ice cream while Jana reached for the knife and ice cream scoop.

"See how well they already work together without a word?" Emma asked, and Jared was pretty sure he wasn't supposed to hear her.

"You're right," Karl replied. "It's almost like they can read each other thoughts. Interesting."

"Yes, very interesting."

After serving their guests, Jana and Jared sat down with their own pieces of pie à la mode. Jared sank his fork into the tender peaches and flaky crust, closing his eyes as the cinnamon-and-spice aroma filled his senses. Then he took a bite and savored the taste. "Oh, Jana, this is so good. I'd fight Trevor again just to have access to this pie for the rest of my life. Do you think he'll go for it?" He looked at her. "Will you?"

"I don't think he'd go for it."

Jared noticed his second question went unanswered, and he saw Emma and Karl exchange "a-ha" glances.

"I love the crust," Emma praised. "You'll have to share the recipe with me, Jana."

"I'd be glad to."

"This is almost as good as my Emma's pie," Karl said, then lowered his voice to address Jared. "Of course, the secret to a long, happy marriage is that nothing is ever as good as your wife's cooking. Things can be almost as good, but never as good as or better than!" He elbowed his young friend in the ribs.

"That's one I'll definitely remember, Karl."

The older man draped his arm around his sweetheart. "Well, my dear, it's time for us to be going. We'll see who can win the race for the remote control. I'll beat you home."

Emma hugged Jana and Jared in turn. "Thank you so much for inviting us over. It was a delightful evening."

Jana returned the hug. "Thanks for coming. Maybe you'd better hurry. Karl has a pretty good head start."

Emma waved it off. "Don't worry. I hid the remote before we came over. He'll never find it." She winked before she headed out the door.

Jana and Jared called after her, "Good night."

⸻

Jared cleared the dessert dishes from the table and started to fill the sink with hot, soapy water. "You really don't need to do that," Jana said, entering the kitchen. "It'll just take me a minute."

"It'll just take me a minute, too. I figure if I leave everything neat and clean you'll be more likely to cook for me again."

"I'd do it anyway," she replied as their gazes locked. He was the first to look away.

He washed the dishes while she busied herself wrapping up leftovers for him to take home. She had lasagna on her fingers when her cell phone rang. "Could you get that, Jared? I need to wash my hands."

"Sure." He answered her phone with a hello. Several seconds later he said, "You're right, Willis. You better not forget it."

Jana's head snapped up. It was Jared's tone that shook her more than his words. He looked at her. "Trevor wants to talk to you."

Nodding, she held up her hands.

"It'll be just a minute," Jared informed Trevor. "She's just finishing something and has to wash her hands."

An awkward silence hung in the air until Jana took the phone and said, "Sorry about that."

"No problem at all." Trevor's voice was artificially cheerful.

"Can I call you back in a little while?"

"I'll be waiting."

Jana smiled as she pushed the button to end the call. "Jared, didn't you just wipe that down a couple of minutes ago?"

"Yeah, but you made a mess again."

Realizing he was upset by Trevor's call, she touched his arm reassuringly. "But it was for a good cause."

"What cause was that?"

"Sending a care package home with you—including lasagna and peach pie."

Jared leaned against the counter with a towel in hand. "That's my kind of charitable cause. You can contribute to the 'Feed Jared Fund' anytime. But I only accept perishable food items."

"I think I can handle that. I was actually hoping it would be a peace offering. Kind of a placation to the vengeful spirit of the volcano."

"It may have worked." He winked at Jana. "But then you know how fickle the volcano spirits can be. It may require constant unburnt offerings to do the trick."

"Unburnt? I'm beginning to wonder if it's worth it."

"I could always just execute my vengeance at the therapy building." He rubbed his shoulder.

She put her hand to her forehead in an overdramatic gesture. "Oh no, sir! Anything thing but that!"

"Muah ha ha ha ha ha!"

She moved her hand to his face. "Seriously, Jared, thank you for all you've done for me. I really don't know how I could ever repay you." As she leaned forward, a stainless-steel bowl, precariously perched on the top of the dish drainer, fell into the sink, shattering the tender moment.

He looked at the sink. "Maybe you should do the stacking next time. And I'm glad to be here for you."

"Well, thanks anyway." She paused a moment and smiled broadly. "Are the volcano gods placated?"

Winking, he reached for the foil-wrapped packages. "Possibly. Is this really for me?"

"Yes, I hope you enjoy it. Jared, can I tell you something before you leave?"

He put down the packages and gave her his full attention.

"It's about something that happened at the cabin. Can we sit down a minute?"

With hands clasped, he led Jana to the couch. "What is it?"

"In the note Trevor left, he said, 'Things aren't always as they seem.'" She looked at Jared's hand in hers. "When I read that, I felt the Spirit whisper that it was true." She looked into Jared's eyes. "I think there's something I don't understand and that I'm being told not to judge Trevor too harshly. That's why I'm allowing him to come here this weekend."

"You have to trust your own feelings, Jana. Go ahead and invite him to stay at my place."

"Thank you for understanding." She stood up. "We'll save the movie for tomorrow night." She hugged Jared and said good night.

After she closed the door behind him, she touched her fingers to her lips. Her mind raced back to his kiss and the feelings it stirred in her. *I can't think about that right now. I have to have a clear mind when I talk to Trevor.* But try as she might, Jared's kiss wouldn't leave her consciousness.

She called Trevor, who picked up on the first ring. "How are you doing tonight? Did Jared leave?"

"All right, and yes. I get the feeling you're a bit jealous." She paced the kitchen, wiping at imaginary crumbs with the towel Jared had abandoned.

Trevor laughed. "Insanely! But I heard a poem I think I'll adopt. 'If you love something, set it free. If it doesn't come back, it was never meant to be. If it returns, love it forever.'"

"I'm seeing a change."

"Good. That's what you're supposed to notice."

"Your voice sounds a little strange. Are you okay?"

Trevor paused a moment. "I'm fine. My jaw is just suffering from a confrontation with your uncle's fist."

"Oh, Trevor! I'm so sorry. Are you okay? That's twice in the last couple of days. You know, Uncle Vince is normally a big teddy bear—unless someone is threatening Aunt Karen or me, of course."

"Forget about it, sweetheart. I deserved it. I assured him it would never happen again, and it won't. So, what did you guys do tonight?"

"Emma and Karl Grant came over for dinner, and we played Uno." Jana turned off the light in the kitchen.

"It sounds like a swinging evening. Who won?"

She cleared her throat. "Yours truly. Jared almost won, but he insisted on house rules and they backfired on him." She sat on the recliner and extended the footrest. "He came in dead last. It served him right. He was being pretty cocky about it."

"Poor guy," Trevor said in a tone devoid of sympathy.

"You're hopeless." Jana kicked her shoes off and they landed with a clunk in the middle of the room.

"But you have to love me, right?"

When she didn't reply, he said longingly, "I wish I were there with you."

"You would've had fun, although you probably would have been even cockier than Jared."

"Of course! But there's a big difference. I would have won. Did you cook or take out?"

Her socks followed her shoes. "I made lasagna."

"Now I'm really sorry I wasn't there. Did you make rolls?" Trevor's words were strained.

"No, I was going to coach Jared in how to make them, but Emma volunteered at the last minute and saved us from his cooking. He did roll out the pie crust, though. My shoulder's still a little too sore to tackle that."

"I'll come down on Saturday. If you need any dough rolled out, I'd be glad to do it then."

"I may take you up on that. I thought I'd make a couple of pies for Jared to freeze. You might be able to sweet talk me into making some for your freezer, too." She stretched her legs while stifling a yawn.

"It sounds like my kind of persuasion. How did Jared do it?"

"Now, now, Trevor. Keep the little green-eyed monster at bay."

"I'm trying. How do you read me so well?" He paused. "So, how *did* he sweet talk you?"

"He didn't. I'm trying to keep him from exacting his vengeance on me at therapy." She rubbed her shoulder.

"Vengeance for what?"

"Well, some lasagna filling mysteriously found its way onto his face." Jana absently twirled her hair around her finger.

Trevor's laughter reached out to erase the miles between them. "That's my girl. At least I'm not the only one getting bombarded with food."

"I still think there may be some hidden in his hairline."

"You're the one who's incorrigible," Trevor said, and she could picture him shaking his head.

"I plead the fifth."

"Ve half vays of making you talk," he replied in a cheesy German accent.

"Fortunately, you're far enough away that I don't have to find them out. How did things go with the missionaries?"

"Great! I put on a couple of steaks, baked some potatoes, and grabbed a salad from the deli. They loved it."

"I'm sure they did."

"They talked to me tonight about families and being sealed together—about temple marriage." Trevor paused. "Jana, is that one of the reasons that you've had such a hard time saying yes to my proposal?"

"Yes, one of them."

"Is a temple marriage something you've always wanted?"

"Yes, Trevor." Jana kicked the recliner footrest down and stood to pace the floor.

"Then you met me."

"Yeah." Jared's kiss flashed into her mind. *Stop that, Jana!*

"Would you be cheating yourself if you didn't get married in the temple?"

Jana pulled her thoughts back to Trevor. She sighed. "Yes, I would."

"Then I think it's pretty much a given. If I can't join your church, it would be best to go our separate ways."

The truth in his statement flooded her senses. "Nothing ever seems quite that cut and dry, but you're right." She bent over to pick up her shoes and socks. With the socks nestled inside the shoes, she placed them in the closet.

"I guess I'll have to pray till I get an answer. Will you pray for me too?"

"Of course—that goes without saying." She walked into the kitchen, opened the refrigerator and glanced inside, then closed it. After picking up the discarded dish towel, she made her way back into the living room and sat down on the couch.

"I want you to know, Jana, that I'm looking into this because it's so important to you, but I won't compromise my principles." Trevor paused and then added wryly, "Even though you might think I don't have any left. If I don't believe it, I won't join."

"I wouldn't have it any other way." She cradled the phone between her ear and good shoulder while twisting the damp dish towel on and off her hand. Her thoughts drifted back to Jared using it to chase her out of the kitchen. She was called back to reality by Trevor's voice.

"I also want you to know that if I do join your church, it doesn't obligate you to marry me. That's a totally separate decision. All right?"

"Fair enough." She was unable to control a yawn.

"You sound exhausted. I'll let you get some sleep now, sweetheart. I love you."

"Good night." Jana threw the towel onto the counter and headed for bed.

Trevor slid from his chair directly to his knees. "Oh, Heavenly Father, this is so important to Jana, and that makes it important to me. Please help me to know if this church is true, and help Jana to forgive me. And help me to be able to tell her everything soon. Amen."

He remained on his knees for a long time, listening.

Eighteen

With the exception of the security guard, Trevor was the only occupant of the building. His voice seemed to echo through the empty halls. "It's Thursday night. I had hoped everything would be over by now. There has to be something I'm missing here." Leaning back in his chair, he reviewed the file on Coleman Industries one more time. He absently ran his fingers through his hair, then stopped short. "That's it!" He slapped his desk and spun around in the chair. His attention returned to the screen. "That's the piece I've been looking for." After highlighting the important parts, he printed the file and prepared to leave.

Trevor's mind processed the new information as he entered the parking garage. *I can get this over to Don, and we can round up the smugglers by this weekend. Then I can start to rebuild things with Jana.* He pushed a button on his key fob to unlock his car door. *When this is over, I'm telling Don to leave me alone. No more "on the side" jobs for me.* Trevor shifted his briefcase to his right hand before opening the door. *This one has definitely been too costly.*

Suddenly, Trevor heard a voice. "Duck!" He turned to see who had spoken and noticed a movement out of the corner of his eye. The voice came again. "Duck!" He attempted to take cover behind the open car door when several loud pops reverberated off the concrete walls and ceiling. He felt a burning in his side and heard a bullet ping the metal of his prized car. *This can't be happening—who will protect Jana?* Thrown off balance, he reached for his briefcase and retrieved a small pistol. A small foreign car squealed around the corner and crashed through the exit gate. Leaning against his GT, Trevor attempted to shoot back, but with his shaky hands, the shot went awry.

The parking attendant hastened toward Trevor, calling 911 on his phone as he ran. "Mr. Willis, Mr. Willis! Are you all right?"

Trevor hugged his side and glanced down to see a red stain spreading over his shirt. Sweat beaded on his forehead, and his vision began to blur. "I . . ." His sigh turned to a shudder, and he slid down against the car.

The uniformed man removed his jacket and folded it for a pillow under Trevor's head. "Just lay back." Then he pulled a handkerchief out of his pocket and held it to Trevor's wound. "Help will be here soon. Just hold on."

———————

A throbbing in his side greeted Trevor as he regained consciousness in the emergency room. A white bandage circled his midsection. His immediate reaction was to sit up and try to get his feet on the floor so he could leave. The tall blond woman at his side stopped him with surprising strength.

"No way, José. You're not leaving this bed until the doctor okays it."

Surprised to see his sister, he complied. "Traci? What are you doing here?"

"I'm the closest relative. I get to make decisions on your care while you're unconscious."

He sat up once again. "I'm not unconscious anymore, so I get to make my own decisions. Where are my clothes?" His feet hit the floor, and a wave of nausea forced him back onto the bed.

"I think you just got your answer, big brother. If you try to get up, *I'll* be making the decisions again—which could very well include sedatives."

"I'm really beginning to regret signing that directive."

"Too bad, Trevor. You already did it."

"I just need a few minutes to get used to my land legs again." His head began to clear. "Where's Don?"

In answer to his question, his brother-in-law poked his head through the gap in the curtain. "Hey there. Getting a bit careless in your old age? You want the good news or the bad?"

"Both."

"The good news is the bullet went straight through without hitting anything—it basically just grazed your side. The bad news is it hit your GT."

Trevor tried unsuccessfully to stand, wincing with the effort. "Why did those creeps want to take me out?"

"You were an easy target. If they wanted to kill you, they would have done it. I figure it was just a warning."

"A warning about what?" Trevor's brain ticked away. As it stopped on the most obvious conclusion, his heart lurched with fear. "Jana!"

"She's fine. Lasky has her covered." Don placed a reassuring hand on Trevor's shoulder.

"I've got to get to her." A small voice in Trevor's head kept repeating, *I'm her only chance.* He gathered his strength, pushed off the bed, and stood by sheer force of will.

"Hey, man, calm down," Don exclaimed. "Your wound isn't bad, but there are quite a few stitches and you lost a good amount of blood. The doctor says you'll be laid up for another couple of days."

Trevor gave an amused snort. "I've always wanted to say this." He cleared his throat and declared in his best John Wayne voice, "Don't worry, little lady." He tipped an imaginary hat. "It's just a flesh wound."

Moving gingerly, Trevor opened the nearby cabinet and grabbed his clothes. "I'm getting dressed and leaving this place right now."

Don shook his head. "There's no need. All the surveillance photos, including the miniature golf course, show no sign of anyone unusual hanging around. Jana's fine."

"I suggest you leave the room, Traci." He pushed past his brother-in-law and threw the clothes on the bed. "And Don, I expect you to help me."

Don shook his head. "No. The boss says you're off this one."

"Remember, I don't work for him—I'm only a consultant. If he wants my cooperation, and my knowledge, for the rest of this operation, he had better butt out. Now, help me get dressed."

Friday afternoon found Jana in the therapy office finishing up the week's files. She had managed to spend the majority of her days with Jared.

He turned out the lights in the main room before entering the office. "Hey, sunshine. Are you about done, or did you need some help?"

"I'm almost done, but you really should be the one doing this. I'm only going to be here one more week." Jana's heart sank as she said it. "You need to see if there's anything you don't understand. Of course, you can always call me with questions."

"This M&M bowl was the best improvement." Jared reached into the candy dish. "Can I call you without questions?"

"I'd be pretty hurt if you didn't."

"Can I ask you the first question right now? Catch." He threw an M&M toward her mouth, but it bounced off her chin.

"No fair. I wasn't ready."

He ate the remaining candy, then took her hand and looked into her eyes. "How are you feeling about Trevor?"

"You sure don't beat around the bush, do you?" Jana turned her head, unable to look at him.

"Not when I want to know something. Do you think you'll be able to forget what's gone on?"

She shook her head. "I know he's changed in some way, but to tell you the truth, I'm still frightened."

Jared took one of the files and opened it, then leaned against the wall. "I have another question. What if he joins the Church? Will that make a difference?"

She blinked back tears. "I'm afraid I might feel obligated to marry him if he does."

"Jana." The quiet urgency in Jared's voice compelled her to face him. "Obligation is not much to build a marriage on— especially a celestial one."

"I know, but he's filled such a void in my life. Without him, I'd be alone."

"You wouldn't be alone."

She sighed. "You don't understand. Before I met Trevor, I was so lost. I had the Colemans, but the pain of losing my parents overshadowed everything."

Jared sat on the desk and held her hand. "Help me understand."

"It had been six years since their accident, and to the rest of the world, I was fine. Trevor saw beyond that and understood me. He filled the emptiness and taught me how to be happy again. I owe him a lot."

"I didn't know that." Jared looked at her hand in his before his brow furrowed. "Wait a minute—six years ago?"

"Yes."

"That's it, Jana! That's why you look familiar."

"What are you talking about?"

"About six years ago, I was visiting Eric and took a drive along the beach. I got out and walked to clear my thoughts."

"I can understand that." She smiled.

"I came across a girl kneeling in the surf and crying. Something about her touched me deeply, and I wanted to protect her from all the dragons in the world."

"That . . . that was you?"

He nodded.

"All I remembered was your eyes," Jana said breathlessly. "No wonder something stirred inside me when I looked into them the first time. I always wished I could find you to say thank you—and return your towel."

"You're welcome." Jared touched her nose. "And you can keep the towel."

She straightened a pile on the desk. "It's funny, but that towel has been a comfort to me. It reminded me of the kindness of a stranger in a time I felt alone in the world. " She paused a while, lost in her thoughts, and Jared seemed reflective too. Finally, she spoke. "You know, I wasn't sure if I could face Trevor, but he sounded so urgent—almost afraid. The thought keeps running through my head, 'Things are not always as they seem.'"

"Don't worry, I'll be there. When will he arrive?"

"Around 6:00. I need to go down to Al's and get my car. He called a few minutes ago, and it's finally ready. I'll be so glad to have it again."

"I'll miss giving you rides, though," Jared said wistfully.

"Who said that would stop? I've enjoyed having a personal chauffeur."

He tousled her hair. "Let's lock up and go."

After retrieving her car, they both drove to the guest house. They got out of their respective vehicles and walked over to the picnic table. "I don't feel comfortable leaving you alone with Trevor," Jared admitted. "But I'll do what you want."

Jana squeezed his hand. "Will you stay around at least till after dinner? I'll suggest a movie if I want you to stay."

"What if Trevor asks me to stay?" Jared said as Jana sat on the picnic bench.

"Do you live in fantasyland? Trevor is very jealous of the time I spend with you, and there will be a snowstorm in you know where before he'd ask."

"Just being prepared for all possibilities."

"Don't tell me, you're a Scout, too."

"All the way to Eagle."

She laughed. "You and Trevor both."

"Really?"

Jana nodded her head.

"Maybe he does have some redeeming qualities," Jared said pensively.

Trevor's classic Mustang rounded the corner. "Here he comes." She squeezed Jared's hand. "Thanks for everything."

———•———

Pulling into the driveway, Trevor took a deep breath to fight the wave of jealousy. The movement sent pain shooting through his side. He looked at Jana and Jared. *Could this guy make her happy like I do? Could he ever understand her the way I do? Can he protect her like I can?* "This is your chance—don't blow it," he said to himself.

He opened the car door and called out, "Hi, you two. How're things going?" The words were a shade too casual.

Jared helped her up from the bench and they met him halfway.

———•———

"Hi, Trevor." Jana looked beyond him to the car. "I thought you were bringing the GT." *There's something wrong here.*

"I have it in for a few repairs. Nothing major."

"You look different. Have you lost weight?" *He doesn't look well, and there's something in his expression I've never seen before.*

"Just a little. I haven't had anyone to take out to dinner or cook me lasagna. I've been left to my own devices." He tried to greet her with a kiss, but she turned her head.

Trevor looked over her shoulder at Jared. "What did you want to do tomorrow?"

Jared closed his eyes. Jana could've sworn she heard him mumble, "Punch you in the jaw again."

"What? I didn't hear you."

"I said we could head to Tillamook and tour the cheese factory. They have great ice cream. Then we could check out a lighthouse or two."

"I like that idea."

"Now, do you want to go out to eat?" Jana asked. "Or I can whip up something. We have to get some meat on your bones." She poked Trevor in the ribs and noticed him flinch as if in pain.

"I won't make you cook—that's for sure. Where would you like to go?"

"We have a great Chinese restaurant in town," Jared replied helpfully. "Would you like to try it?"

"Sure. I'll treat tonight." Trevor placed Jana's arm in the crook of his. "Tillamook ice cream is on you tomorrow, Jared."

"Sounds like an even trade." Jared rushed to her other side and offered his arm.

"Let's get takeout and come back here to eat," Trevor said. "I'd like to be able to talk to you both about some things I've learned about the Mormon Church."

Jared smiled at Jana's stunned silence and winked at her before answering for both of them. "That sounds good." He whispered in her ear, "Seen any snowflakes lately?" He held out his palm up while looking to the sky. He was out of punching distance before she had time to react.

Trevor ignored their banter. "Great! Let's go. I'm feeling hungrier than I've been for the last week."

Sitting around the coffee table a short time later, Trevor amazed them by offering a blessing on the food. As they began to pass around the containers, he started the conversation.

"The missionaries mentioned the first four principles of the gospel. Faith, repentance, baptism, and the gift of the Holy Ghost."

"That's right." Jared helped himself to some sweet and sour chicken.

Trevor explained that he wanted to talk about repentance, so Jared and Jana each gave their thoughts, and then Trevor asked questions.

An hour later, Jared got up to leave, his questioning gaze on Jana. "I'll say good night now."

"Yeah, it's getting late." Trevor stood as well. He looked exhausted. "I'll follow you over to your place right now, Jared. Did you say Zack and Caitlyn were joining us tomorrow?"

"They had plans for the day, so it'll just be the three of us. Caitlyn invited us to dinner afterwards."

Jared looked away as Trevor kissed Jana's cheek.

"I'll see you in the morning."

She averted her gaze from Trevor. "Jared, what time should I be ready?"

He looked at his watch. "I have a couple of patients in the early morning, but they should be done by 9:00."

"Trevor, maybe you could roll out those crusts while waiting for Jared tomorrow morning."

"It would be an honor to help such a lovely lady. Say at the crack of 7:00?"

"Sure." Baffled, she watched the two men who meant so much to her leave. There was a definite change in Trevor that could be attributed to the gospel, but he was also hiding something. *Is he afraid I'll discover what it is if we're alone? Of course,* she thought as she remembered Jared's kiss, *we all have our secrets.* She sat on the couch with her head cradled in her hands, rubbing her temples. *I'll just put everything in Heavenly Father's hands.*

Jared unlocked the stained-glass front door and stepped back for Trevor to enter. In realtor's terms, the house would have been described as cozy. The living room was sparsely furnished in bachelor style with a small, quilt-covered couch, a comfortable recliner, and a large flat-screen television. A weathered end table held a supply of remote controls and a variety of magazines, including several physical-therapy journals and the latest issues of *Sports Illustrated* and *ESPN.*

Trevor put his leather suitcase on the floor before sitting on the edge of the couch. "I appreciate your opening your house to me, Jared."

"No problem." He looked his guest squarely in the eye. "I figured it was the best way to keep you in my sights."

Trevor nodded. "You know, Carpenter, someday we may be friends."

"Not very likely."

"Where do I crash tonight?"

"Follow me." Jared headed down the hallway, passing a kitchen that was last remodeled in the 1950s. Lights reflected off the lemon-yellow walls, illuminating the hall. "Just help yourself to anything you want for breakfast."

"Thanks." Trevor hauled his bag with some effort.

"Here's the bathroom. Extra towels are in the cabinet."

Trevor looked in at the claw-foot tub surrounded with a pink Swiss dot shower curtain on an oval rod that was suspended from the ceiling. "Whoa, I haven't seen anything like this since I left Massachusetts. Some of the cape-style homes built in the 1800s had bathroom fixtures like these."

"I don't think this is quite that old, but it might be close." Jared opened a door across the hall from the bathroom. "Here's your room. I'm sorry about the bed—it's the same one I've had since I was a boy. The mattress is kind of lumpy."

"No problem. I'm so beat that nothing is going to bother me tonight. Thanks for everything."

Jared nodded and turned away. An irksome thought buzzed in his head. He tried to swat it away, but it persisted. His guest headed toward the bathroom with a towel over his shoulder, clutching his toothbrush and toothpaste. Jared realized sleep would elude him until he addressed his concern. He glanced upward, shaking his head and muttering under his breath, "Okay, okay."

He pivoted toward Jana's friend and cleared his throat. "Ahem. Trevor?"

"Yes?"

"Have you been feeling well?"

Trevor's hand paused on his side, and he refused to look Jared in the eye. "Just a little sore the last few days. It happens when you get socked in the jaw a few times."

"Have you checked with a doctor?" Jared watched the man shake his head as a mask of confidence fell into place.

"I haven't been to a doctor since I was eighteen. I've always been healthy as a horse."

Jared frowned in exasperation. "Look, you may think you've hid it well, but Jana knows something is up."

Trevor walked through the bathroom door before facing Jared. "Really, it's nothing I can't handle."

"Well, good night." Jared pointed to a door at the end of the hall. "That's my room, if you need anything."

"Thanks again." Trevor switched the toothbrush and paste to his left hand, then extended his right hand to his host.

Jared woke Trevor minutes before he left for the therapy office and noted his ragged appearance. "Are you okay?"

"I'm fine." Trevor beamed as he swung his legs over the side of the bed. "In fact, I'll be much finer than you, because I get to spend a couple of hours alone with Jana before you even get there! Thanks for the bed."

Once Jared left the room, Trevor looked down to his side to make sure no blood had seeped through the dressing. His facade melted as he groaned in pain.

Nineteen

The bold knock reverberated through the guest house. Trevor entered at Jana's prompting. "Hello, sweetheart." He walked up behind her and kissed her neck as she worked at the kitchen counter, but she sidestepped away from him.

"Good morning." She turned to glance at him and gasped. "Trevor, you look like something the cat was afraid to drag in." She put her hand to his forehead. "What is wrong?"

"Nothing's wrong. This is me without my morning coffee."

She rummaged through the cupboard. "It's a good thing I found out about this before I made any commitments. I think I have some hot chocolate. Would that help?"

"No, that would only lull me to sleep. Put me to work. They say it's good for the soul." He chuckled. "I think we all agree that my soul can use all the help it can get."

His comment brought a smile to her lips. "Come here, and I'll show you how to roll out the crust." She placed a ball of dough between two sheets of wax paper and carefully rolled it out from the middle. After watching Trevor give it a try, she said, "You're pretty good at that. I might have to hire you."

"Sure thing. I'll sign on for the rest of my life and beyond." He leaned against the cupboard and dried his hands on a towel.

Jana's emotions rose to the surface as she remembered Jared leaning there a few short days ago, holding a dish towel.

She quickly wiped a tear from her eye. "No commitments right now."

Trevor held his arms up in surrender. "Understood." He cocked his head to the side and pointed his index finger in the air. "But it doesn't mean I can't use subliminal advertising, does it?"

"You're incorrigible," Jana said quietly, shaking her head. "So, I talked to Sue this morning."

"Everything okay?"

"Yes. She was just checking in. I talk to her every few days. It helps me to keep current with events at work."

Jared's knock coincided with the timer as the last pie came out of the oven. "Mmm. Things sure smell good in here. Do we need to do something with those pies before we go?"

Jana pulled her focus from Jared's handsome face to the desserts. "No, they need to cool down before I can freeze them anyway. They'll be fine till we get home tonight."

"Okay, then let's go!"

Trevor got up from the couch. "Why don't you drive today, Jared?"

"Sure thing. Have you ever seen a cheese factory?"

"I may have toured one in Vermont as a Cub Scout or something. That was a few years ago."

Jared chuckled. "I think I did the same thing."

Trevor opened the front door for Jana and then got in the back seat. *Wow—letting Jared drive and having me sit up front. Maybe Trevor really has changed,* she thought.

"Well, the Tillamook Cheese Factory is one of the best in the world," Jared began. "There's a visitor's center with films on cheese making, and interactive kiosks. They have a café and gift shop, and of course, the ice cream counter. They have more than forty flavors."

"Move over, Baskin-Robbins," Trevor remarked.

Jana swiveled around in her seat. "I forgot to tell you, Trevor. Jared is a great tour guide."

Sure enough, Jared maintained the narrative for most of the trip, with Trevor occasionally adding a comment.

At one point, Jared said in response to a question from Trevor, "Well, with Tillamook, it's actually not a company. It's a co-op."

"Really? That's an interesting concept."

"It started in 1909. It's now owned by about 130 independent family farms."

"Great idea," Trevor replied. "I wonder if there is some way to incorporate that principle with my suppliers. Go on."

"We're here now. You can check it out for yourself." Jared pulled into a parking space.

The three young people entered the visitor's center. They picked up a map and started their self-guided tour with the informational movie. After convincing a passerby to take their picture as they posed by the cow statue in the entry, the trio watched the cheese-making process. Trevor asked several questions about the production phase, and then he and Jared and Jana continued to the cheese-tasting room.

Once they tried the samples, she spoke up. "My favorite is the vintage white medium cheddar. What did you think of the cheese curds?"

Trevor wrinkled his nose. "They tasted a bit rubbery. I'm with you, though—I think the vintage white cheddar is the best."

Jared rolled his eyes. "I disagree. My vote is cast for pepper jack. By the way, the curds are called squeaky cheese. Did you like the story of the guy experimenting with the process?"

"Yeah," Jana said. "It would have been fun to see it hopping off the shelves."

Trevor took her arm. "I'd like to see those forty flavors of ice cream."

Jared looked between the ice cream shop and the café. "Should we decide life is short and eat dessert first? We could stop for lunch after the lighthouse, or eat here and finish off with some ice cream before heading to Cape Meares."

"The ice cream is awfully tempting," Trevor replied, "but we should probably eat something substantial before we indulge. I've heard good things about the café." He veered to the left, his hold on Jana never wavering.

A loud crash, followed by the tinkling of broken glass, shattered the calm in the room. Trevor immediately pulled Jana to the floor, sheltering her between himself and the wall.

"Trevor, what are you doing? Someone just dropped a tray of glasses." Jana noticed the alarm in his eyes as he perused the surrounding area.

Jared rushed to her side and wrapped an arm around her. "Jana, are you okay?" When she nodded, he turned to Trevor, who leaned over, clutching his side. "Are you crazy, Willis? What has gotten into you?" Jared led Jana to a chair.

Trevor followed with a glass of water. "Here you go. I'm sorry, sweetheart. I guess I've been a bit on edge." He clapped his hands together. "Are you ready for lunch? Do you think the clam chowder will be as good here as it is on the East Coast?"

Both Jana and Jared looked at him as though he had just landed from Mars.

He ran his hand through his hair. "You can both wait here, and I'll order everything."

Lunch was filling, but they managed to save room for ice cream. The three drove toward the coast and parked in the visitor's lot. They headed down the trail to the Cape Meares lighthouse, stopping abruptly as they caught their first glimpse of the red crystal in the tower. They continued their downward journey, and Tour Guide Jared took over.

"This lighthouse is the shortest one on the Oregon coast at only thirty-eight feet."

They checked out the view from the tower and walked around the grounds before heading back toward the car, stopping at each overlook to let Trevor catch his breath. *This is strange,* Jana thought. *I usually have to run to keep up with his walking pace.* They crossed the parking lot and headed toward the Octopus Tree. The trail was only about one-tenth of a mile, but the grade sloped sharply upward. Trevor seemed to exert all his effort at putting one foot in front of the other. Jared continued his commentary as the massive tree came into view.

"They estimate it was a sapling around the time the Savior walked the streets of Jerusalem. It was shaped by strong winds on the coast and is called the Council Tree by local Indians. The circumference at the base is approximately sixty feet."

"Wow! I would have liked a tree like this to climb when I was little." Trevor looked on in awe, leaning over the surrounding fence for a better view.

Jana circled the tree to see it from different angles. "Yeah, we never had anything like this in New Hampshire either."

After the obligatory pictures, Jared suggested they head home. "It's getting late, and I'm beat. It must be all this sea air. We can relax a bit before we go to Caitlyn's."

Trevor sighed. "You won't get an objection from me."

They piled into Jared's Corolla and headed home. As the trio entered the guest house, they were greeted with the smell of peach pie. Jana walked into the bedroom and put her purse on the dresser. When she returned to the living room, she noticed Trevor's pinched expression. She put her hand on his arm. "Why don't you come and sit in the recliner and put your feet up? You're not looking very good."

"I must admit I enjoy it when you fuss over me, honey, but you better be careful or you'll damage my ego." He squeezed her hand.

"Your ego will survive—it's you I'm worried about."

"I'm fine."

"Well, like I said, put your feet up and close your eyes for a few minutes while I take care of those pies."

Jana entered the kitchen and saw Jared with a knife poised

above one of the pies. He rotated the dessert as if in search of the perfect cutting spot.

"Jared Carpenter! What are you doing?"

He jumped back, dropped the knife on the counter, and clutched his hand to his chest, guilt etched in his features. "You scared me to death! Didn't anyone ever tell you not to sneak up on someone holding a knife?"

"That doesn't count if he's about to cut into a pie." She lowered her voice. "I'm worried about Trevor. I think there's really something wrong, but he won't say."

"I'll go talk to him. Take care of these pies before I can't resist anymore."

Jared walked into the living room, where Trevor sat on the couch with his head back and eyes closed. A protective arm covered his midsection. In that unguarded moment, Jared watched a flicker of pain cross his face.

"Willis, what's wrong? Not that it matters to me, but Jana's concerned."

"Nothing. I'm just a bit tired. When do we head over to Caitlyn's?"

"In about an hour."

"I'll just rest until then." Trevor turned his face away and seemed to fall asleep in an instant.

Jared went to sit at the kitchen table. "Jana, what do you know about Trevor's background?"

She put the pies in the freezer and joined him. "All I know is that he grew up in a small New England town and attended Harvard business school. He moved out here after graduation and started his own business."

"Was he ever in the army?

She thought a moment. "Not that I know. Why do you ask?"

Jared took a breath before plunging ahead. "His reaction this afternoon. His reflex was one of a bodyguard—like someone in special ops or secret service."

Jana thought a moment. "I guess there are things I don't know about him." *And those things scare me.*

The hour's rest seemed to help Trevor, and the trio headed over to Caitlyn's for dinner. After the meal ended, she brought out four spoons and a deck of cards.

Trevor gave her a puzzled look. "Is this some strange after dinner custom?"

"It's spoons," Caitlyn informed him.

"I can see that. What are they for?"

"Spoons."

"It's a game, Trevor," Jana said with a chuckle.

"Oh, okay. Is this what you Mormons do for fun?"

Zack put his hands on Caitlyn's shoulders. "Yeah. Usually something that doesn't cost a lot of money."

"Especially now," she continued. "We're trying to save up."

The couple looked at each other, and Zack said, "For when we get married in three months."

"Oh, I'm so happy for you both!" Jana jumped up to hug Caitlyn.

Jared shook Zack's hand and slapped him on the back. "I guess this explains the air of mystery around you two. I never thought you'd take the plunge, Zack."

"Congratulations," Trevor put in. "Now, who's going to explain this game?"

"You want to get four of a kind—four kings or aces, etc.," Jared started. "When you get that, you take a spoon. Once the first spoon is gone, the others are free game. It's kind of like musical chairs, except with spoons and cards instead of chairs and music.

The first round, Trevor concentrated so hard on finding four of a kind that everyone else had a spoon before he even realized they were gone. "Hey, what happened?"

"The trick is to keep one eye on the cards and one on the spoons!" Jana declared.

The next few rounds, Trevor kept a close watch on Jana, and if she got a spoon, so did he. He finally found a happy medium of watching and grabbing. During the last hand, both he and Jared had hold of the final spoon, with neither one exhibiting an intention to let go.

"Jana, did Al say what caused your accident?" Zack asked suddenly.

"No, he said I must have collided with some sharp object. There were metal fragments in the tire, and it was completely blown out."

Trevor dropped the spoon and allowed the round to go to Jared. "You never told me that," Trevor said, his face going even paler.

"I didn't think it mattered."

Everyone looked at him in astonishment, but he just smiled. "I guess it really doesn't."

Zack chuckled. "It might have been a surveyor's stake. Knock. Knock."

"Zack! You promised." Caitlyn said.

He whispered back to her, "You'll like this one."

Caitlyn sighed. "Okay. I'll play along. Who's there?"

"Lettuce."

"Lettuce who?"

"Lettuce eat pie!"

Trevor laughed. "I like that one."

Jared whispered to Jana, "We'll see how my pie-rolling skills compare to Trevor's."

"Trevor was faster," she teased.

Trevor puffed out his chest and smiled cockily, then blew on his fingernails and rubbed them on his shirt.

Jared looked at Jana. "But mine was much more artistic, right?"

"Oh, brother." She rolled her eyes.

Both men walked her to her door. Trevor unlocked it and stood back to allow her to enter.

"Did you guys want to come in?"

Jared glanced at Trevor before meeting Jana's concerned gaze. "I think I'll head on home. Are you coming, Trevor?"

"Yeah. I'm exhausted." Stroking Jana's cheek, he seemed to have something to say, but must have changed his mind. "Good night, sweetheart. I'll see you in the morning."

After gingerly climbing the few steps to the front door, Trevor followed Jared into the house. "Can I talk to you before I head off to bed?" Trevor asked.

"Sure. Have a seat. Are you going to let me know what's wrong?"

Trevor lowered his body onto the couch. "I'm fine."

"Sorry, but you'll have to erase those dark hollows under your eyes to convince both me and Jana."

"I just want to know what I need to do to get baptized."

The heartbeat of a mouse could have been heard in the ensuing silence. "Why do you want to get baptized?" Jared asked finally. "Is it just so Jana will marry you?"

"No. From all the things I've learned, I think the gospel is true. Jana told me how she feels the Spirit. I've felt the same thing when I've prayed about the Church." Trevor looked down at the floor. "I've also had times where I felt the Spirit told me to do something. I want to be able to have that all the time."

"Why are you asking me and not Jana?"

"I don't want Jana to know yet. I'm afraid she'll feel an obligation to me." Trevor ran his hand through his hair. "Anyway, can I have anyone baptize me, or can only missionaries do that?"

"Anyone who is at least a priest can perform the ordinance. You do need to talk to the missionaries and be interviewed."

"I can take care of that when I'm back in Portland." Trevor paused a moment. "Jared, would you baptize me?"

"Me? Why?"

"Because you're Jana's friend, and I really don't know anyone who could, besides the missionaries and Zack."

Resentment, anger, compassion, and resolve warred inside Jared before he could reply. "Yes, I'd be honored to baptize you."

It seemed to take great effort for Trevor to get off the couch. "Thanks. I'll let Jana know soon."

Jared noticed something red on his guest's side. "Is that blood on your shirt?"

Trevor looked down at the stain. "It must be ketchup from lunch." He headed toward the bathroom.

"You had clam chowder."

Trevor waved his hand in a dismissive gesture. "Night."

———

A shadowy figure picked the lock at Al's Garage. With a furtive glance over his shoulder, the man entered the dark building. In the pile of old tires waiting in the recycling bin, he found what he was looking for. He pulled the blown steel-belted radial from the discards and carefully checked the interior. The hole might have been made from a sharp object in the road, but the metal fragments imbedded in the rubber made it clear the offending object was a bullet. The resulting crash had been anything but accidental.

Twenty

The incessant ring of his cell phone pulled Trevor from a deep sleep. "Yeah, what is it, Don?"

"The shipment was made today. With the information you discovered on Thursday, we were able to pull the Colemans into protective custody about five minutes ago. The whole thing could explode within the hour."

All traces of sleep dissolved. "Okay." Trevor sat up quickly, wincing at the pain the movement brought.

"Trevor, Lasky did some investigating around the body shop tonight." Don's strained voice carried an urgency. "He discovered bullet fragments in Jana's tire."

Trevor's blood ran cold. "I'll get her out immediately."

"They probably have a pretty good idea of where she is. When they discover the Colemans are missing, you've got an hour or two at the most before they come after her."

"Not if I can help it." Trevor ended the call and began to gather his things. He silently opened his bedroom door and crept into the hallway. His hand was on the doorknob when a voice from the couch caused him to spin around in surprise. "What?"

Jared sat up. "Where do you think you're going?"

"Look here, Carpenter. I don't have time to argue with you."

"From where I sit, we have all night. I can always invite the sheriff over for this visit, too." Jared cradled his cell phone in his hand.

"You might have all night, but Jana doesn't."

Jared jumped up and lunged at Trevor, grabbing his collar. "What do you mean by that? You better start talking right now."

Trevor gave an exasperated sigh. "Let me give you the quick rundown. Some bad guys just decided it's time to come after Jana. She knows nothing about her uncle's actions that have put her in danger. The men who caused her parents' deaths will not hesitate a moment to use Jana as a bargaining chip to ensure Vince Coleman's cooperation. The longer you keep me here, the less chance there is of Jana getting away safely."

Jared released Trevor's shirt. "So, you are protecting her? I'm coming with you."

"No! It's safer to travel with just Jana and me."

"Have you taken a look in the mirror? You're not exactly in prime shape right now."

"That's because these guys took a shot at me on Thursday night. The only reason I'm here right now is because I had a strong impression that without me, she doesn't have a chance. I took her out of harm's way last weekend, and I'm going to do the same thing right now."

Jared murmured as if to himself, "Things are not always as they seem." He paused for several seconds. "Okay, Willis. I'll do as you suggest, but you better let me know where you are, and how I can reach you."

"Fine. We have to hurry. I'll tell you on the way to Jana's."

Jared grabbed his shoes and jacket and flew out the door on Trevor's heels. "You can also tell me why Jana slept for hours in the mountains."

Trevor stopped in mid-stride. "It was for her own good."

"You don't believe that, do you?"

"No, not for one minute, but I didn't have a choice."

As they got in the car, Jared asked, "Why didn't you tell Jana about this?"

"The Special Agent in Charge suspected her of being in on it. I was forbidden from telling her a thing." Trevor gripped the steering wheel hard. "Heaven knows, it probably cost me the woman I love. Her crash was not an accident. As far as we know, they're unaware of her exact location, and that's probably the only thing keeping her safe at the moment. It won't take them long to find her, though."

Upon arriving at the guest house, the two men exited the car in silence. Trevor retrieved his suitcase from the back seat and pulled out a cell phone. He handed it to Jared. "Here—use this to call if you need to reach me."

With Jared standing behind him, Trevor knocked quietly on the sliding glass door.

"Jana," Trevor whispered, then repeated her name louder.

A disheveled Jana peeked through the blinds and cracked open the door. "What are you doing here?"

He grabbed her hand and pulled her toward the darkness. "Listen, honey. We have to leave right now. You're in danger, and I need to get you out of here."

She fought against his grip. "I'm not going anywhere with you. Let go of me."

Jared stepped into her view, and she stopped struggling and ran into his arms. "It's all right," he said quietly. "You need to listen to Trevor."

Looking at Jared with eyes full of trust, Jana nodded her head. "All right. Are you coming with us?"

"Not right now, but you know how to get in touch. If you need me, call and I'll drop everything. Let's get your things together."

Within five minutes a bag was packed and they were heading for the car. Just before Trevor closed the door behind them, an impression hit him. "Jana, where's your cell phone?"

"In my purse. Why?"

"I think you should leave it here."

Puzzled, she looked at Jared. After a slight nod from him, she rummaged through her bag and handed the phone to Trevor.

They dropped Jared off at his house. He embraced her and said, "Everything will be all right. I'll see you soon."

She continued to watch and wave until they were out of sight. Then she turned forward. "Trevor, what's going on?"

"Honey, try to sleep. We'll talk when we get to the cabin."

"I think not!"

"Please, Jana." He reached out to touch her hand. "Trust me on this one. I'll tell you everything when we get to the cabin."

Closing her eyes, she raised her thoughts in prayer, and soon she felt a peace descend upon her.

An hour later, Karl Grant woke to the sound of glass shattering. He and Emma sat up in bed. "What was that?" she asked.

He quickly ran to the window and peered out. "It looks like there's someone by the guest house."

Emma gasped. "Jana!" She reached for her robe and hurried for the stairs.

"Wait! You can't go out there alone. Let me call the sheriff."

He made the call to the dispatch, and within minutes police sirens blared. Karl and Emma saw two people leave the cottage and speed away in a car.

The older couple rushed across the lawn just as the sheriff's car arrived. "We saw them leave, Sheriff," Emma said. "It was a small dark car. They headed that way." She pointed toward downtown.

"Calm down, Mrs. Grant. Let me call that in so someone can start looking." The uniformed man leaned into his car and relayed the information, then told Karl and Emma to stay there while he went to check out the interior of the guest house.

"But Jana's in there!"

The sheriff put a hand on Emma's shoulder. "Yes, and I've got to see if she needs assistance."

Karl embraced his wife and nodded to the sheriff. With his gun drawn, the officer cautiously peered around the shattered sliding-glass door to the interior of the bedroom. After an eternal pause, he entered. The Grants watched as light flooded the room and spilled onto the lawn. Slowly, each light in the house came on, illuminating the lawman's progress. As he exited the front door, he waved to the couple and they hurried over to the house.

"Is she all right?" Emma asked worriedly.

"There's no one in there. Could she have left earlier?"

"Jana's car is still here," Karl answered. "Maybe she's with Jared Carpenter. Do you want us to call him?"

"Please do, Mr. Grant."

Jared answered the phone before the first ring finished. "Jana?"

"No, Jared. It's Karl Grant. We were hoping she was with you."

"No, she's not. What's wrong?"

"You might want to sit down, young man. Someone broke into her house and she's missing."

"I'll be right there, Karl. Did you call the sheriff?"

"Yes, he's here."

"Good."

———————

At the cabin, Trevor rolled down his window and spoke to the two men guarding the gate. "Everything okay?"

"Seems to be."

"Good. If you notice anything out of the ordinary, call me immediately. This is not a drill."

"Yes, sir. We'll be ready."

When Trevor continued driving, Jana faced him. "I think it's time to tell me what's going on."

"Just another couple of minutes, sweetheart."

"As soon as we're in that cabin, you better plan on talking up a storm."

He smiled and patted her hand. "I promise."

After their last trip here, Jana was not about to let her shoes out of her sight, so she walked to the porch on her own. They entered the cabin and she confronted him with arms crossed. "Start spilling your guts, Trevor. You might want to begin with why you're in so much pain."

He put his arm around her and led her into the living room. A welcoming fire burned in the hearth. Unbuttoning his shirt, he revealed a white bandage with dark red seeping through it. "I was shot on Thursday."

Color drained from her face, and she stumbled backward onto the couch. "Why? What happened."

"Word on the street says it was a warning for me to keep away from you."

"Who would . . . oh no!" Jana shook her head slowly and spoke with her hand over her mouth. "No, it can't be. Please tell me it wasn't."

He knelt down in front of her and stroked her hair. "I'm so sorry, sweetheart. It's true."

"I should have never told him about last weekend!" She reached out to touch Trevor's face. "Can you forgive me? Ever?"

Trevor blinked back tears. "There's more." He let out a slow breath. "It all started about six years ago."

"That's . . . that's when my parents were killed." Her body began to tremble. "Uncle Vince couldn't have had anything to do with that."

"Indirectly, honey. It was another warning for him to cooperate or else."

Terror coursed through Jana's veins. "Cooperate with who?"

"The Chinese government. They wanted him to develop—"

"Infrared imagers." She looked toward the ceiling. "That's why there was a problem with the invoices."

"What?" Trevor stared at her. "You know something?"

"Not really. Only that we had about fifteen imagers unaccounted for. I pointed it out to Uncle Vince the day I left. He said he'd take care of it."

Trevor kissed her full on the lips. "Thank you, sweetheart. You may have just shortened the whole process."

"But I can't testify against my uncle."

"You won't have to, if I can help it. Is there anything else you can think of?"

"Is this why you started dating me?" she asked Trevor point blank.

"It was until you made me dinner the first time. At that point, I knew it would be impossible for me to keep things strictly business."

"And why you wanted to marry me so quickly?" Jana squeezed her eyes shut, trying to keep the tears back.

Trevor flinched. "Yes. I wanted you near me so I could protect you and get you away from Vince. The timing was because of this case." Trevor looked at her tenderly. "The desire wasn't." He shook his head as if to clear his mind. "Can you think of anything else about the infrared imagers?"

"No, that's all I know."

"Okay. Okay. Let me think." He stood and paced the room.

"Trevor, why am I here right now?"

He sat next to her on the couch, took both of her hands in his, and looked into her eyes. "You're in danger. We've just taken Vince and Karen into protective custody. If they can't get to Vince, they'll come after you." Trevor got up again and turned away from her, rubbing his temples. "Honey, your car accident wasn't an accident."

She stood up and planted herself in front of him. "Who is 'we,' and what do you mean it wasn't an accident?"

"There were bullet fragments in the tire. It didn't blow. It was shot out. 'We' is the FBI. Don's in charge—"

"Don's not a private detective?"

"No. It's a cover when he needs it."

"Why didn't you tell me this before? How much more have you kept from me?" She gave him an accusing glare.

"I just found out about the tire tonight, although I suspected." Trevor looked down. "There's a lot I've kept from you. I was under direct orders not to say a thing. The Special Agent in Charge thought you might be involved."

"I see."

Trevor's cell phone rang, and when he checked the screen he connected immediately. "We're here and safe, Jared." Trevor paused, his expression growing troubled. "Was there anything unusual about the phone?" He listened again, then replied, "You're right."

The cabin's front door burst open, and one of the agents from the gate sprinted through it. "Mr. Willis, we're under attack."

Trevor ended the call and jumped into action. "Where are they, Lou?"

"We're holding them at the front gate."

"Jana, we need to leave now." Trevor grabbed a waiting backpack, hoisted it onto his shoulder, and reached out to her. She clutched his hand and they ran out the back door. He called back to the agent, "I'll let you know when we're safely away."

They hurried across the meadow, the sound of gunfire urging them toward the cover of the woods. Trevor pushed Jana through the forest ahead of him. Suddenly, he jerked forward, his grip on her hand slackening.

"Trevor, what happened?"

In a controlled voice, he answered, "Nothing. Keep going straight on this path."

When he stumbled, Jana twisted around. With the moonlight filtering through the leaves, she saw a dark stain spreading across his shirt. "You're hurt!"

"Keep going, we're almost there." They entered a clearing where a dark-blue four-wheel-drive Jeep Grand Cherokee waited. Trevor pulled a key from the pocket on the backpack. "Get in."

Jana took the key and opened the front passenger door. "You're in no shape to drive."

After a pause, Trevor hefted the backpack into the car and climbed in. Jana got in the driver's seat and started the engine. "Where do I go?"

"Follow that road. It leads to the highway." He seized the backpack, and Jana saw him pull out a first-aid kit. "I think this one might be more than a flesh wound," he said with a groan.

She glanced over as he pressed a large gauze paid against his shoulder. "Oh, Trevor! Where's the nearest hospital."

"No hospital! It's the first place they'd look for you. Keeping you safe is the most important thing." Trevor's breathing was labored.

"I'm pulling over right now. I have to look at your shoulder."

"Don't stop until I say it's safe!"

She tried to keep him talking. "What did Jared tell you?"

"Some . . . someone broke into the guest house. They smashed your cell phone."

"My cell phone? Why would someone do that?"

"Something about a homing device. I had a strong impression you should leave it there."

"Trevor, I remember something from the crash."

"Is it important?"

"I think so. After the car stopped, I reached for my cell phone. I vaguely remember someone taking it from my hand before I lost consciousness." Jana talked more to herself than to Trevor. "The police insisted the 911 call came from my number. The man must have put the bug in it and then thrown it in the back seat where Al found it."

"Then how did they know to look for you at my cabin? Not many people know about it."

She gripped the steering wheel with white knuckles. "Uncle Vince."

"Honey" —Trevor reached over with his right hand and caressed her hair— "I know Vince has done a lot of terrible things, but he'd never purposely put you in danger."

"But if he connected us when he asked them to give you a warning, they might have assumed I was with you."

Trevor grunted. "And a simple check of property records would have led them directly to my cabin. Oh! If I ever get my hands on him . . ."

"We're at the highway," Jana pointed out. "I'm going to take care of that before we go any farther."

She pulled over and dug through the first-aid kit to find the scissors, then gingerly cut away Trevor's shirt sleeve. "I don't remember bullet wounds being covered in first-aid class at girl's camp."

"Do your best."

She cleaned the wound and applied antiseptic to both the entry and exit wounds.

"Isn't that the Boy Scout motto?"

"Close. Cub Scout."

Jana reached back into the kit. "Trevor, you saved my life. If you hadn't pushed me into the woods, this would have been my head."

Maintaining an iron grip on the arm rest, he only nodded.

She applied gauze to the fleshy part of his upper arm and wrapped it with the stretchy tape. "I'm not sure what to do next."

"Get moving," Trevor said with a groan, then made a call on his cell. "We're on our way, Lou," he said into the phone. "Have Lasky ready to take over."

Jana threw the SUV into drive. "I need to get you to the hospital."

"Take me back to town. Doctor Grant can deal with this, and we have someone there. I can pass you off to him."

Soon, Trevor's breathing slowed as he fell into a restless sleep.

Oh, great, Jana thought. *First I'm a pawn to be moved at will, and now I'm a football to be passed around. Trevor's got a lot more questions to answer!* She looked at the quiet form and realized how much he had risked for her. She stroked his arm, her agitation melting away. "Thank you, Trevor. I owe my life to you. Please, please hold on."

Twenty-one

Night dissolved into dawn as Jana pulled up in Jared's driveway. She slipped from the car, quietly made her way to the back door, and knocked. Footsteps sounded before he opened the door.

"Jana." With one look at her, the relief in his face turned to concern. "What's wrong?"

"Trevor's in the car. He's been shot, and I can't move him alone. Can you help me bring him in?"

Together they managed to carry Trevor into the living room. Jana made him as comfortable as possible on the couch while Jared called Doc Eric. A short time later they heard a car pull in behind the Jeep, then heard voices as the occupant climbed out.

"Hey, Doc, wait a minute. I have to talk to you before you go in."

"I'm in a hurry, Zack. I have an injured man in there."

"I know." He reached for his wallet and flashed a badge. "I'm with the FBI. It's important you don't let word of this reach anyone. It's a matter of national security." He looked toward the house. "And life and death."

Eric looked at him soberly. "Understood. Let's go in."

When Jared ushered in both men, Jana frowned and asked, "What are you doing here, Zack?"

"With Trevor unable to protect you, you're being passed off to me."

"You? You're the man who's been watching me all this time?"

"Zack Lasky, FBI, at your service." He bowed to her. "Now that all the niceties are over, I need you to come with me so I can take you to a safe location." He grasped her arm.

She slipped away from him. "Not until I know Trevor will be all right."

"Doc, would you please tell her he's going to be fine, so I can get her out of here?"

The grave look on Eric's face stopped Zack in his tracks.

Jana stepped closer. "Tell me what's wrong."

"He's lost a lot of blood with this wound and the last one. If we don't get him to the hospital right now, he may not make it."

Zack paced back and forth, scratching his head. "Okay, okay. He has to be checked in under an assumed identity. We can have a surgical team in Astoria in fifteen to twenty minutes to assist you. As far as anyone knows, this is appendicitis."

The doctor stood gaping at Zack. "In his shoulder?"

"We'll arrange for around-the-clock care for him while he's there, so no one else will know anything about it. He'll just be an eccentric wealthy patient who insists on private care."

Eric growled. "Okay, okay. Whatever it takes. Time is of the essence."

Once again, Zack grabbed Jana's arm. "Let's go."

"No!" She dug her heels in. "Not until I know he's out of danger."

"Jana." A weak voice came from the couch.

All attention turned toward Trevor, who mumbled, "I'm not leaving for the hospital until I know you're safely away from here. Go with Zack. Now."

"Trevor. I can't go without—"

"Now, Jana." His jaw was set and there was no arguing with him.

A siren sounded in the distance. She looked in that direction, then back at Trevor. "I . . . I . ."

Jared stepped up. "Will you feel better if we give him a priesthood blessing before we go?"

Closing her eyes, she nodded.

Doc Eric turned toward his patient. "Trevor, I need your permission to be treated and a power of attorney for Jana, or whomever, to make decisions as to your care."

"I . . . I already have one on file for my sister. Unfortunately, she's been using it too much lately." Trevor looked pointedly at Jana. "Lasky, I don't want Jana anywhere near the hospital." It obviously took an effort to speak each word.

"I'll get her to the safe house."

Jared and Eric gave Trevor a blessing before the paramedics arrived. They started an IV, then loaded him into the ambulance.

Jared held Jana in his arms and promised Trevor would be okay. "He's too stubborn to let anything keep him down." He looked heavenward in prayer before he helped Jana into the Jeep.

From the driver's seat, Zack looked at her with compassion. "Don't worry. They'll be able to get in touch with me at any time. Traci and Don Townsend are already in Astoria, so Trevor won't be alone. And the FBI has a team of doctors and nurses on their way to the hospital."

She nodded as Zack put the SUV in reverse. "Oh! I forgot my purse in the house. I need to get it."

Zack watched the ambulance turn the corner. "All right, but hurry."

Jana hopped down from the Jeep and ran in the back door.

———•———

After a few minutes, the men looked at each other. Jared was the first to speak. "She's had enough time to pack a picnic lunch." He rushed into his house calling her name, checking every room before returning to Zack. "She's gone."

"I should have known something was up," Zack growled. "She came with me too easily. Where do you think she is?"

"My guess is halfway to the hospital by now."

Jared hopped into the SUV, and they headed toward Astoria. They spotted Jana's Camry in the distance and sped up.

"Unless you want me to run her off the road, I suggest we just catch up and follow her to the hospital," Zack said.

The span between the two vehicles began to diminish when Jared saw the flashing lights in the rearview mirror and heard the accompanying siren. "Argh! What else could go wrong?"

Jana drove quickly, determined to allow no one to stop her before she arrived at Trevor's side. The blue Jeep followed, gaining slowly on her. She laughed when she glanced in her mirror and saw them being pulled over by the highway patrol.

After what seemed like ages, she drove up to the emergency entrance at Columbia Memorial Hospital in Astoria. Without bothering to find a parking spot, she stopped in the drop-off zone directly in front of the medical center and threw the car into park. Knowing Zack and Jared were close behind, she rushed into the ER and spotted Traci and Don Townsend.

"What are you doing here?" Don shouted.

She ignored him and ran directly to Trevor's sister, who embraced her.

"How is he?"

"Holding his own. The bullet missed all the important stuff, but chipped a bone. They'll have to wait till he's stronger to attempt surgery. After he's stabilized, they'll move him to a private room. He's going to be fine."

Don looked over his wife's shoulder, and Jana turned to see Zack sprinting into the lobby. "What's she doing here, Lasky? Get her out of here right now!" Don pointed to the exit. Motioning to a man waiting by the entry, he barked out orders. "Jana, give me your keys." She looked at his outstretched hand with defiance before she finally placed her keys in his hand. He handed them to his agent. "Get her car out of sight."

Zack pulled on her arm to lead her outside, but she maneuvered away from him again. "I'm not leaving until I see Trevor and know he's going to be all right."

"She's just as stubborn as Trevor," Don grumbled. Then he addressed the nurse at the receptionist desk. "Is there someplace we can talk in private?"

A minute later, Don led the small group into a conference room and shut the door behind them. His expression softened as he placed a hand on Jana's arm. "You've not only put yourself in danger by being here, you've put Trevor in danger, too. You have to go with Lasky before anyone else gets hurt. Do you understand?"

Tears spilled from her eyes. "Please, Don. I just have to see him."

He sighed, looking between Jana and his wife. "Just a minute, then you'll go?"

"Just a minute. Cross my heart."

"I've got to give Zack some last-minute instructions," Don explained, "so I'm putting you in the care of Agent Murray."

Murray escorted Jana and Jared as they followed a nurse through the hospital. Jana noticed various agents waiting for word on their comrade, and others watching the exits.

When they arrived at the treatment room, the nurse pulled a curtain aside and stepped back, allowing Jana and Jared to enter. "I'll come back in a couple of minutes to get you."

"Thanks." Jared guided Jana into the room, while the agent waited outside.

"Oh, Jared, he looks so pale."

At the sound of her voice, Trevor opened his eyes and weakly spoke her name.

"I'm right here, Trevor. Don't try to speak." She took his hand.

"Please go now, sweetheart," he said with surprising strength. "You don't have a lot of time." He closed his eyes and fell back against the pillow. "Jared."

He stepped forward. "Yes?"

"I'm putting her in your hands. Take care of her."

"I'll guard her with my life."

"Goodbye, Trevor," Jana said before she left with Jared.

He placed a protective arm around her shoulders as they walked back toward the waiting room.

"I'm so worried about him. What if he doesn't pull through?" Tears sprang from her eyes. "Without him, I'd be dead right now. That bullet was meant for me."

"Where's your faith, Jana? The blessing we gave him promised a full recovery. I'll tell you, it was one of the strongest promptings I've ever received while giving a blessing. He's got a lot of good to do in this life."

"Do you really think so?"

"I know so. Why don't you go in the restroom and wash your face, and then we'll leave. Okay?"

She managed a small smile. "Thanks, Jared."

————•·•————

He pushed her toward the bathroom and watched her as she disappeared. He was serious when he told her how he felt as he laid his hands on Trevor's head. Any ill feelings toward Trevor had evaporated. *If when we look at another human being, we could see what our Heavenly Father sees, I wonder how much more peaceful this world would be? I wish I could look into the future to see what part Jana plays in his life . . . or in mine.*

Jared walked a few feet down the hall to a water fountain, while Agent Murray continued on to the waiting room. Wiping the drops of water from his mouth with the back of his hand, Jared turned toward the bathroom and froze in his tracks.

Jana exited the restroom with a stocky Asian man. He held her right arm in an iron grip, with a small gun jammed into her side. Fear filled her eyes as he pulled her toward the back of the hospital. Jared followed from a safe distance, reaching into his pocket for the cell phone Trevor had given him. He scanned the list of contacts and found a number for Don. He pushed the call button and waited for someone to pick up.

"Don Townsend here. Who is this?"

Jared whispered into the phone. "Jared Carpenter. They have Jana. I'm following them down the corridor toward the rear of the building. He's got a gun on her."

"Okay, Carpenter. Keep her in your sights, but don't do anything. I'll send my men to cover all exits."

Just before he ended the call, Jared heard Townsend giving instructions to his men. "Fan out around the building. They've got the Clawson girl, and they're heading rearward."

A prayer filled Jared's heart. *I can't live without her. Please help me.*

The gunman exited the building, looking around before he pushed Jana toward an empty ambulance with its engine idling. The paramedics were just inside the hospital, talking to the nurse at the supply desk. The kidnapper hauled Jana to the emergency vehicle and pushed her through the driver's door and across to the passenger seat. Then he climbed in after her.

As Jared sprinted toward the exit in an attempt to catch them, he ran into an orderly pushing a gurney. Stumbling against the cart and then going around it cost Jared precious seconds. When he saw the ambulance leave the curb, he slapped a support pillar in frustration. At that moment, Zack rounded the corner in the Jeep, stopping long enough for Jared to jump in the passenger side.

"If Townsend knew I brought you with me, he'd probably shoot me first, and then fire me for good measure."

"Just follow that ambulance." Jared pointed to the speeding vehicle turning right on the next street.

Zack picked up the radio and called Don. "Sir, I'm following them in an ambulance heading east on US-30."

"Keep them in your sights. We'll try to set up some kind of a road block."

———•———

The FBI team gathered in the hospital conference room. A county map covered the rectangular table. Don turned to Agent Murray. "Is there any place we can set up a barricade?"

"If we move quickly, the best place might be here." The agent pointed to a spot on the map. "You have this curve between John Day and Fern Hill. They won't see anything till they're right on top of it."

Don nodded his head. "Make it happen." He paced the floor, muttering under his breath, "Now I'm the one who's going to have to tell Trevor we let him down. How can I do that?"

A hand on his arm brought him back to the present. "I'll go tell him," Traci said. "You need to be out here coordinating efforts to stop them."

"Thanks, Trace. I'll be there as soon as I'm able."

———•———

Traci Townsend approached her brother's room with consternation. She nodded to the guard before she poked her head through the curtains separating Trevor from the other patients. He appeared to sleep soundly, so she moved quietly to the chair next to his bed. She closed her eyes and leaned her head back. A tear escaped from the corner of her eye.

"Hey, Sis. Don't cry." Trevor reached his hand out to her. "Everything will be fine."

"I know. How are you feeling?"

"Much better after that nap, especially knowing Jana is on her way to the safe house."

Traci bit her bottom lip and squeezed her eyelids shut, attempting to stem a flow of tears.

His eyes narrowed. "Jana is on her way to the safe house, isn't she?"

His sister opened her eyes and shook her head, causing the tears to fall.

"Traci, talk to me. What's happened?"

"They . . . they got to her after she left your room."

"Where is she now?" All traces of weariness were gone from Trevor's voice.

"Lasky's following them down Highway 30."

Trevor pushed the covers aside and pulled himself to a sitting position. "Where's Don?"

"In a conference room here at the hospital."

"Traci, get me a robe and have them bring a wheelchair."

She sprang up. "Trevor, you need to lie down. You've lost a lot of blood."

"If you don't bring a wheelchair, I'll walk there on my own. This is Jana we're talking about. I am going to be in that room where her future is being decided."

Traci sighed. "All right. Just don't move until I get back."

He called to her retreating form, "I'm counting down! Ten . . . nine . . ."

With a hospital-issue blue robe in hand, she scurried back to her brother's side, while a burly agent pushed a wheelchair into the room. After Traci helped Trevor into his robe, the guard helped him into the chair.

"Let's get to the control room." Trevor leaned on his right arm, while his injured left shoulder hung in a sling.

———•———

All heads in the conference room turned toward the door as Trevor entered. Don looked up from the map and commented dryly, "So much for anyone thinking you're in here for appendicitis. We've got a barricade set up, with traffic diverted off the highway." He pointed to a bend in the road. "Right there."

"Good spot," Trevor said. "How long before they reach it?"

The radio crackled. "Lasky here. Suspect is still heading east on 30. We're closing in on the barricade—ETA ten to fifteen minutes."

"Roger, Lasky. Keep your eyes peeled for an opportunity to rescue the target."

"Yes, sir."

When the microphone rested on the table, Trevor spoke up. "Fill me in, Don. What's going on?"

"With Coleman and his wife in protective custody, we completed the raid and have rounded up the majority of the players. We have a few loose ends, and one of those loose ends decided to take revenge on Vince the best way he knew how—"

"Jana."

"That's right."

"If we don't get her back right away, her life is worth nothing." Trevor ran his good hand through his hair. "How secure is the barricade?"

"It's in a heavily wooded area just around a bend. It'll be pretty hard to get through. The only cars on the road will be

FBI and local police. As they approach the blockade, cars in front of them will slow down. Hopefully, Lasky and Carpenter will be able to get her away."

Trevor closed his eyes and bowed his head as if in prayer. All noise in the room hushed. Finally, with moisture shining in his eyes, he said, "They will."

"Don," Lasky's voice boomed from the radio, "we've reached the bend, and cars in front of us are slowing—almost stopping."

"You know what to do, Lasky."

"Yes, sir. Over and out."

Twenty-two

Jared locked his eyes onto the vehicle in front of them and gripped the door handle, ready to move. "When they slow down enough, I want you to move carefully to the passenger side while I approach the driver," Zack instructed. "Keep low and under the sight of his mirrors."

Jared gave a single nod of his head.

The ambulance slowed to a crawl, and Zack threw the Jeep into park. With his voice steady, he commanded Jared, "Now."

The two men quickly moved near the ground to either door of the other vehicle. Jana glanced in the side-view mirror, and Jared knew she'd caught a glimpse of him. With her kidnapper distracted by the slowing traffic, Jared watched Jana release her seat belt, fling the door open, and launch herself out onto the ground. He rushed to help her up, then pulled her, limping, toward the heavy growth of trees, where they blended into the shadows.

Zack ran to the driver's side, threw open the door, and aimed his gun at the abductor's head. "Slowly put your hands up and don't make any sudden moves."

With pistols drawn, officers swarmed the stolen ambulance. The kidnapper exited the vehicle, his hands raised, and Zack immediately forced him to the ground. Once other agents took over, Zack pushed his way through the crowd of law enforcement personnel to the edge of the road.

He cupped his hand and called, "Jared! Jana!" He paused to listen. "It's safe to come out."

A voice called from far away. "You better come down here and bring a first-aid kit."

"I'm on my way. Keep calling so I can find you."

When Zack found them, Jana sat with her back propped up against a tree. Jared knelt next to her, probing her ankle.

"Hey, guys, you ready to go?"

Still poking her ankle, Jared answered, "I think we might want to carry her out."

"Jared, I'm fine." Her voice trembled. "Help me stand, and I can climb up on my own power."

"Okay, we'll try."

The two men managed to get her to her feet. When they let go, her legs buckled under her.

The portable radio crackled in Zack's pocket. "Lasky, we have the paramedics coming down to examine Miss Clawson. They're bringing a stretcher to transport her."

"Good thing. She's pretty shook up." He turned to his friends. "You heard that, I assume?"

"Yes. Maybe she'll listen to them." Jared gave a stern look.

After examining Jana, the paramedics strapped her to the basket, and the four men carried her.

As they struggled up the hill, Zack asked, "Why don't spies go into the forest?" He paused. "Too many bugs."

"Take me away—please!" Jana implored the paramedic.

A new ambulance stood next to the getaway vehicle, its doors open. "I think we should bring her to Columbia Memorial and have a doctor see her," one of the paramedics said.

Zack put a hand on his shoulder. "That's a negative. Her life would be in danger. Let's situate her in the back of the Jeep and we'll get a doctor to see her at the safe house."

Jared helped a shivering Jana into the back seat, enfolding her in his arms and reassuring her. Then he looked at Zack. "We're ready for you to take us anywhere you want. Jana promises not to give you any more trouble, right?"

She lifted her head from Jared's shoulder and nodded her assent.

"To a safe house and beyond!" When Zack spoke into his cell phone several seconds later, his voice sobered. "I have the packages and am proceeding as planned, sir."

"Get them out of there, now!" Don yelled.

"Yes, sir." After ending the call, Zack told his passengers, "I don't think he's very happy with any of us right now."

Darkness closed in as they pulled into the yard of a decaying yellow farmhouse outside of Canby, Oregon. Zack pressed a code on his phone, and the weathered gate opened silently on well-oiled hinges. The exterior gave the impression of neglect, but a closer inspection of the property would dispel the illusion. Beneath the deteriorating piano on the front porch lay a strong framework. The peeling paint around the dirty windows hid the thick double panes.

Zack parked near the back door and got out of the car. His eyes scanned the surroundings, his hand resting on the gun in its holster. Then he opened the car door and helped Jana out. Jared followed and put a protective arm around her.

"Go right through that door," Zack instructed. "I'll be there in a minute."

Favoring her right ankle, Jana leaned heavily on Jared to climb the steps. They entered the house, and she gasped at the modern kitchen and beautiful interior. "Wow. What a contrast from the outside."

Jared chuckled. "Yeah, I thought I'd have to chase the rats away and lift you over broken floor boards."

At the sound of running footsteps, Jana turned toward the stairway. A familiar voice called her name. "Aunt Karen?" Scarcely believing her eyes, Jana limped toward her. "I'm so glad to see you."

Karen Coleman took her niece into her embrace and held her tight. Jared guided them to the couch.

"Oh, Jana. We've been so worried about you. You look like you've been put through a wringer. Are you okay?"

"Yes, I'm fine." She watched her uncle Vince slowly descend the stairway, his shoulders sagging in weariness. He refused meet Jana's gaze.

Compassion welled up in her at the sight of her beloved uncle, now a broken man. She was upset with him, but she couldn't hate him for wanting to protect his family. She put an arm around him to lead him to the couch, then coaxed him to sit.

Tremors shook the large man. "I'm so sorry for what I did, for everything I put you through. I know you'll never be able to forgive me."

"Of course I will. It's just taking a little time. I know you didn't mean to cause anyone harm. I love you, Uncle Vince."

"Because of me—oh, pumpkin . . ." He choked back a sob. "It's because of me your parents are gone. I . . . I tried to tell them no, but then they killed Charles and Eileen. Then they threatened to hurt you and Karen. I couldn't bear for that to happen, so I did what they asked." He held his head in his hands. "I'm sorry."

"I know all about it, Uncle Vince. I wish you had gone to the police instead of caving in to their threats."

"Yes, that would've been the smart thing to do, wouldn't it?" He paused, shaking his head. "And that wasn't all." He rubbed his hand along the stubble on his jaw. "I sent them to give Trevor a warning."

Jana sighed. "Yes. I know. He could've been killed, Uncle Vince. Fortunately, he'll make it through this."

With a new resolve to his features, Vince stood and helped Jana up. "I'm going to make this right."

———•———

Within a week, thanks to the information provided by Vince Coleman, the police and FBI rounded up the entire network of operatives. Jana and Jared traveled across Oregon in the blue Jeep, with Zack at the wheel.

Involuntary shivers ran up her spine as the hospital came into view and terror-filled memories flooded her head.

Zack looked in the rearview mirror at his passengers. "Well, we're here. Jana's car is in the parking lot. Trevor's out of surgery and in his room now." He pulled up near the front entrance.

Jared helped Jana out of the vehicle. "Thanks, Zack. I'll talk to you in the morning." Jared began to close the door.

"By the way, Jared . . ."

He leaned back into the Jeep. "Yes?"

A smile burst out on Zack's face. "Did you hear about the man who fell into an upholstery machine? When he came out, he was fully recovered."

Jared laughed and shut the door. Jana clasped his arm and they walked into the hospital, her limp now barely noticeable.

When they reached Trevor's room, she paused outside the door. Jared gave her a reassuring squeeze.

Trevor glanced up as they entered. "Hey, you guys. Thanks for coming." He paused. "Jared, would you please give Jana and me a few minutes alone?"

"I'll be just outside."

Jana watched the door close, then turned to face Trevor. "What is it?"

"Come sit and hold my hand. I have something to tell you, and it's not going to be easy." He winced as he reached out to her. "I'm not sure you'll ever forgive me for this one, but I've already waited too long to tell you." The crooked grin was back. "Besides, I figure you'll be less likely to hit me in my present condition."

"What are you talking about? You're scaring me, Trevor."

He took a deep breath. "Remember how you slept so long at the cabin? You thought you must have been exhausted."

"Right, I was. But . . ." She dropped his hand and glared at him. "What are you saying?"

Trevor sighed. "I slipped something into your milk. I didn't have a choice, Jana. The cabin was the only place you'd be safe, and I had to leave. I was under orders."

She collected her thoughts and took a deep breath. "Okay. I can understand that. You were trying to protect me."

"You understand? Is there hope for us then?"

"I said I understood drugging the milk."

He closed his eyes. "Uh-oh. What comes next?"

"You were angry with me at the guest house, for absolutely no reason."

"Sweetheart, I thought someone was outside your window. I had to pull you out of the way."

"But you didn't have to get so angry."

He looked away. "You're right. It was inexcusable, and I apologize." Silence hung in the air for a long time before he went on. "As long as I'm confessing, I might as well bring everything into the open."

"What else is there?"

"It's about your parents."

Jana frowned. "My parents?"

"I knew your father very well. Do you remember me telling you about a mentor in high school?"

"Yes." She drew out the word.

"It was your father. He helped me get through college. I met your mother a couple of times." Trevor smiled. "You're a lot like her."

"Why didn't I meet you?"

"I didn't come into Keene much. Charles was very influential in my life, maybe even more than my own father. His beliefs about the sanctity of marriage helped keep me morally clean."

"I had no idea."

"He's also the reason I don't drink."

Jana stood and walked to the other side of the room. "Where do my parents fit into this?"

"The Chinese who approached Vince tried to get to your dad, too."

"Dad would never . . ."

"I know. I'd been recruited by Don for the FBI, and because of my ties to your dad, I was assigned to find out how deeply he was involved. I agreed so I could prove his innocence. That's why I was at the Pumpkin Fest in Keene."

"And?" Jana motioned for him to continue.

"And I proved it. Your father convinced Vince to refuse them. The Chinese decided Charles was too much of a liability—he would never waver. He was killed as a warning to Vince."

The day of the accident rushed back into Jana's mind, leaving her trembling. She returned to sit in the chair by Trevor's bed.

"Jana." He waited until she looked at him. "By the time I discovered the plot to kill your parents, it was too late to warn them. I was too late." He paused. "I know this has been hard for you, but I have one more thing to tell you. Remember the Desert Rose pitcher I gave you?"

"Yes."

Tears brimmed in Trevor's eyes. "It had a listening device attached to the bottom. I'm sorry."

Suddenly, Jana felt nauseous. She stood. "What? Why? How could you do that to me? Was that an order from the FBI too?"

He closed his eyes. "No, it wasn't."

"I . . . I . . ."

"Jana, I want you to go home and think about everything," he said firmly, the tears now flowing freely down his cheeks.

Jana turned and left the room in silence. She heard a faint "I love you" before she closed the door.

———※———

Trevor watched Jana leave the room. His sister entered a few moments later.

"Hey, Trev, how are you feeling?"

"Like death warmed over."

"I won't keep you long. I saw Jana leave."

"I sent her home. Visiting hours are almost over anyway."

"She looked pretty spent."

His tears fell silently. "I may have lost her for good this time."

"Trevor, are you delirious?" Traci raised her hands in a question. "She risked her life to make sure you were all right."

"I told her everything. You . . . you should have seen the look on her face. I . . ."

"Trevor, it's okay. She'll come around." Traci stroked her brother's hair.

"Not this time. I can feel it."

"I'll pray for you both."

A knock sounded at the door, and a nurse appeared with a small paper cup containing a pill.

"You better go now, Sis. Here's my pain pill. I should sleep blissfully through the night."

She kissed him on the cheek. "Remember, Trevor, it's all going to work out. I love you."

"Love you too."

How will I survive without Jana? he thought. *Maybe, just maybe, she'll be able to forgive and forget this and let us start new. Maybe, but not very likely.*

Jana's own tears began their silent journey down her face as Jared escorted her to the car. After handing her a box of tissues from the back seat, he closed her door and walked around to the driver's side.

"Where to, Jana?"

"The beach."

He nodded. "I know just the spot."

They reached the coast and parked. Jared pulled a blanket out of the trunk, and he and Jana walked wordlessly toward the water. They spread the blanket on the sand, then sat to watch the sun slide soundlessly into the horizon.

Jana stared at the glow cast on the rock formations jutting out of the ocean. "This has been one of those days you wish never happened. I don't know what to think, Jared. I feel like I've been socked in the stomach. It's as though I can't catch my breath."

"Lie down on the blanket. Just listen to the waves while I rub your shoulders a bit."

A sigh escaped her as she began to relax. "It's sure nice to have a physical therapist as a friend. It would be nice to get a back rub like this every day."

"What I wouldn't give to be able to do this every day." The wistful words were lost in the wind.

"What did you say?

"I said, just relax and let the tension float away."

He must have rubbed her back and shoulders for half an hour before she turned over and sat up. "I've said it before,

Jared Carpenter, you're a miracle worker." She got up on her knees and faced him. "I don't know what I would have done without you." She closed the gap and kissed him.

The darkness hid his blush as he responded to her kiss and held her in his arms. Finally he pulled away. "I'm sorry, Jana. A lot has happened, and you don't need me to complicate matters." He cleared his throat and helped her up. "Let's go home."

He turned to fold the blanket, and Jana took off at a run toward the parking lot. "Beat ya to the car!"

Jared was never one to resist a challenge and sprinted after her, the blanket flying in the breeze behind him. Her head start was a little too much, and she beat him by inches. "Cheater!" he said, leaning over with his hands on his knees, trying to catch his breath.

"All's fair in love and racing to the car."

"You mean 'All's fair in racing to the car and therapy.'"

"You wouldn't dare!"

Jana rested against the car while Jared faced her, leaning with his arms on either side of her. He double-arched his eyebrows in a challenge. "Just wait and see."

Jana ducked under his arm. "Didn't you ever take an ethics class that told you not to threaten patients with revenge?"

"No, I don't recall that scenario coming up."

"Could I coerce you with a root beer float?"

"You think that just because bribery worked once, I'll fall for it again?"

She grinned sheepishly. "Yes."

"I'll have to think about it." He helped her into the car.

They were silent for a few minutes before Jana said quietly, "All's really not fair in love, is it? What Trevor did wasn't fair at all."

"No, it wasn't."

"Things might be over between us."

"What are you going to do?"

She looked up at him and shrugged. "I'll go back to Portland when he goes and take care of him as best I can. When he's fully recovered, and I can slug him a time or two" —she smiled— "then I'll make the final decision."

"Makes sense."

"Will I get to see you again?"

"Just try to stop me."

"Thanks, Jared."

When he pulled up at the guest house, he said, "It's pretty late, Jana, but would you like to watch a movie? I think *Seven Brides for Seven Brothers* is still in the car."

"Let's try it. I don't want to be alone right now."

He captured her hands in his and searched her eyes. "Would you rather talk?"

She shook her head. "No, I really don't want to think about it, either. I'll veg now and be like Scarlet O'Hara and ponder the situation tomorrow."

Jared smiled. "Then let's make root beer floats and watch the movie."

Twenty-three

As Trevor began to mend, something weighed heavily on his mind. This was his chance to show himself he had changed, and no one else needed to know about it. He picked up his phone, took a deep breath, and phoned his office.

"Mr. Willis's office. May I help you?"

"Brenda, it's me."

"I didn't expect to hear from you so soon after your surgery."

"There's something I need you to do. I want this top secret—no one is to know. Okay?"

"Yes, sir."

"You know that file on Jared Carpenter?"

"Yes. It's still on your desk where you left it a week ago."

"Well, he's got a loan application filed with Tom Weaver. Tom mentioned he was going to deny the loan. Give him a call and let him know I will personally guarantee the loan. There's only one condition—he can't let Carpenter know anything about my part in it. Understood?"

"Understood. You sure wouldn't want word to get around that you're a nice guy."

Trevor chuckled. "It would sully my reputation. Listen, you can reach me on my cell phone. Today, just emergencies. Tomorrow, just important stuff. All right?"

"Check. Feel better now. That's the secretary giving the boss orders."

"Thanks, Brenda."

———•———

Jared had dropped Jana off at the hospital while he ran some errands. The door to Trevor's room stood open. Jana entered and put her hand out to pull back the privacy curtain, but stopped when she heard him mention Jared's name. She paused a moment to listen to Trevor's side of the conversation and realized he was sticking his neck out to help Jared. *Wow, that's certainly unexpected!* She filed the revelation away and called out, "Knock, knock."

"Come in." Trevor looked haggard, but he smiled when he saw Jana. "Hello, beautiful."

"Good morning. How did you sleep?"

"Pretty good. They gave me a sleeping pill, and I don't remember anything until about 6:00 AM. At that point, there was a lot of pain, but it's under control now. Come sit by me."

She walked across the room and sat in the chair nearest his bed. "I didn't sleep very well last night."

"I know who's to blame for that. I'm sorry, honey."

"Too bad you were in here. We had root beer floats. After all the revelations last night, I think a float would have looked good on you, literally."

Trevor flinched. "I guess I deserved that. I still haven't had anything more substantial than green Jell-O. You'd think we were in Utah."

"Nah, in Utah you'd have a much larger variety of Jell-O—green, yellow, orange, red, pink, and blue."

"Thanks." He held Jana's hand and rubbed it absently. "How are you doing?" He wouldn't meet her eyes.

"I'm alive."

"Can you forgive me? Telling you was my last step to repentance—unless you count being able to forgive myself."

"I don't have a choice. You know the scripture—'I the Lord will forgive whom I will forgive, but of you it is required to forgive all men.'"

Trevor smiled. "Okay, let me rephrase that. Is there a chance I can make this up to you and we can overcome this obstacle?"

"I honestly can't say. I feel like I've had the wind knocked out of me and can't catch my breath."

He kissed her hand. "You deserve so much better than me. But I can promise you that I've changed. Do you believe me?"

She thought back to the overheard conversation. "Yes, I do. Is Traci coming?"

"She'll be here shortly."

"What are your plans? Will you go home when you're released, or to her house?"

"I'm not sure. What are you going to do?"

"I'll still be heading home next weekend," Jana replied. "If you'll be there, I'll do what I can to help you. I'm not sure what kind of work I'll have to go back to, though."

"Don said that, for the moment, things are business as usual. The district attorney is working on a deal with Vince. It'd be a shame for all those people to be out of work."

"Yeah, I have some money from my parents, so I'll be fine either way. But not everyone is so lucky."

Trevor cleared his throat. "Jana, I have something I want to tell you. I thought about waiting a little longer so it wouldn't influence your decision, but this incident reminded me that life is short. I have to seize the trout."

"Seize the trout? What are you talking about?"

"It's a long story Zack told me, something about stunned trout and a small dock. Remind me to tell you about it sometime." Trevor patted her hand. "Anyway, I had a close call and I don't think I can afford to wait any longer."

"Well, tell me then."

He beamed. "I want to be baptized into the LDS Church."

Jana gasped. "What? Oh . . . that's wonderful, Trevor! But where have I been when all of this was happening?"

"I decided about a week and a half ago, but everything broke loose before I could tell you. Are you happy for me?"

"Of course I am. I'm just surprised."

"Jared agreed to baptize me."

"Jared? Really? Well, that's great." Jana paused. "Who were you talking on the phone with when I came in?"

"Just Brenda. I may be out of it, but the business never stops."

"That, or you can't stand to let anyone else handle things."

"Ah! You know me too well."

"Sometimes I think I don't know you at all. Do you need help with anything? I'm told I'm a decent personal assistant."

"Vince said you're the best he's ever had."

Jana waved her hand dismissively. "Whatever. I'm through with therapy and Jared's books for the day. So, here I am at your disposal."

"Okay, go ahead and sit right here."

She took the chair next to the bed. "All right, what do you need me to do?"

A huge grin appeared on his face. "Just let me look at you. That's all the medicine that I need."

"I must say your charm is quickly returning."

"You're my inspiration. Why don't you read to me?"

"All right, what did you want me to read?"

"How about 3 Nephi?"

Smiling, Jana opened the Book of Mormon and began reading the first chapter of 3 Nephi. After a few minutes, she realized Trevor had fallen asleep. She looked at his unguarded face and felt a tenderness creep over her. *He's made some major mistakes, but he is a good man. Do I have the right to hold those*

mistakes against him? Oh, Heavenly Father, what should I do?
Tears trickled down her cheeks as she prayed.

———•◦•———

Saturday morning, Traci and Don Townsend arrived to take Trevor back to Seattle. Jared and Jana were there to say goodbye, along with Zack and Caitlyn, who gave Trevor a gift bag with a deck of cards and a box of plastic spoons. "So you won't be bored," Caitlyn explained. "I also put in some homemade applesauce cookies."

Jana glanced at the bag longingly. "They smell so good."

Caitlyn smiled. "Don't worry, Jana. I made enough for you to take some home, too."

Trevor inhaled the aroma from the cookies. "Thanks, guys. I appreciate everything. You've been great."

"Just get well soon." Caitlyn hugged him, her eyes filled with tears.

Zack extended a hand to Trevor. "We'll see you in a few weeks for the Dunkin' Trevor Festival. Should we have Dunkin' Donuts for refreshments?"

Trevor just shook his head. "I'm looking forward to it." He turned to Jared. "What can I say, brother? You've taught me a lot, and I'm humbled to know you. You will be there for the baptism, right?"

"Wouldn't miss it for anything. I gave my sister, Dani, your phone number. She said she'd try to stop in. Traci's house isn't far from her school in Seattle."

"Good. Thanks again for everything. Words aren't very adequate, are they?"

"Not coming from my mouth." Jared reached out his hand to Trevor, who took hold of it.

"Jared, take care of her for me, okay?"

"I will."

Trevor held Jana's hand as they headed toward the hospital exit. "I'm worried about you driving home alone tomorrow," he told her.

"Don't worry. I'll call you when I get home."

"Never thought I'd say this, but . . ." Jared shook his head. "I agree with Trevor. I'm not too crazy about you driving home alone tomorrow."

"I'll be just fine! You don't have to worry."

"Just the same, I'd feel better if I went with you," Jared said.

"He's making sense, sweetheart." Trevor squeezed her hand.

"Don't be silly. How would he get back?"

Zack walked over to them with Caitlyn in tow. "We could always drive Jared's car down while he drives with you. It'd be nice to have Caitlyn alone for the drive. Since we announced our engagement, her mom won't let us have a minute to ourselves."

"I hate to put you all out like that."

"The peace of mind will be worth it," Jared added.

Jana chuckled. "With all of you ganging up on me, I guess I don't have a choice."

Trevor let out a relieved sigh. "Great! It's all settled then."

Traci set up a make-shift bed in the middle seat of her minivan. Jana helped fluff the pillows and tuck the blankets around Trevor.

"It sure seems weird to be going home," Jana admitted as she leaned through the van door. "It feels like I left a lifetime ago, instead of just four weeks."

Trevor looked up at her. "A lot has happened, hasn't it?"

"Yeah. We both need to do a lot of soul searching and praying over the next week."

Trevor caressed her cheek. "You're right. I'll see you on Saturday. Be careful, and call often."

"I will. See you."

He reached up and tucked a piece of hair behind her ear. "I'll call you when I get to Traci's."

Jana waved as she closed the sliding door. Jared came up beside her and together they watched the van pull away.

———

The next afternoon, Jana said goodbye to her new friends and drove with Jared, while Zack and Caitlyn followed. Jana waved until the Grants were just a dot in the distance. Then she turned to face forward, wiping tears from her eyes. "I feel like I'm leaving home again. Isn't that crazy?"

"Not really." Jared glanced at her from the driver's seat. "I feel like you're going out into the cold, cruel world. I wish I could be there to protect you."

"Thank you. You've really been there for me. How will I get through my days without you?"

"You'll have Trevor," he mumbled.

Jana closed her eyes and drew a deep breath. "I'm not sure about that."

"I'm only a phone call away. Less than two hours driving—unless it's rush hour. I'll be back for Trevor's baptism."

"And I'll have to come for Caitlyn and Zack's wedding."

Jared smiled. "And the position of secretary is still open . . ."

Jana's laughter filled the car. "I'll think about it—who knows how long I'll have a job. In the meantime, you'll come up to Portland to go to the temple frequently, won't you?"

"You can be sure of that. We can write, and you can send me cookies." Jared grinned.

"All you need to do is get Mrs. Gardner to make you cookies, and you won't miss me a bit."

"I'll miss you more than you know, Jana."

She looked down at her trembling hands and replied quietly, "Me too."

———

After everyone left, the silence and loneliness of Jana's apartment was almost too much to bear. She changed into pajamas, brushed her teeth, and washed her face before lying down on the bed to call Trevor. She got under the covers, then reached for the phone. He picked it up on the first ring. "Hello, sweetheart."

"Hi, Trevor."

"You sound tired."

"I am. It's been a long day. Everyone left about fifteen minutes ago. I'm in my warm, fuzzy pajamas, snuggled under the covers."

"Sounds cozy. I'm in my warm, fuzzy sweats and snuggled under a blanket on the couch at my sister's house. I felt pretty good today, and I'm going to try getting home this weekend. I think I'll be ready to be baptized in a couple of weeks. Can you make arrangements with the missionaries and Jared?"

"I'd love to. Would a Saturday be good for you?"

"Whatever works for all concerned."

He cleared his throat. "By the way, Jared's sister, Dani, came by today. She's helping me hone my skills at spoons. I can already beat Traci's kids."

Jana tried to stifle a yawn. "Uh-huh."

"Well, I should let you go get some rest, even though I'd rather sit here and talk all night. I'm not the one who has to get to work tomorrow."

"I am feeling pretty worn out, so I'll say good night. Sleep well, Trevor."

"Sweet dreams, honey."

Jana hung up the phone and turned out the light. Kneeling beside her bed in prayer, she asked for guidance in the decision she had to make, and for the strength to follow through with the answer.

Trevor arrived home, and the week passed quickly. He and Jana met with the missionaries, made plans for the baptism, and at Trevor's insistence, spent time together to find out if their relationship could be rebuilt.

On Saturday afternoon, Jared, Dani, Zack, and Caitlyn met Trevor and Jana for a tour of Portland. After dinner, the group returned to Jana's apartment.

Sitting at the table, Trevor pulled out the cards. "Jana, go ahead and get the spoons. I'm ready for a rematch." He made a big show of shuffling the cards with his best imitation of a card shark. "I'm almost unstoppable now. Right, Dani?"

She rolled her eyes and shook her head. "Of course you are. Beating the five-year-old was especially difficult."

"Hey!" He tossed an M&M across the table, barely missing her head.

"Okay, no food fights," Jared declared.

Dani gave him a sassy little sister grin. "Yes, Daddy dearest."

Zack interrupted. "Hey, we're told to honor our father and mother. Is there a commandment on how to treat our siblings?"

Dani answered in a heartbeat. "Yes. 'Thou shalt not kill.'"

Laughter erupted around the room as Jana returned with the spoons. Things got pretty intense because neither Trevor nor Jared gave up easily. The situation disintegrated even more when Trevor captured a spoon after tickling Jana till she fell out of her chair.

Still giggling, Jana got up from the floor. "No fair, Trevor. You're cheating."

"That's how he beat the seven-year-old," Dani explained.

When Jana announced ice cream sundaes for dessert, the guys cheered, and everyone headed for the kitchen.

Jared joined Jana as she began scooping ice cream into bowls. "Here, let me do that for you," he said. "You can concentrate on the hot fudge."

Their hands brushed as he took the scoop from her. Jana rubbed the spot where he'd touched her, then looked in his eyes.

Trevor cleared his throat. "What can I help you with, Jana?"

"Um, let's see. The toppings are in the corner. Put them on the table and we can all help ourselves."

After the sundaes, Jana pulled some bundles out of the hall closet and unrolled the flocked vinyl air mattresses. She handed Trevor a manually powered pump. "Before you go, maybe you three could help blow up these air mattresses."

Trevor cleared his throat and bowed gallantly. "Anything you ask."

After about ten minutes of one-handed pumping, he turned it over to Jared, who approached it as he would the hammer and bell of the strongman contest at a county fair. He lasted fifteen minutes. Zack intertwined his fingers and stretched out his arms to crack his knuckles, then took his turn.

When Trevor finished his next turn, he muttered under his breath, "You'd think she would invest in an electric pump."

Jana overheard him and smiled sweetly. "I did."

All three men swung around to face her, exclaiming in unison. "What?"

"I said I did invest in one. I just thought you men would like a chance to show off your strength and endurance." She ducked as three pillows flew across the room toward her.

A disgusted grunt came from Trevor. "We better head back to my place and leave these three to their slumber party. We'll pick you up for church, and don't forget the baptism follows immediately after the meeting."

Opening the door to leave, Trevor came face-to-face with Sue as she raised her hand to knock. "Whoa, Sue. I didn't expect to see anyone here. Is everything all right?"

"Oh, mercy, I didn't expect anyone to walk out, either." She fanned her face with her hand. "Everything's fine. I just had a few things to show Jana."

"Well, she's right inside."

"Thanks. How's your arm? I can't believe all that was going on at work. I thought I knew everything that happened over there." Sue shook her head.

"Well, sometimes even the shrewdest fox gets outfoxed." He patted her shoulder. "Have a good evening."

"You too, Trevor." She walked into the living room where the three women were making up their beds for the night. Caitlyn sat cross-legged on her neatly tucked in blanket. "I can't believe you made the guys pump this up by hand."

Dani shook out the sheet over her air mattress. "I've never seen anyone get the best of Jared like that. It was great."

Jana picked up the other end of the sheet, still chuckling over the men's reaction. "It was rather brilliant, if I do say so myself. Dani, tell us what Jared was like growing up."

"He was a good brother—a bit infuriating at times," Dani replied. "No matter what I tried, I could never goad him into getting mad. Except once."

"What did you do?" Caitlyn asked. "I've never—"

Sue cleared her throat, catching Jana's attention.

"Oh, Sue. What are you doing here so late?"

"I needed you to glance over a few things before I can close out the journals this week. I have them in the car."

"Okay." Jana looked at her friends. "I'll be right back. Save the story for me." She followed Sue out the door. "Thanks so much for your diligence. I know all of this has put quite a burden on you. What does your husband say about all your extra hours?"

"Oh, Lee's been keeping me company all day," Sue said as she guided Jana to the van her husband had double-parked outside the apartment building. "He didn't want me traveling around the city alone. You know, I heard a woman was snatched right off the sidewalk tonight."

"Oh, that's terrible. Where did it happen?"

The older woman opened the door, and Jana began to climb into the back seat. "Right here, dear."

With surprising strength, Sue pushed Jana into the interior, hopped in, and slid the door shut behind her. "Willis thinks he's so smart. We'll see which fox has been outfoxed."

Twenty-four

The van careened from side to side through the Saturday night traffic in downtown Portland, keeping Jana off balance with each sharp turn. She braced herself between the driver's chair and the back seat. "Sue, what's going on here? Where are you taking me? Why?"

Sue turned in her seat to look at Jana. "Stop whining. Do you think I've enjoyed working at Coleman Industries all these years? I did it for my family."

"Your family? I don't understand."

"My husband's uncle is the representative of the Chinese government. He's the one behind the effort to procure the infrared imagers. Even Vince didn't know about him."

"But why kidnap me?"

"Vengeance. What better way to strike back at Coleman for double-crossing him?"

Another sharp turn from Lee threw Jana against the side of the van.

"There's no way to escape this time. We made sure of that."

"Sue, I thought you were my friend."

"Family comes first," she declared.

Jana looked to the floorboards. "I assume since you're telling me this, they plan to kill me."

Sue refused to meet her eyes.

A tear threatened to break free, but Jana blinked it back. *What would Jared do? He'd look for a way to escape. At least I have my hands free.*

Sue must have read her mind. "It'll be a bit of a drive, so I'll have to restrain you. No telling what that FBI agent taught you." She pulled out a pair of handcuffs. "First, get off the floor and fasten your seatbelt." She shackled Jana's wrist to the seatbelt mechanism. "You might as well rest. We won't be there for a couple of hours."

Maybe I can talk my way out of this—appeal to our friendship. "So, it was you who keyed them into my location that night?"

"Of course. Vince had nothing to do with it. He thought he was calling the shots, but in reality, he was the doormat."

"Enough!" Lee's command from the front seat hung in the air, effectively halting the conversation.

Sue crossed her arms and stared straight ahead.

———

At Trevor's apartment, sleeping bags covered the middle of the living room, crowding the couches against the walls. Jared exited the bathroom with a towel around his shoulders and his shaving kit in his hand. "Trevor, did Jana mention Sue coming over tonight?"

"Not that I remember. I guess she just dropped by."

"Is that normal?"

Trevor thought a moment. "Not that I know of, but then I monopolized a lot of Jana's time. I know they did things together before we started dating. It's been hard to tell what's normal during these last few weeks. Zack, did you do a background check on Sue?"

"Yes. Just after you took Jana out to lunch the first time."

"Anything unusual?"

"Nope. How does a mouse feel after a shower? Give up? Squeaky clean!"

Trevor snapped, "Will you be quiet? Something is wrong here."

"I agree with you." Jared pulled out his phone. "I'm calling over there."

After a few rings, his sister answered the phone. "Dani, let me speak to Jana."

"She's not here. She went out with someone from work right after you left and hasn't come back. We were about to call."

"Just a minute." Jared placed his hand over the mouthpiece. "She's not there."

Zack and Trevor froze, staring at him.

"We'll be right over." Jared hung up.

Trevor reached for his keys and started for the parking garage. "If anyone's coming with me, you better be fast." Once he got behind the wheel, he made a call. "Come on, Don. Pick up the phone," he said impatiently.

After several rings, Don answered sleepily, "Townsend here."

"Don. Jana's gone."

Don seemed to shake himself awake. "What do you mean? How could she disappear with so many people around her?"

"Sue Williams."

"The secretary? Why would she want her?"

"No clue."

"I know." Jared's matter-of-fact tone startled Trevor.

"What do you know?" Zack asked.

"I think I know why Sue would kidnap her."

"Well." Trevor drew out the word. "Please feel free to clue us in."

"Sue's mother-in-law is from China. There must be some connection."

"Lasky, why didn't you know that?" Trevor barked.

"I just checked Sue, not her husband's family."

Trevor spoke into the phone. "Did you hear that, Don? We have a possible connection with her husband's mother."

"I heard, and I'll get on it right away. Where are you?"

"On our way to her apartment."

"Good. Talk to people there. Maybe someone saw something. Meet me at headquarters when you're through."

The Dodge Caravan approached an older neighborhood in Astoria. Jana woke with a start, her arm numb from its elevated position cuffed to the seatbelt anchor.

Lee approached the sliding door with a gun pointed at their captive and handed Sue a miniature silver key. After she unlocked one end of the handcuffs, Sue released the seatbelt and helped Jana out of the van. Her husband held out his hand for the key before using a flashlight to point toward the back of a dilapidated, nineteenth-century Queen Anne home. They climbed the stairs to the wraparound porch and opened the door.

Crooked hooks clung to the wall of the mudroom, and water-spotted wallpaper curled near the ceiling, threatening to lose contact altogether.

Lee shone the flashlight into a butler's pantry furnished with a single wooden folding chair. "Sit."

When Jana hesitated, he pointed the gun at her chest. With no other choice, she complied.

"Cuff her to the pipe."

Sue bowed her head toward him and obeyed.

He stepped to the light switch and turned the antique knob. With its light no longer needed, he extinguished the torch. Jana watched him open a cupboard to remove a bundle covered in soft cloth and tied with a narrow red braid with gold tassels. After loosening the braid, he drew out a long, thin knife with ornamental carvings on the hilt. Jana gasped.

"I want a picture of this," Lee said to his wife. He yanked Jana's head back to expose her neck and positioned the blade under her chin. "Take the picture now. Do not include my face."

Sue did his bidding. When he took the blade away, she drew a deep breath.

"Now, send this message and picture to Mr. Willis." Lee gave her a piece of paper. "My uncle will be here shortly, and we must be ready. Keep a close eye on her." The knife was returned to the cloth, and Lee left the room with the bundle in hand.

Trevor and Zack flashed their badges at the front desk of FBI headquarters. A burly security guard blocked Jared's access.

Without slowing down, Trevor called over his shoulder, "He's with us—Don Townsend's authorization. Get him set up and then escort him back."

Jared paced the floor, his frustration mounting with each passing minute. He threw his arms up in the air, addressing the stone-faced man at the desk. "She's too trusting. She would never be suspicious of anyone. She believes everyone is as good as she is."

The desk phone rang. After a short conversation, the agent buzzed him in and handed him a visitor's badge. "Follow me, Mr. Carpenter."

He was taken to a conference room with a briefing already in progress. Don Townsend stood at the end of a long table with at least a dozen FBI personnel clustered around it. He held a dry-erase marker and paced in front of a whiteboard.

A woman looked at her notebook. "We have a police report saying that an older man, possibly Asian, was approached in front of the victim's building. He was double-parked and the officer requested him to leave. He did so immediately."

"Do you have a description of the car?" Don asked.

"Yes, sir. A late-model dark-blue Dodge minivan. No license plate number."

Trevor raised his finger. "That matches the doorman's description."

Don wrote it on the board. "We have a vehicle. Now—"

A woman with a stack of papers in her arms came through the door. "Here are the pictures you requested."

"Thank you, Carole." Don returned his attention to the group of agents. "These are driver's license photos of Sue and Lee Williams." He passed them around the table.

Suddenly, Trevor pulled his phone from his pocket. As he glanced at the screen, his face went white. "Don," he croaked almost inaudibly. The room went silent, and everyone turned to Trevor.

Jared grabbed the phone. The photo showed Jana in a chair with a knife at her throat. The words were equally chilling as he read them out loud. "'Willis, bring Coleman to the following address within three hours—no police, FBI, or weapons. If you do not comply, you will never see Miss Clawson alive again.'"

Trevor closed his eyes briefly and said, "I'll head out there right now and—"

Don took the phone. "You're putting the horse before the cart. Carole, have Coleman brought here immediately."

"Yes, sir."

"Trevor, they'll search both of you. See Hamilton. Find out what he can do for you to even the odds."

"No way. I'm not carrying anything that might jeopardize Jana's safety."

"All right. They have a new wireless listening device. It looks like a button. At least we'll be able to hear what's going on. Meet back here in twenty minutes." Don turned on his heel. "Mr. Carpenter, we can't have you in the way. Murray, Weston." He beckoned them with an incline of his head. The two men stepped up. "Take him into custody."

Jared struggled against the two agents as they escorted him out of the room. "You can't do this, Townsend. You have no right." A well-placed elbow to Murray's midsection incapacitated the man. Jared then dropped to the ground, using a Russian coffee grinder move to sweep Weston's legs out from under him. He neutralized a couple more agents before several guns were drawn and pointed at him. Trevor stared dumbfounded at the scene before him.

Don looked down at Jared. "I hope you'll reconsider and allow us to usher you into custody."

Jared yanked his arm away from a security guard and complied.

———◆———

When the door closed, Don faced the rest of his men. "Murray."

"Yes, sir." The man still held his stomach.

"What can you tell me about the homes surrounding the meeting location? We need a place nearby to set up our team without arousing suspicion."

"The Flavel House Museum is within a block or two of that location. I'm sure we'd be able to set up in the carriage house."

"Make it happen. Carole, do you have the surveillance photos of the area?"

"Yes. The home is in an advanced stage of deterioration. There is a small shed in the back. We might be able to hide someone in there as a wild card."

"Good idea." Don paused with his chin held between his thumb and forefinger. "I wonder . . ." He snapped into action. "Carole, arrange immediate transportation for the team. We need to be ready in fifteen minutes. Also, have a helicopter ready for me. Where's Coleman?"

"He should be here any minute."

"Fill him in on the situation. I'll meet the team in Astoria." He headed down the hall to the detention cell and a conversation with Jared Carpenter.

———•———

Jana watched Sue pacing across the kitchen and decided to try again. "Sue, why are you doing this? I thought we were friends."

The woman paused in front of the door. "You've seen my husband. If I don't do what he says . . ." She drew her index finger across her neck.

With the memory of the knife against her skin, the gesture chilled Jana to the bone.

"If you help me get away, maybe the FBI could hide you."

"Yeah." Sue gave a derisive laugh. "They sure did a great job with your parents, didn't they?"

"I'll help you. Please."

Sue's eyes darted toward the stairs. "I . . . I can't do anything about it. I'm sorry." She walked out of the pantry, leaving Jana behind.

Jana's thoughts raced. *I might never live to see the dawn. And I might never see Jared again.* Realization slammed into her. *I love him.* A tear made a track over her cheek, and her mind screamed a message she hoped would be caught from across the miles. *I love you, Jared.* She saw headlights break the darkness through the kitchen window. *Could Trevor and Uncle Vince be here this soon?*

Sue glanced out the kitchen window. "It's my husband's uncle." She leaned closer and squinted to see though the glass. A lopsided grin appeared on her face and she turned to wink at Jana, then opened the door and bowed. "Welcome, my uncle. I am going to the shed to get more rope to secure our hostage."

His wrinkled hand reached out and touched her shoulder. "That is good. The time is at hand. When you return, bring her into the dining room." He reached into his pocket and produced the spare key for the handcuffs.

Sue rushed outside while the old man addressed Jana. "I apologize for what is going to happen next," he said calmly, "but it is, indeed, necessary." Jana shivered when he reached out and stroked her cheek. Then he lifted her chin to look into her eyes. "It is a shame that in this world, sometimes the most beautiful and delicate things must be sacrificed for a cause."

The old man left the room. Sue returned and unlocked the handcuff from Jana's wrist, leaving the other half dangling from the pipe. Looking behind her, Sue nodded toward the back door. Then she clutched Jana's arm and pulled her up. "Let's go." The close proximity allowed a quick hiss of a message. "Help is here."

Jana's mind raced to Trevor, Don, or even Zack. *If anyone can help me, it's them. I just wish Jared was here.*

Twenty-five

The Jeep rolled up to the deserted century-old home near Astoria. Trevor and Vince stepped out, each looking furtively around. Ragged curtains flapped in the breeze through the broken windows. The stair creaked and bent under the two men's combined weight. Through the open front entrance, they saw a single light shining from underneath a door in the back of the house. With great caution, Trevor took the lead toward the golden beam, with Vince following close behind. Trevor reached for the doorknob but stepped back when it creaked open.

"Come in, Mr. Willis. We've been expecting you."

The voice belonged to an ancient Chinese man in a gray suit, holding a sharp, thin blade to Jana's throat. She sat bound by rope on the edge of a sturdy narrow wooden table in front of a swinging door. "I assume Mr. Coleman is right behind you."

"Yes, he is."

At this prompt, both men entered the room.

An ornate chandelier and built-in china cupboards decorated the old dining room. Worn mahogany paneling and tattered brocade curtains hinted at the room's former elegance. Lee and Sue Williams stepped into view. Lee aimed a gun at Trevor and Vince.

"I am Mr. Wong," Lee's uncle said. "I am told you have kept your part of the bargain. There are no agents in sight."

"You have us, now let her go." Trevor moved forward.

The man tightened his grip on Jana. "I will ask you to step back, Mr. Willis. In case you have doubts as to the sharpness of this blade, all I need to do is apply slight pressure."

The terror increased in Jana's eyes as the action brought forth a trickle of blood. Trevor retraced his footsteps.

"Lee, search them both thoroughly," Mr. Wong ordered.

Sue's husband obeyed, then bowed respectfully to the old man. "There are no weapons, my uncle."

"Good. Now make sure they do not move." He turned to Trevor. "While I am grateful you have kept your end of the bargain, I am afraid I cannot keep mine."

Before Trevor had a chance to react, Mr. Wong moved the knife from Jana's throat to position it above her heart. Just then, a figure burst through the door of the butler's pantry and grabbed the old man by the arm, preventing the weapon from hitting its mark.

"Jared?" Jana gasped.

Mr. Wong flung him against the wall. In the resulting confusion, Lee's attention turned from the men he guarded. Vince seized the moment and lunged toward Jana, shielding her from the assailant's blade, which was brought forcefully down into Vince's back. Sue grabbed Lee's arm and fought for control of the gun. When it exploded, she fell backwards, blood oozing across her white blouse. Trevor dove toward Lee, taking him to the floor. His fist ensured the man would offer no further resistance. Trevor found some rope to tie him up before he ran to Sue's side.

He turned back to see Jana watching Jared and Mr. Wong circling each other, their gazes locked. Every few steps, the older man slashed at Jared with the knife. With her hands still tied, Jana wriggled off the table. Trevor gasped as she rammed her shoulder into Mr. Wong's arm. It was enough to turn the tables and give Jared the advantage. He hit the man with an upward thrust of his palm and swung his leg around to knock him off his feet. His foot stomped on the hand holding the knife, eliciting a scream of pain. Jared pulled the defeated man up, dragged him to the pantry where Jana had been held, and slipped the man's uninjured wrist into the handcuff hanging from the pipe.

Hands still bound in front of her, Jana sat with her uncle's head cradled in her lap. Trevor saw the tears in her eyes as she pled with Jared, "Can you help him?"

"I . . . I don't know. I need something to stop the bleeding." He picked up the knife and cut the rope from her wrists.

Trevor removed his shirt and tossed it over to Jared. "Here, use this. An ambulance is on its way, and the rest of the team will be here in seconds. Jana, you better come over here."

She looked toward Trevor and saw Sue on the ground. "What happened?"

"She took a bullet meant for me."

Jana left Vince in Jared's care and went to kneel by Sue. "Will she be all right?"

Remaining silent, Trevor refused to look Jana in the eye.

"Will Zack be here?" Jared tore the shirt and used half of it to apply pressure to Vince's wounds.

"I think so."

"Good. We can give them both a blessing."

Sue reached for Jana's hand. "I'm free now."

Jana patted her dying friend's hand. "I know."

"No, Jana. You don't understand. I am free now—forever." Sue closed her eyes while the pain faded into peace, and her last breath came as a sigh.

With tears trickling down her face, Jana bid a final goodbye.

Trevor pulled her away as FBI agents swarmed the house. Once Don deemed the building secure, the paramedics followed. They covered Sue's body with a sheet. Jana watched with Trevor and Jared while the paramedics worked to stabilize Vince.

A spare paramedic dressed the small wound on Jana's neck.

Trevor approached. "That was a foolish thing you did, Jana. You could have been hurt."

"It was the only way to save Jared."

Trevor's anger exploded. "Jared can take care of himself. I'm putting you in protective custody immediately."

"You'll do no such thing!" Jana said indignantly. "I am not a pawn to be pushed around at will, and I won't have you telling me what to do anymore." She turned as the paramedics pushed the stretcher out the door. "I'm riding in the ambulance with Uncle Vince." She left without another word.

A flabbergasted Trevor stared after her. "I never would have thought she had it in her."

"I knew she did," Jared replied.

They sat on a couch at the hospital, waiting for word about Uncle Vince.

"I'm a little confused, Jared." Trevor stood up. "Although I've never been happier to see anyone, I thought the FBI had you in custody."

"After my little, uh . . . demonstration of my abilities, Agent Townsend came to talk to me. He discovered my background in the military and made an executive decision. I was someone the Chinese would have never thought to watch."

"Ah. So Don got you out here quickly, and you were able to hide."

"Sue helped me, too. She really was a hero."

"It's all my fault." Jana's tears threatened to fall again. "If I hadn't . . ."

Jared took her hand, bringing her gaze up to his. "You can't blame yourself. She made her choices. Remember the scripture, 'Greater love hath no man . . .'"

Warmth spread through Jana as she listened to his soothing voice, and she nodded.

At that moment, Dr. Grant appeared in the hallway, still clad in his surgical scrubs. Jana sprang up from the couch and hurried to him, her eyes questioning.

"Vince is a tough old bird," the doctor said. "It looks like he has a good chance to pull through. When he's stabilized, we'll airlift him to Portland."

Jana let out a long breath. "Thank you so much."

She turned back to the men in the waiting room, rushing past Trevor into Jared's embrace.

Twenty-six

When Jana and Jared arrived at the hospital room, his way was blocked by the two FBI agents. "I'm sorry, sir. Only Miss Clawson is allowed in. Special Agent Townsend's orders."

Jana placed her hand on his arm. "It's all right, Jared."

"I'll wait for you in the lobby."

She stepped through the door and pulled back the privacy curtain to peek in at her uncle. "Knock, knock."

A weak voice came from the bed. "Who's there?"

Jana moved closer. "Olive."

A faint smile touched his lips. "Olive who?"

"Olive you, Uncle Vince." She learned over and placed a kiss on his forehead.

"I love you, too, darlin'." He clasped her hand in his.

Squeezing back, she looked at him with tears in her eyes. "Thank you for saving my life."

"Yours is a life worth saving, darlin'. After all the things I've done, mine isn't worth a plug nickel."

"Please don't say that. You've made mistakes—we all have. What was it Pumbaa said? 'You have to put your behind in the past.'"

Her uncle's smile shone in his eyes. "Thank you. They worked a deal with me. I have to sell the company and retire. I'll be on probation for several years, but I won't go to prison."

"That's good." Jana patted his hand.

Trevor pulled aside the curtain. "They're coming in a few minutes to take you to the helicopter, Vince. Karen will be waiting for you at Legacy Emmanuel in Portland."

"Thanks, Willis. Take care of my girl, okay?"

Trevor put his arm around her waist. "I'll do my best."

She moved away from him. "Uncle Vince, I'm not going back to Portland right now." The two men gaped at her. "I'm remaining here on the coast for awhile. The Grants said I could stay at the guest house."

Vince frowned. "What are you talking about? I thought you would help me get the company ready to sell, and then Aunt Karen and I are heading back to Texas. I hoped you would come with us—at least for a little while."

"I'm so sorry, but everything at the office is ready. Anyone can come in and take care of the final details. It's time for me to make a life for myself, and I've chosen to make that life here. Texas was never home to me."

"Are you sure, darlin'?"

"I appreciate all you've done, but it's time for me to follow my heart. I have to stay here."

The curtain parted with a brusque movement as a couple of orderlies came through the door. The taller young man spoke. "Mr. Coleman, the helicopter is landing. Let's get you ready to go." Within a few minutes, the team had transferred Vince from his bed to a gurney.

Jana took her uncle's hand again. "I love you. Tell Aunt Karen to call me, okay?"

"I will. You have a place with us anytime." He kissed her hand. "'Bye, darlin'."

She started to follow him, but the shorter man stopped her. "I'm sorry, ma'am. This is as far as you go."

Her gaze followed Uncle Vince out the door, and she wiped at the tears with her palm.

"Sweetheart, he'll be all right." Trevor put his arm around Jana's shoulder. "Maybe we should sit down." He gestured toward the small sofa bed. It slid backward into the wall when they situated themselves on it.

"Whoa. This thing doesn't seem very stable." He held his hands out for balance.

"You can say that again. I've been thinking about us, Trevor."

"I'm sorry for telling you what to do yesterday. I'd like to say it won't happen again, but in truth, it's very likely to happen again."

She chuckled. "Knowing you, it would. You can't help yourself."

"You didn't have to agree so readily." Trevor touched her hair. "There's something else I discovered in preparing for baptism."

"What's that?"

"Sometimes, even when you want something so badly that you ache, the Lord's answer can still be no. I've begged and pleaded to have things work out for the two of us, but I keep getting this feeling that Heavenly Father is telling me it isn't what you want."

A tear fell from Jana's eye. "And He would be right."

"Besides, I'm afraid I would smother you, and that as we became 'us,' you would be lost."

"You're a good man, Trevor, and you've been a blessing in my life. You helped pull me out of the sadness from my parents' death, and you were there for me."

A nurse rushed through the curtain with a cart to prepare the room for the next patient. Her cheerful whistle died on her lips, and she came to a standstill. Like a catapult, Jana jumped up from the couch.

"I'm s–sorry," the woman stammered. "I thought this room was vacant."

Trevor stood. "Don't worry. We'll just be a few more minutes." He ushered the nurse out the door and drew the curtain.

Jana felt drawn to the window as the helicopter rose from the ground.

"You know, many women would sell their souls to be Mrs. Trevor Willis," he said quietly from behind her. "But you're not like other women. You would never sell your soul—for anything. You're a lot stronger than you think." He pulled Jana around and into his embrace. "If you ever need anything, let me know, and I'll do everything in my power to help you. You'll always have someone to turn to."

"Thank you. I'll remember that." She took a step back.

Trevor looked into her eyes. "This may not have worked out the way we planned, but I wouldn't have traded my time with you for anything. You've brought the gospel into my life and helped me to be a better person. You will be at my baptism?"

"I wouldn't miss it for the world. See you then."

As Jana grasped the curtain to pull it aside, he said her name.

She turned back. "Yes?"

"If it doesn't work out with Carpenter, give me a call." Trevor winked and chuckled.

She shook her head as she left the room, muttering a quiet "Incorrigible."

Jared rose to meet her when she entered the waiting area. "Everything okay?"

Warmth enfolded her, and she inclined her head. "Yes, everything's good."

"There's something different. What happened?"

"Trevor and I broke things off. We agreed it wasn't right."

Jared draped his arm around her and gave her a squeeze. "Let's go then. To the beach?"

"Of course. How did you guess?"

Jared put the car into park and touched Jana's hand. "Wait here for a sec."

"Sure. What's going on?"

He wiggled his eyebrows. "You'll see."

She watched him unlatch the trunk and remove something. He continued around to open her door. After a glance at her feet, he shook his head. "Those shoes aren't exactly beachwear."

She strained to see what he held out of her sight. "What are you hiding, Jared Carpenter?"

His smile erupted when he revealed the surprise.

Jana's hands flew to her mouth. "My flip-flops!" She gasped. "I can't believe you kept them." She reached out for the yellow shoes, talking through her tears. "Jared, my mom bought these for me the day before the accident."

Jared crouched down and removed Jana's shoes, slipped the flip-flops onto her feet, and helped her out of the car. Hands clasped, the two headed for the shore.

They reached a sheltered cove as the sun began its descent in the western sky. Varying shades of orange and red shimmered in the water. Sitting on the blanket Jared always kept in his car, they stared into the distance. Jana hugged the worn towel around her shoulders and reclined against the safety of his arm. The sun sank lower on the horizon as the minutes passed.

Jared reached into his pocket and pulled out a coin. "A penny for your thoughts."

She studied the copper disk as she turned it in her hand. "I've learned a thing or two through this all."

His silence encouraged her to share in her own time.

"I found out you can't take life for granted. It might be over before you know it."

"Anything else?" he asked.

Jana closed the penny inside her hand and placed it against her chest. "I learned this is home. It's where my heart is."

With his face inches from hers, Jared looked into her eyes, straight to her soul. "Are you sure?"

The coin fell from her grasp when she reached around his neck. Her lips met his, and all strands of doubt melted into the ocean as the sun cast its final rays of light.

About the Author

Born in Illinois, Donna Fuller has lived in a variety of places and currently resides in Newberg, Oregon, with her husband. At times, she feels like a Ping-Pong ball—bouncing from coast to coast. She has always been involved in writing, from journals to plays for Cub Scouts, to short stories for her children and as a reporter for a small newspaper. Donna has won awards for her writing and has also taught in writing workshops. *A Strand of Doubt* is her first novel.

4